# FACING THE FIRE

CALLE J. BROOKES

FACING THE FIRE

Copyright © 2021 by Calle J. Brookes

For information contact:

www.callejbrookes.com

Book and Cover design by C.J. BROOKES

First Edition: AUG2021

# PROLOGUE

Clint Gunderson hadn't wanted it to end like this—but this…

*This* was the expected outcome.

Live by the gun—die by the gun.

It was about damned time.

And he was tired of living by the gun.

That it was at an end felt more than just surreal—it felt damned impossible. Far too many months of his life had gone to this case. It had cost him more than any other case ever had. Tonight, it had almost cost him his closest friend, too.

He couldn't live like this anymore. Clint just couldn't.

Now it was over. Clint was finished. He never wanted to work law enforcement again.

He never would.

He'd made that vow as he'd watched his truck burn to ashes more than five months earlier—after the son of a bitch who now lay dead at his feet had placed C4 beneath his back seat.

The back seat where his infant daughter normally rode. It had been luck that had had his baby at home that day.

*Never* would someone he loved be targeted because of what Clint did ever again. He'd made that vow and meant it.

Clint was a man of his word.

He looked at the man standing next to him. His supervisor appeared mean and hard and ready to chew through nails—as an appetizer. To be followed up with a main course of razor blades and glass.

Rexford Weatherby was just as dangerous as he looked.

Rex was one of the only close friends Clint had ever had. These past six months or so had just made that even clearer.

At times, the only one he'd been able to trust at all had been Rex.

Clint didn't take that lightly.

It had come too damned close for Rex with this one, too. Clint had pulled him out of the way of a bullet at the very last moment. It hadn't been in time—but it had kept Rex alive.

"I can handle the rest of the details," Clint said, hoping the man would take the hint. Knowing he wouldn't.

Rex nodded. The man looked completely out of place in the meth lab where their suspect had been hiding. Rex's dark three-piece suit stood out from the filth. As did the dark stain growing on the man's shoulder. "Thought this was never going to end. But we got every damned lackey and mule and runner out there now. It's finished."

Clint hadn't looked that close at Rex in the heat of the moment. He did now. And cursed.

"You need to get that taken care of. Now." Ambulances

were on their way. Backup had arrived fifteen minutes ago. Clint could handle things from here.

Clint knew better than to even say more than that. The man wasn't stupid. He'd get medical care when he was damned well ready. Nothing Clint said would change that.

Rex was damned stubborn at times.

"You leaving town soon, I take it? Do I need to stop by and grab the dog until you get back?"

"I'm leaving as soon as possible. Taking Kody to Dusty Talley to board him for a few days. My...family...is out there. Somewhere. I've waited long enough to find them."

His baby girl was out there without him. His Violet. She was almost fifteen months now.

His world.

He had no idea where she was. Had no idea if she was safe, happy...alive. He had no clue where she was or whether she needed him right this very moment.

That knowledge had eaten at him every single night she had been gone.

Worry for her hit him hard.

He hadn't let himself focus on what he was missing. Not for almost six months now.

He hadn't been able to, or it would have destroyed him. He had had to make things *safe* for them all again. Violet and...

*Maggie.*

A sweet, beautiful woman with red hair and big blue eyes. Who had once looked at him like he mattered.

He missed them. More than he would have ever thought possible.

The two people he loved most in this world were out there where he couldn't get to them.

So they would be safe from his damned *job*.

His job had cost him more than five months of his daughter's life and the time with Maggie when he could have been convincing her of how he felt about her.

Convincing her that what they'd had together was *real*. And not the stupid lies he'd told her back then to protect himself.

She had to hate him now, for what he'd caused.

He hated himself for that, too.

"I'm going to go find my family," he said as the sound of sirens split the cold mid-March air. "And bring them *home*. Where they belong."

# 1

HOME WAS CALLING HER REAL HARD TONIGHT.

Maggie Tyler couldn't answer. She couldn't even decide whether she *wanted* to go home, either.

Someone knocked on her suite door. She hefted Violet up and put the toddler on her hip, ignoring the twinge in her back at the movement.

Moving around while being the size of a whale was a whole lot difficult and a whole lot awkward. Violet was getting bigger and bigger every day as well. It was becoming a little difficult to maneuver the toddler all the time.

Maggie had to pee again, too. No surprise, she always had to pee now.

But first, the door. Whoever was out there could hold Violet while Maggie took care of more pressing business. Like waddling to the bathroom. For the three hundredth time in the past hour.

If she had to hide herself away, at least, she was hidden in a place that had multiple staff members who could *help*.

Not exactly how she'd imagined this whole pregnancy

thing going, but it could be worse. She was seven and a half months along now. She looked closer to ten. Or one hundred.

Clint Masterson made *big* babies. His baby number two had permanently settled on Maggie's bladder. Where he liked to do tae kwan do. Plus, gymnastics.

"I didn't want to disturb you," Mel said, once Maggie opened the door. Mel had been her savior these past five months. Without her and Mel's cousin by marriage, Brandt, Maggie would have fallen to pieces months ago. "But there is someone at the gates looking for you. Demanding to be let in. Not going away. Once I got a good look at him, I figured you'd want to know. This man... long, tall, and cowboy gorgeous. Looks like he belongs on a western romance novel cover somewhere—and can give any woman the shivers. The good kind of shivers. He could almost give my husband a run for his money. Says he's here for his woman and his baby and we'd better give them to him now. Was rather insistent on that. Since you're the only one with a baby here right now...process of elimination."

There were very few possibilities.

*He* was here.

"Should I have security let him in?" Melody Beck Barratt's husband was one of the richest men in the United States. They were currently at his property in Finley Creek —well guarded behind his stone gates. If she said no, no one would ever be able to get in to her. But...that was just delaying the inevitable. Clint had come for his daughter. He wouldn't stop until he got Violet. "Or do you want me to chase him off?"

Maggie and Violet were safe here. Houghton and Mel

had protected her and the baby—when they had not had to.

She would never be able to repay them for that. But… there had always been an *end* in sight. She'd just somehow thought there would be more planning to it than this. She'd thought there'd be a phone call, and her uncle Phil— a good friend of Mel's family—would come get her, she'd meet Clint at the airport and return Violet to him.

As simple as that.

Then she'd head back to her brothers' ranch, where she'd stay until she gave birth. With five more than overprotective brothers hovering over her, watching every move she made.

Or she'd fly home and introduce Clint to his son. She'd had nightmares that the baby would be born before Clint found her again, and she'd have to pick the name herself. To take that away from him, too.

Before she went home with her brothers. Back to the eight-by-ten room she'd spent most of her life in. At least until she could find a place of her *own.*

Maggie had never had that. A place that was just hers. A place she could decorate, could put *her* mark on. The way she would want it. Maggie had never had that.

She wanted that now. So much.

"It's Clint, isn't it? He's finally here."

He had been bound to find her sooner or later.

Well, he had been bound to find *Violet.*

Clint Gunderson wouldn't have ever bothered looking for Maggie. Except for one thing—Maggie had basically abducted his daughter.

He was in for a nasty shock when he got a good look at Maggie. He'd come for one baby—surprise!

Clint was getting two.

She'd never had a chance to tell him about his son, that she was pregnant.

He would hate her forever when he realized what had happened after that one night they'd slept together.

It had just been one night.

Her she was—the punch line of a very bad made-for-TV melodrama.

"I knew he'd find Violet eventually."

"You're sure it's just for her he's here?" Mel asked. "The first words he said to the guard were 'I've come for my *woman*. My family.' But the 'my woman' was pretty clear. Heard it on the security replay myself. That is one determined man out there."

"He means Violet. She's the only blood family he has left."

"He said *woman*, Mag, not baby. There aren't a whole lot of possibilities here."

"I'm not Clint's woman. I never have been. He's…into women like Miranda. Not women like me." Maggie was just a simple ranch girl who'd never gone to college, would never be anything like Clint's ex. Miranda was some bigwig with the biggest, best branch of the FBI possible. Miranda Talley was the type of woman men wanted, loved.

There was no way mousy Maggie Tyler would have ever been able to compete with Miranda. The other woman was tall, vivacious, gorgeous, smart, successful—and genuinely kind. More than that, Clint opened up with Miranda far more than he ever had Maggie.

Clint trusted Miranda. Let her get close to him in ways he would never have let Maggie. She'd had five months to figure out what that meant for her.

She would always come in second to Miranda with

Clint. Well, she'd come in third—his late wife, Amy, and ex-girlfriend, Miranda, were far ahead of Maggie, nothing more than his housekeeper, in his heart.

They always would be.

She'd finally come to terms with that.

Clint had lost his first wife to a fast cancer that she had chosen not to fight so that Violet would have a safer chance at surviving the birth. Amy had been a casual friend of Maggie's for years, one of those women who were genuinely nice and kind.

Shortly after, Clint had lost his only brother.

Maggie hadn't fallen for Clint until after she'd seen how his brother's death had affected him.

Maggie had fallen for him even more as time had passed. She'd built dreams she shouldn't have about the broody, mysterious loner who watched her with heat in his eyes.

She'd let him in.

The stupidest mistake of her life.

The stupidest—and the best—mistake of her life.

Her free hand brushed against the spot where Clint Gunderson's son rested beneath her heart.

She would *never* regret the baby she carried. No matter what happened with his father. "Can you take her? I really have to…"

"I'll hold her. Go." Mel slipped into the room and settled on the couch. Mel always sat down to hold Violet. She was careful not to drop the baby. Mel wasn't as strong physically as she liked people to think.

A .38 caliber bullet too near Mel's spine had partially paralyzed the former police detective, who was now married to the extremely sexy, extremely wealthy Houghton Barratt.

Maggie had made it a part of *her* job to make certain Mel didn't overdo it, either. She liked her life here in Finley Creek County, Texas. Mostly.

It wasn't Masterson.

But Maggie had been able to find a part of herself here—standing on her own two feet as much as she could behind guarded walls—that she doubted she'd ever have been able to find in Masterson, surrounded by overly protective dominant men everywhere she turned.

Tyler men were worse than stone walls for hemming a woman in at times.

In Texas, Maggie had figured out who Maggie *is*.

Maggie just didn't know what that meant for her future.

She knew one thing to the bottom of her toes.

Clint Gunderson wasn't about to let *his son* stay in Finley Creek without him.

Once he learned the baby even existed, that was.

Maggie walked with Mel to the elevators after freshening up in the bathroom of her suite. The two had spoken about how Maggie felt concerning Clint dozens of times. There wasn't much left to say now.

Maggie still hadn't fully figured out just how she did feel about him.

Eight months ago, if someone had asked her if she was in love with Clint Gunderson she would have not hesitated to say yes.

She hadn't known Clint well enough to love him. It had taken her a while to understand that. She'd loved the idea of him, loved how much he loved his daughter, loved how kind he had been to her, but she hadn't loved *him*.

Not the way she had thought.

He was the second man she had slept with. It had only been the one night. They had used birth control.

The baby never should have happened.

But he had. That was what she and Clint would have to focus on.

Going forward.

Maggie would move on with her life. She'd felt like she had been in stasis for five months.

That ended now. It was time to go home.

To start really living.

Violet rested her head on Maggie's shoulder, patting one small hand against Maggie's protruding belly.

It was almost time for Violet's nap.

There was a nursery on the first floor. Violet could sleep there—while Maggie dealt with the child's father.

She just hoped she was ready.

Now or never.

She walked with Mel to the family room on the first floor. A man stood there by the fireplace, staring out the expansive window that overlooked the back garden. He turned, a tall, broad-shouldered, dark-haired man who had once been the center of her world. And he hadn't even known it.

"Clint."

## 2

PREGNANT. IT WASN'T A DREAM OR A MISTAKE. IT WAS FOR real—the evidence tech who had told him Maggie was pregnant after finding the pregnancy tests that day she and Violet had almost died had been right. The evidence hadn't lied.

Maggie was pregnant. Clint just...stared. Like a complete idiot.

She didn't say anything to him. Maggie stood in the doorway and watched him. Clint stared right back. He studied every single inch of the woman he had dreamed about each night for almost eight months.

Longer.

He'd been dreaming about her far longer than that.

Since about a month after she had moved into his home. His wife had only been gone four months, and he had been lusting over his housekeeper.

Not exactly admirable.

He couldn't bear to look her in the eye now.

Maggie would see every failure he'd ever had. Every way he had let her and Violet down before.

He had failed Maggie so badly it made him sick to even think about it.

Clint turned to the baby in Maggie's arms, instead. Tears hit his eyes, but he blinked them back. He'd missed his daughter so damned much. She didn't look the same at all.

"She's gotten so big." Clint looked at his baby for the first time in five and a half months. There had been so many changes. Her hair was quite a bit longer. Thicker. She had her mother's golden curls, having lost the bit of red she'd been born with. Now it was spun gold. So beautiful.

Violet chattered at Maggie, shooting the woman holding her a smile.

Amy's smile.

It was his late wife's smile. Full of mischief and joy, just like Amy's had always been. Damn, that hurt. So much.

A pang of grief stabbed right through him.

They hadn't married for love; both had admitted that just a few months into the marriage during a heated argument he'd always regretted. They had cared a great deal for one another. They'd decided to work together to have a successful marriage, to build a good life together as friends. And they had. Would have continued to do so if they'd had the chance.

Amy had chosen to give their baby girl life.

He would always mourn her. Always love her.

But Maggie…Maggie was the woman he wanted now. The woman he wanted to spend the rest of his life with. He just had to get her back to where she belonged first.

"Da, da, da!" Violet babbled, waving a chubby little hand at him.

Like she recognized him.

"I've...shown her your picture every day. Talked about you so she wouldn't forget you. Hello, Clint," Maggie said quietly as the woman who'd walked in with her stepped out of the room and pulled the large, hand-carved doors shut, giving them privacy.

Maggie carried Violet further into the room and sank onto the overly large couch. She placed his daughter on the floor.

The baby sat at Maggie's feet, yanking on the tassels of the couch and banging on the knee of Maggie's cream trousers. Playing.

Perfectly content right where she was.

There were baby toys in one corner of the family room they were in. Toys for his daughter, as if she belonged right there.

Perfectly comfortable in the home of a billionaire.

Clint had rarely felt intimidated as an adult—but where he was now...it was a totally different kind of world than what he was used to.

He couldn't give his child *this*.

Either of his children.

He looked at Maggie again, cataloging every tiny change her pregnancy had made. She was the most beautiful pregnant woman he had ever seen.

"Maggie, honey..."

Clint's gaze fell. To the rounded stomach where his baby was growing, very obviously. Emotion slammed into him.

Maggie hadn't lost the baby or gotten sick or hurt or any of the other fears that had run through his head at his weakest moments. Every crazy scenario possible had tormented him for months. Haunted him.

That was over now.

Maggie Tyler was definitely pregnant with his baby.

Clint hadn't realized how much he loved her until she was gone. That love threatened to send him to his knees at her feet right now.

He'd been terrified something would happen to her during her pregnancy, just like it had Amy. Terrified he'd lose her and never know. Terrified that she needed him and he couldn't get to her.

Would find her too late. Or not at all.

He'd been afraid he'd never see her again. But there she was. Perfect. Beautiful.

He'd beg if he had to.

## 3

Nothing was ever that simple for Clint.

He'd packed up her and Violet's things and now watched as she told her Texas friends goodbye. He was about to whisk them away in his rental car.

Just like that.

She hadn't said much to him. Just nodded when he'd said he was there to take her home. She hadn't acted happy, or excited—just nodded.

Clint knew he had no right to tell her where she had to go. Even with the baby growing in her being half his, too. If she'd wanted to stay with her rich friends, she would have been able to.

All she had to do was say the word—the security guards would have booted him in an instant. Then dragged his body off with that damned ATV.

It was because of Violet that she was cooperating. He had no doubt about that. Clint held his daughter in his arms while Maggie was hugged repeatedly by the rich man's wife. Both women were teary-eyed when Maggie finally pulled away.

He felt like a monster ripping her away from her friends forever.

Then it was Violet's turn. The billionaire himself seemed ready to cry when he told Clint's daughter goodbye and hugged her close, rocking her gently as if he'd never let her go.

He'd spent time with Violet—it was obvious. Violet told him, "Bye-bye, Ho-ho." And gave him a sweet little wave.

Clint was torn between jealousy that another man had been there with his daughter for the last five months and gratitude for what Houghton Barratt had done for them, provided for them.

Gratitude won out. This man had kept his daughter and Maggie safe behind guarded walls. Protected them when Clint hadn't been able to.

Clint would never be able to repay that.

He shook the man's hand and thanked him again.

Houghton Barratt just nodded. "Anytime. We'll miss them around here. I wouldn't be surprised if Melody didn't suddenly want to visit Wyoming in a few months. She's adopted Maggie as one of her little sisters, I think. Wants to be there when the baby comes."

Ten minutes later, they were in his rental and Maggie was attempting to get comfortable. Clint just wanted to sit there and stare. At the beautiful woman next to him, at the beautiful baby in the backseat.

He finally had them back with him. Where they belonged. Words couldn't adequately describe what he felt right now.

He controlled himself. Barely.

"You ok?" Worry for her was at the forefront of his mind.

It probably always would be.

Damn, he wanted to touch her. To kiss her. To just tell her how sorry he was for being such a total asshole seven and a half months ago. He should have tracked her down that first morning when she'd run back to her room. Followed her and made her understand why he'd gotten stupid. Scared.

He should have lifted her into his arms and made her understand that he was an idiot and hadn't meant a word he'd said. Should have kissed her and apologized and just held her for hours. If she'd let him.

He'd told her there was no future for them—and told her he'd lied about how he felt for her. Destroyed everything they could have had with two minutes of stupid words.

He'd *known* the first moment he'd touched her that he had strong feelings for her.

He'd just let his cowardly self convince him he didn't.

"I'm fine. It's hard to get comfortable sometimes."

Clint looked at her stomach. A boy. She'd told him they were having a son. He couldn't quite wrap his head around it. It was real. "You...doing ok?"

"The baby is healthy. And I'm doing fine. You don't have to worry. I'm not sick or anything. Perfectly healthy pregnancy."

Her tone was so impersonal. That gave him pause. She'd never spoken to him like that before. "I can't help but worry, Maggie. I care about you."

"I'm sure you do. But like I said, the baby is fine," she said before turning toward Violet and checking the baby quickly. His daughter was still in a rear-facing car seat; he could hear her giggling, though. The most beautiful sound in the world.

"I do. More than I told you. Then."

"Clint…I…am not going to do this. I am going back to Masterson because I left things, my life, hanging there. I want to see my brothers and my cousins and my friends. But I've had a lot of months to think about what happened between us. I'm not the same woman I was back then. You need to understand that. Everything is different now. I'm no longer your housekeeper. I won't be again. My life is going in a different direction—one I'm very happy with now. We have a few things to work out between us, for the baby's sake. That's it."

He bit back the panic. There was too much finality in her tone.

"I'm not the same man, either." Hopefully, he was a better one. He needed to make her see that. Fast. "I hope you'll let me have a chance to show you."

She just watched him for a long time, out of those Tyler blue eyes of hers. Those eyes had seared into his soul the one night he'd had with her. He'd never be able to erase Maggie's eyes from his memories.

Nor that night.

She kept the distance between them for the rest of the journey back to Masterson. Even on the flight.

Maggie was so busy with taking care of Violet he didn't even attempt to have a more serious conversation.

Clint just attempted to help with the baby and tried not to stare—at either of them.

When they left the airport, he carried Violet to his truck, marveling at how she felt in his arms. She was asleep again.

Tonight, she would sleep in her own bed for the first time in five and a half months.

Where she belonged.

Maggie would be just down the hall.

If...she went back to the ranch with him at all. He'd been stupid. Just assumed he would go get her and Violet, take them back to the ranch, and everything would just go back to the way it had been—with two major differences.

One—the baby would be there in a few months, and two—he would make things right with Maggie, and she'd love him again. He'd be able to make things right with her.

He should have known better.

He thought about the options as he led the way to his new truck in the airport parking lot.

"I...are you coming home with me?" He asked it, after they'd been on the road for a few minutes. "All of your stuff is there. I wouldn't let your brothers take it. Even though they wanted it. Fought me several times to get it. I had to call Rex out to threaten them once—so they probably still hate my guts. They've harassed me weekly since you've been gone."

She winced. "I'm sorry. For whatever they did or said while I was gone. They can be total idiotic Neanderthals sometimes."

"They weren't too bad." Other than Michael breaking Clint's nose for refusing to tell him where his sister was. Clint would have a permanent bump on the bridge of his nose because of that. Would remember how he'd gotten it every time he looked in a mirror.

Or at one of Maggie's brothers.

It was only Phil Tyler showing up at the last minute and making it clear that *no one* knew where she was that had kept the other four brothers from breaking every bone in Clint's body that day.

They'd just wanted their sister back. Hell, Clint had understood.

He'd wanted their sister back, too.

He hadn't been about to share that fact. *Michael* was considered one of the *nicer* of Maggie's brothers. It would have been more than his nose the Tyler brothers broke that day. Clint wasn't stupid. "But I'm definitely not their favorite person around Masterson. They've...made their thoughts clear."

"No. I suppose you wouldn't be. Did you tell them anything about the baby?" she asked evenly. She had asked him if he was angry with her about the baby. Asked if he had known for long.

How could he ever be angry with her over their son?

He'd told the truth; he'd known almost from the moment she'd been taken from him. Had worried and missed her just as long.

He didn't know if she'd believed him at all. Maggie was more guarded with him than she had ever been.

Clint shook his head. "I didn't want that information getting out. I didn't want to give anyone any more ammunition to use against me. I had to keep you safe."

"Thank you." She watched the countryside roll by for a while. Then she turned back to him, a resolute look on her beautiful fairylike face. "I...was afraid you'd hate me, you know."

"For what? I could never hate you."

"I took Violet and ran, Clint. I basically kidnapped your daughter that day."

"Bull. If you hadn't taken her, Maggie, she would have been hurt or killed. I know that. You protected her and cared for her and loved her. I will always be thankful to you for that. Hell, if you hadn't gotten her out of town, she would have been with me the day those bastards bombed my truck. It would have been your day off, honey. You saved her. I'll never forget that. There hasn't been day that has gone by since that day that I've not thanked God you were there with her, and Miranda there to get the two of you out of the state. I...you and Violet and little Clint Junior there are my everything."

Clint reached out and snagged one small feminine hand where it rested between them.

He just wanted to touch her. Maggie jerked slightly. As if his touch burned.

Clint decided to just go for it. To get it out there between them. "I've had a lot of time to think over the last five months. Longer. I was a fool. A coward. I never should have run from you that morning. Now that you're back, I'm hoping you'll give me a chance to show you."

"Show me what?" She shot him a wary look, one that stabbed him in the gut.

Maggie didn't trust him any longer.

"Let me show you how much you mean to me. I hope you'll give us a chance. Things will change now. I can promise you that. I'm going to be the kind of man you deserve. And I'm never going to be a coward where you are concerned ever again."

She just stared at him as he drove.

Clint was afraid to hope. Afraid he'd acted too soon. Afraid she was going to tell him to just drop her off at her brothers', or at the Talley Inn right there in the middle of Masterson. She had friends there who wanted her back, too.

He didn't know if he could do it.

He couldn't lose her again.

## 4

Maggie stared at the man driving next to her. Clint was dead serious. But she had his measure, knew the truth.

He couldn't get away from her fast enough that next morning all those months ago. Just a little time hadn't changed that.

No. He'd convinced himself he loved her. Probably as a coping mechanism for his worry over Violet.

She wasn't naive anymore. Nor was she a fool.

Clint did not love her. He wanted the *idea* of her. That was all. It couldn't ever be anything else. She had kept his home clean, kept his baby safe and cared for, kept food cooked on his table, kept him in clean clothes—and one fateful night, she had kept his bed warm.

She'd been so *convenient* for him, after all.

That was exactly what he'd said.

He'd made love to her that night because she'd been convenient.

Never again.

He'd run away like his boy part was on fire. All she'd

seen of him for weeks after was his *backside*. Yes, it was a nice backside, but still...

She thought about exactly what had happened as he drove to his place a good thirty miles north of town. She'd had nothing but time over the last five and a half months to think about what had happened between her and the man next to her.

Nothing much had changed between them.

Maggie wasn't going to be *convenient* for him ever again.

She almost ordered him to stop at the inn when they drove through Masterson.

That would have been the easiest choice.

To have him just leave her there with the Talleys. Dusty and Marin were two of her closest friends. Daisy and Meyra were her friends, too. She would have been perfectly fine right there with them for a few days or so—and had more than enough cash to pay for a room for a week or two. Until she could decide what to do next.

Violet fussed in her sleep.

Violet.

The precious baby girl had Maggie not making that exact demand.

Violet needed her tonight. Violet needed, deserved, to be with her father after so many days apart, too.

Maggie would never do anything to cause Violet pain. Ever. She loved that baby girl so much.

The eight weeks after she and Clint had slept together had been filled with the two of them avoiding each other as much as possible. She'd cried herself to sleep every night for almost a month. Thought about quitting as the nanny and leaving forever a thousand times a day.

Only Violet had kept her in Clint's home back then.

Violet had needed her, and Maggie loved her so much. Otherwise, she'd have run right back home to her brothers. And stayed there.

Probably forever, knowing her. That would have been the worst thing she could have done. For herself.

New Maggie wouldn't have ever existed if she'd run home to Martin and Michael and the rest.

No. She wasn't going to hide from life any longer. Not even for a moment.

She would admit that, freely. She would have run from him—once. He wouldn't have done anything to even *try* to stop her. She knew that down to her bones.

"Tell me what you're thinking, Maggie. I can't stand the silence. I...missed you."

Of course, he had; she had something he wanted now. Her hand touched her stomach, where their son was doing his cartwheels. Dr. Kaur had told her he was a big boy. Strong and active.

Looking at his father, she had no doubts why. Strong and active definitely described Clint. All six foot, four inches of him.

The man looked strong and fit and active, all right. He looked perfect, though his warm brown hair was in need of a haircut again, his blue eyes were tired, and there was a new scar on his forehead she hadn't seen before.

The rest of him looked as strong and hard and lean as it always had been. Probably from the work he'd put in on the ranch, even after his shift with the Wyoming Highway Patrol would end.

He was one of the hottest men in Masterson County; that was something she would never argue.

No matter how her hormones were screaming she was *his*, Maggie was resolute on one thing.

Maggie wasn't about to be something convenient for a man ever again.

"We both know that you didn't want more between us eight months ago. I don't see how anything has changed. Yes, it was months ago, but to me…it wasn't. I've had a lot of time to think about…us. Or the *us* that has never existed. It shouldn't have happened. I don't regret it, for the baby's sake, but…we slept together because it was… convenient. I can't be that again."

"No, Maggie. That's not it. The biggest regret I have is that I was an idiot the next day. I should have followed you down the hall and…been honest. I've thought about nothing else since you and Violet were taken away from me. I—"

She couldn't stand it. Not now. It wasn't right. Fair.

She'd dreamed of him saying these very words—more than seven months ago, long before she'd even known about the baby.

Maggie knew Clint down to his toes. Knowing his baby was growing in a woman would make him feel that responsibility. He'd feel obligated to try to build a future for them—no matter how Clint really felt about her.

He'd convince himself that there were feelings there— so that he could do the right thing.

He'd had almost six months to plan how to do the right thing.

That just wasn't good enough for her.

She didn't want to be some man's *right thing*.

She wanted to be loved—not be someone's responsibility.

She knew exactly what it was like to be someone's responsibility when that man hadn't asked for it.

Her brother Martin had *never* once complained about

keeping her when she'd been fourteen, but she'd seen what the strain had done to him. He'd ended his long-term relationship because the woman involved hadn't wanted responsibility for Maggie. He'd stopped running around with friends of his. Stopped being *Martin* for a while there, just to take care of her.

It had hardened him in ways she couldn't define. Closed him off from the rest of the world. Closed him off from hurt.

She'd never be a man's *responsibility* like that again. She'd stand on her own two feet, no matter what.

Clint carried responsibility better than anyone she'd ever seen. She knew exactly what that man was planning —this was one of those scenarios she and Mel had discussed many, many times.

She wasn't going to let herself get dependent on him for anything. That way lay only heartache.

Maggie held up a hand. "I'm sorry, Clint. I don't really want to hear this anymore. I…I'm not interested in a relationship just for the sake of the baby. I want more than that. I deserve more than that. I deserve a man who loves me completely. No strings or ties. And I'm willing to wait for that."

She'd just spent the last five months surrounded by couples who were so deeply in love with one another that she'd almost been able to reach out and touch the connections that ran so deep between them.

Mel and her husband Houghton had a connection that was meant for the movies, it was so strong.

Mel had told Maggie in a particularly weepy moment that she'd kick Maggie's butt if she settled for anything less than the real deal.

Maggie was worth it. She didn't know why she hadn't ever had that thought before.

Growing up with her brothers, she'd never had much time to reflect on hopes and dreams and what she wanted from life. It had always been a matter of just getting by. Getting things done. Practical, purposeful—do what you had to do to keep things going for just another day. After she'd been fourteen, it had been even more intense. She hadn't allowed herself to mess up at all.

Make no waves, just *do*.

To keep the social worker away. There had been one particularly vile social worker who had had it out for their family—especially her brother Michael.

Because of some girl they'd fought over when they'd been teenagers. That social worker had loved terrorizing Maggie whenever he could. Telling her she'd be sent away to another county—or a group home.

She'd learned quickly—don't rock that boat.

Settle for what you could manage or get and just move on.

She was a lot like her brother Martin in that way. After they'd lost their parents, he'd tightened the reins on himself so intensely that he hadn't resembled the big brother she remembered at all.

None of them had been allowed to mess up at all.

Maggie had been terrified that if she made a mistake, it would destroy everything for all of them. It had been a real possibility with that social worker.

Losing her brothers had been her greatest fear back then. *That* was when she'd first started running, hiding from life.

No more.

She and Mel had discussed that in detail, too. Mel was

a practical person down to her bones. She'd lost her mother in her early twenties and had stepped up to help her father with her younger sisters.

Mel understood.

Mel had told Maggie to throw all that out the window for once and *dream*.

To figure out what it was that would make *her* happy. Her. Maggie.

No worrying about her brothers or Violet or even the baby. What would make Maggie happy?

Maggie had just stared at her for a long moment, like a total idiot. She didn't have time to dream. She had a baby coming.

A baby who deserved the best possible life she could give him. *That* was what would make her the happiest. There was no question about that.

Mel had said she understood that. But eighteen years was a long time for Maggie to wait and make do. To settle.

She'd told Maggie to just stop accepting that she had to *settle*.

Mel had told her something about fear keeping her from what she deserved.

It had taken a while—but Mel had had all those months to work on Maggie. She'd made Maggie her personal mission. Maggie had figured that out pretty early, too.

She would always be thankful to Mel for what she'd done for her. Because of Mel, Maggie understood something about life that she hadn't before.

She didn't have to *settle* for anything again. And she wasn't going to. She would raise her child with Clint, however best they thought, and she would have her career, too. For herself.

She would be happy. No matter what. Eventually, if the time was ever right, maybe she'd find a man she loved the way Mel loved Houghton.

A man who loved *Maggie* just as much in return.

There was an entire world out there, and Maggie wanted to be a part of it. She didn't want to be hidden away from the world on Clint Gunderson's ranch in Masterson County—raising his children, doing his laundry, cooking his meals, and being…forgotten about.

Being invisible.

She wouldn't be his convenient wife.

Maggie feared she'd just disappear forever if that was what she became.

Nor would she be his way of assuaging his conscience or his honor. "I'm not interested in something more with you, or with anyone. Not…now. I just want to focus on getting settled back home in Masterson. I'll need to find a house for me and the baby. I have a good job—a well-paying job that I intend to keep and can easily do virtually. I've already worked out the details to do just that once the baby is born. I want to nest for a while. We can discuss visitation and things in a week or two."

"You're not staying on the ranch with me? I know you were scared last time you were there. But I've repaired the place. Repainted. It's a good place now. Plenty of room for the babies. And any more you want to have after this one."

Dear heaven, he meant it. He just expected her to go right back out there and just…be there.

Talk about a totally clueless man.

Having his arms around her but him not truly loving her—that would slowly drain the life right out of her. She couldn't do that to herself.

It would be different—if he really loved her. If they had

had a chance to actually fall in love with each other. If it was real—instead of convenient.

The man was clueless. Completely clueless. "I...no. I don't think that's a good idea."

"What about Violet?"

She shot a look into the rear seat, to the safety mirror clipped above the car seat. Violet was sound asleep now, her little fist jammed up next to the tiny mouth that was identical to her father's. "What about her? She's almost home now."

And it was breaking Maggie's heart to imagine leaving her. She felt sick just thinking about it.

Violet was Clint's daughter. Not Maggie's. Violet belonged with her father. She'd told herself that multiple times each day in Texas.

Violet wasn't hers, no matter how much Maggie loved her.

"She thinks of you as her mother. Anyone can see that; and it makes perfect sense that she would. You have taken care of her for nearly her entire life. You can't just leave her now. She's far more bonded with you than she is me right now."

"I don't want to leave her. But I seriously doubt you'll let me just keep her." She wished he would. More than anything, it was breaking her heart to even imagine leaving Violet.

Violet was the daughter of Maggie's heart and always would be. No matter what happened between Maggie and Violet's father.

"She belongs at home, in her own room, in her own bed. With me. But she belongs with you, too. All I want is what's best for my baby—for both my kids. Help me make that happen. Stay at the ranch with me, Maggie. At least long enough for Violet to get settled in. A few weeks. Please? I'm asking you for my daughter. After that, we'll figure this out. What's best for both kids. And for us, too."

He was a master manipulator—he was going to use every tool in his arsenal to get her right where he wanted her.

In his house, caring for his children, and probably—very conveniently for him—in his bed warming his sheets. No doubt making that bed the next morning, too, before cooking him breakfast, patting him on the head, and sending him out on adventures without her. While she kept the home fires burning and tended his children.

Just waiting for him to *really* love her. She'd be waiting forever for that to happen. She just couldn't do it.

Maggie's eyes closed for a moment as she took in the sight of Masterson County. Of home.

He'd said the one thing she'd known he would. The one thing she couldn't resist.

*Violet.*

Maggie loved her so much she'd do anything to ensure the little girl was safe, happy, and whole.

Maggie wanted some time in her own home to get settled in before the baby came. That meant... "Two weeks. Not a moment longer. In two weeks, I want to be in my own house in town and preparing for the baby. That'll give me four weeks before he comes. That's all I'm agreeing to. Period."

She opened her eyes and looked into Clint's lighter blue ones. That's when she knew.

She'd just played right into that man's far too skilled hands. He had her right where he wanted her.

## 5

CLINT FOUGHT THE URGE TO CROW. HE'D WON THIS ROUND, and he knew it. There was no way in hell he was letting this woman get away from him. And not just for the babies' sakes. He'd had a lot of time to think over the last five months.

If he had been any kind of man back then, he would have faced her the morning after they'd slept together. Instead, he'd closed himself off and told himself—and her —that he had to focus on his caseload. That he couldn't do anything stupid.

Well, telling her that had been the stupidest thing he had ever done.

Now he was paying the price.

He had to fix that. Two weeks wasn't much time, but he was going to do his damnedest. "That sounds reasonable. And when the time comes, I'll help you get your new place ready for the baby. All I want…is for all of us to be happy, honey. All of us. Not just the babies."

Her hand stroked over her abdomen, and she winced. Worry hit him.

Maggie was around five five and thin. All of the Tyler women he'd ever met were on the smaller side. The baby looked huge on her narrow frame. "Are you ok? You and the baby? Everything…healthy?"

He couldn't lose her. Not like he had Amy.

Losing Amy had been horrible; to lose Maggie now would damn near destroy him.

The mere thought of losing Maggie had had him waking in a deep sweat more nights than he could count. Only that she had been with the one other woman on the planet he'd absolutely trusted had kept him sane at all. He'd known Miranda would protect her and Violet. But that hadn't really mattered.

Losing Maggie was his nightmare.

The Maggie next to him now wasn't the Maggie in his memories.

Not really. There was a strength of will that hadn't been there before.

He found her even more fascinating now than he had all those months ago.

Clint had been obsessed with her. Every move the woman had made in his house, near him, right in front of him had…fascinated him. Made him want to touch her. Hold her. Taste her. Over and over again.

He'd had no choice; to keep his sanity, he'd had to stay the hell away from her.

"Why don't you lean back a little, rest some until we get ho—back to the house?"

He wanted her to see what he'd managed to do with the place since he'd lost her and Violet all those months ago. Wanted to make her feel like it was her home now, too. He'd even painted the living room in the colors she had suggested months ago. He'd wanted to make it a dream home for her.

For Maggie.

No more of that housekeeper and nanny bullshit. She was far more than that.

She dozed off beside him as they drove the remaining miles through the light snow to his place. As he slowed and pulled into his driveway, he looked at her. Really looked at her, more than he had on the plane.

She was gorgeous. Beautiful in that natural way some women had.

She'd cut her hair a bit. Styled it. Before, she'd had long strawberry-red hair she'd worn pulled into a ponytail most days. Now it was sleekly styled—and very expensive looking.

No surprise; she'd spent five months playing besties with a billionaire's wife. Even if that woman was a former cop, she was the playmate of one of the richest men on the continent. She was expected to look great and well put together at all times. Probably had her own hair salon in the basement, or something.

He tried not to let insecurity flare again.

Maggie had probably hobnobbed with the rich and famous for months. The Barratts of Texas—the damned Barratts who were in the celebrity news and tabloids all the time. Hard to miss that in the damned grocery store line with the tabloids right there in front of him.

Maggie had no reason to want *him* after being around men like that.

She was gorgeous enough, smart enough, loving enough, perfect enough to have any man in the world falling at her feet.

Especially in Masterson County, where men outnumbered women by a factor of three. He'd been lucky some other guy hadn't already snatched her up and away from him. Clint wasn't stupid.

She had no reason to want a man like Clint.

He reached out, intending to touch her gently. To wake her.

Instead, his hand lingered on her narrow shoulder.

He glanced in the rearview mirror, checking where his daughter slept in her car seat. Gratitude to the Man Above filled him.

He had been convinced five months ago that he'd never have the chance to tell Maggie how much she meant to him. To make it up to her and Violet.

But that part of his life was in his past. As was his stepfather, his brother, and the WHP and CID and IA in general.

He was free.

Free to do what he had to do to build the family he wanted.

Violet fussed in her sleep, calling for her Mag-Mag. He would see that shifted to *Mama* soon.

He had two weeks. Fourteen short days.

He was going to use them wisely.

Clint saw the two ranch trucks parked in front of his porch when he rounded the last curve in his drive too late to turn around and hightail it back to the inn.

Trucks he recognized.

Dread filled him immediately. Hell, no. Not tonight.

He was probably about to get his ass kicked seven ways to Sunday.

Maggie's brothers had found out she was coming home. And now they were here to get her.

Probably there to kill him, too.

Phil Tyler wasn't there to save his ass this time.

"Maggie? Time to wake up." He shook her awake firmly. "Honey? Your brothers are here. Time to wake up."

# 6

MAGGIE HEARD HIS WORDS, BUT IT TOOK A MOMENT FOR THEM to register—and for her to remember where she was and who she was with. She squeaked in surprise. Which was ridiculous. Twenty-five-year-old women should not *squeak* when facing the father of their unborn child.

But she had. Damn it.

She saw Clint next to her—and then she saw the two trucks parked in front of the porch.

And five tall men she'd always recognize anywhere. They were all there, from Martin all the way down to the younger twin, Reese.

Her brothers had come to call—every one of them: Martin, Michael, Chandler, Kaece, and Reese.

No. They'd come to get her and take her home where they thought she belonged. So they could build a wall of Tyler men around her and see to it that she never got so much as a scraped knee again.

Or a broken heart.

It was about to get really interesting around here. This was not good. So definitely *not* good.

Not good at all.

Her uncle had probably found out she was on her way home and had called her brothers. Phil had told her himself he was staying in Finley Creek for a few days at his business partner's ranch. Good friends of Mel and Houghton—family connections. They and her Uncle Phil had helped Miranda Talley smuggle Maggie and Violet out that day.

That traitor. Her uncle had to know what her brothers would do with that kind of information.

Maggie let out a small curse—words she never would have said five months ago but she'd learned from Mel—as the five men who'd raised her from the age of fourteen straightened and glared at Clint's truck.

Five tall, strong, broad-shouldered Tyler men dressed in winter coats and braced for war.

Fire was on five Tyler faces. This was not going to be good.

Her brothers were glaring.

At Clint.

Phil had said her brothers blamed Clint for her sudden disappearance five months ago. No wonder. Her connection to him was to blame.

They were about to blame him for a whole lot more. And all it would take would be one *look* at her to have that happening. Her brothers were baboons, but they were smart. They'd figure it out fast.

"Well, it's time for the reckoning." Maggie winced as she said it. Time to face the music. "There's something I should probably tell you...before we get out and face the fire."

"What is it?" He parked in his customary spot and killed the engine.

The big yellow dog Kody darted out from the porch, tail wagging. Maggie's heart melted seeing the big doofus. He was almost enough to distract her. Almost.

She'd thought he'd been killed that day in a hail of bullets and had grieved him, too. He had always been so lovable. She'd poured her heart out to that dog quite a few times after that one night with Clint.

"I never told my brothers."

He shot her a look of surprise. "What?"

"I never told them about the baby. About us. They don't know I'm pregnant. And they don't know about... you...and what happened. They aren't going to be very happy about this at all."

Clint flinched. He understood what she was saying. That was clear in his lighter blue eyes. "Then it's time to face that fire and put it out. If they beat me to a pulp, tell Violet when she's older that her daddy loved her. This baby, too. More than words can say."

Maggie pulled in a deep breath and nodded. Now or never. A few of her brothers were reasonable men, even if they did all have reputations for being hotheaded.

Something that could be laid directly at Clint's stepfather's feet.

Clive never had liked the Tylers. No one knew why.

He'd harassed her brothers for years; Clive had even arrested several of the Tylers a few times on trumped-up charges that never stuck.

Her brothers had been furious she'd taken the job as Clint Gunderson's housekeeper, simply for that very reason. They'd made it clear she had no business anywhere near him, or any other Gunderson.

But...she'd known Amy Gunderson, too. And the idea that Amy's daughter needed someone...well, it had brought Maggie to the ranch that day to interview for the position as his housekeeper. Just to help, to be there for that little baby and the man who had been grieving the woman he'd loved.

She had never intended the position to be a long-term one.

She had also never intended to be the woman he used to help him forget.

Everything had changed that day.

Time to deal with the repercussions. So she could move on.

She opened her door first. And slid from the passenger seat.

Maggie faced her brothers straight on as they came toward her, keeping her eyes locked on Martin.

They stopped. Stared. Cursed. Loudly.

One hand dropped to her stomach, an unmistakable challenge to the five tall men staring at her. Her baby was her priority now. They were her family—but the baby was her everything now.

The baby and Violet.

Maggie took the first step toward them.

This was the first test of showing the world who *Maggie Tyler* was now.

She wasn't going to back down from anyone telling her how to live *her* life ever again. Maggie had found a backbone in Texas—and she fully intended to use it.

Starting with the six men surrounding her.

## 7

SHE LEFT HIM TO TEND THE BABY.

Clint wondered if that was a conscious choice to keep her brothers from ripping into him immediately or what.

He stepped around the truck.

He wasn't going to hide behind his daughter.

Or behind Maggie.

He kept half his attention on what he was doing as his daughter was waking—and half his attention on his woman and her brothers.

He didn't know them well—he didn't think her brothers would ever hurt her, but *he* was about to be toast as soon as they put one and one together and realized that in this case it added up to three.

Martin Tyler, that mean son of a bitch who Clint had tangled with a time or two in his early twenties, was the well-known leader of his brothers. Around the same age as Clint, Martin had raised Maggie after their parents had died.

Rumor had it Martin wasn't too pleased with what had happened. And was blaming Clint for every bit of it.

Martin had said as much to Clint right in the middle of the IGA four months ago.

No surprise; everyone blamed Clint for it. Including Clint.

But that was in the past. It was time they faced the future.

He had two weeks to win Maggie back. He wasn't going to let Martin or any of the rest of her brothers stand in the way of that. Even if Michael did pack quite a punch.

Martin came toward Maggie first. Clint pulled Violet onto his hip and watched Martin like a hawk. One wrong move toward Maggie and Clint would kick the asshole off his property faster than Martin Tyler could blink.

Or any of the other four men.

Martin scooped his sister close, lifting her off the ground gently. Like she was he most precious creature in the world.

No words were said.

He just held her, a look of love on his face that surprised Clint at the intensity, the open expression of how the man felt.

Martin Tyler had a reputation around Masterson as being a real fiery badass. Half the town was afraid of him because of his legendary temper.

He didn't look like that now, rocking his pregnant baby sister in his arms like that.

Maggie's arms snuck around her brother's waist, and she held him close for a long moment.

Then Martin was passing her to the next brother, Michael, who held her just as long. The hugs just kept going, until every brother had hugged her. Sometimes twice.

Clint envied them their closeness. He had never had

that with Jay. Not even once. Clive hadn't encouraged closeness—he'd encouraged competitiveness from the moment Jay learned how to walk. Then he'd arrange things so Jay would always win. And Clint lose. Time and time again. Just so that Jay would feel special.

"We were worried, Mags. No matter what Uncle Phil said, we were worried. You needed to be home where you belonged," Michael said firmly. Clint stiffened.

He'd been right. There were there to take her away.

"No," Maggie said even firmer. "I needed to be in Finley Creek more. I needed to find who I am. That was the greatest gift I could have been given. No more searching for who Maggie Tyler is."

"And this kid?" one of other brothers asked. "Who is the father?"

Five men looked right at Clint. It was obvious Maggie was more than five months along.

No one there was an idiot.

Tylers were hotheaded—but they weren't stupid.

They were doing the math quickly.

And not liking the answer.

Maggie had told him once herself that the biggest issue her brothers had had with this job had been *Clint* and what he might try to do.

With her.

Exactly what Clint had done.

Clint stepped up behind her and put his free hand on her shoulder. He looked at Martin and nodded. "The baby is mine."

And so was Maggie.

It was time they all knew that.

**8**

---

IT TOOK HER TWO HOURS TO GET HER BROTHERS TO SETTLE down. Even longer to get the pack of buttheads to leave. Not a one of them was happy with her being with Clint. At all.

They hadn't liked her taking the position of his house-keeper a year ago, but she'd needed the job. And the inde-pendence from them. They were good men, the best she had ever known, but they took overprotective and smoth-ering to the next level.

She'd eventually just out-stubborned the lot of them.

Now they had no choice but to back down to her.

She had a place in Texas she could run away to if they got to be too much trouble.

Them...or Clint. She'd told them all that—repeatedly. It had finally gotten through. She thought. It was hard telling with her brothers.

Her brothers could overwhelm a rock when they were in agreement on something.

She'd had to get out back then. She realized that now.

They had been driving her crazy. Every job she'd had,

other than the one she'd had at the diner—which she had stunk at, they had found some objection to. Half of those, they'd managed to get her fired from somehow.

She hadn't wanted to work at the diner or the Talley Inn forever. She'd known that. They'd wanted her to.

Because in their minds the Inn and Masterson Diner were safe places for her to be.

Heaven help her if she bucked what they expected of her back then.

She'd heard Clint had had an opening for a live-in housekeeper. It had seemed like the perfect answer to her problem of five overbearing brothers who were keeping her from having any kind of a life.

If nothing else, Clint's ranch was in the opposite direction of her brothers'. A good seventy miles separated them. Distance would keep them out of her business—or so she'd thought.

She'd lived at her childhood home until the day she'd moved into the small room at the end of Clint's hallway. She'd felt stifled but hadn't been able to put that into words—until she'd met Mel and the woman had practically forced her to discuss every feeling Maggie had ever had in her entire twenty-four and a half years.

It had helped. Knowing that her feelings were valid had…mattered.

She'd very rarely stood up to her brothers before. She'd been afraid of causing them problems at first, and then it just became a habit.

It had taken her two months to get them to stop "casually" swinging by Clint's place just to say hi. And check on her. Protect her from Clint.

As a teen, she'd mostly been afraid the social worker

would decide her two eldest brothers had had no business raising her.

Foster care had been a very real fear for her, even though several of her aunts and uncles had made her promises that that would never happen. At one point, it had looked like she'd have to move in with her uncle Phil and his family.

She would have been happy there—she'd spent hundreds of nights with her cousins as a child—but she was happier at home with her brothers. Her home.

Until it had started to smother her as an adult.

A part of her had feared Martin—who she hadn't been super close to at the time, considering the eleven-year age difference between them—would have not wanted to deal with her any longer if she caused him too much trouble.

But he had. And he had loved her. Would always love her.

No matter what happened.

One thing had been made abundantly clear though—all five of her brothers wanted to tear Clint apart. Into teeny tiny pieces for daring to touch their sister.

Only her warning to keep things civil or she'd take her baby and disappear again—this time forever—had had the six men behaving at all.

Clint was just as bad as Martin and Michael and all the rest. Half the things he'd said tonight had been designed just to infuriate her brothers. Almost taunting them.

Jerks.

He was ready to fight for what he wanted. He had made that known to everyone tonight. He'd fight the world to get what he wanted.

What he wanted was her.

What he truly wanted was the baby she carried.

His son.

She was just the incubator when it was all boiled down to the lowest common denominator. She'd moved from convenient one-night stand to convenient incubator.

It had felt surreal stepping foot back into the ranch house after so long away. It had taken her a moment to get her bearings.

He'd kept her things exactly as she had left them.

Now…now she was alone. Back at Clint's ranch again.

He was outside, feeding the horses, cattle, and Kody like he did every night. She finished feeding Violet and gave her a bath. It was easy to settle back into their routine. Just their surroundings had changed. Violet seemed to be doing ok.

As long as she could see Maggie, that was.

But finally, it was time for the little girl to go to bed for the night.

Clint came back in, just in time to give Violet a good-night kiss and cuddle her. He wanted to be the one to put her down in her crib. Maggie definitely understood.

Maggie stood at the door and watched. Tried not to think how perfect the man looked with the little girl held so close in his arms.

When she'd first taken the position, he'd still been awkward with the baby. That had changed in the months between that day and when she and Violet had been spirited out of the state. Now, he couldn't keep his hands or eyes off his baby.

It was obvious he'd missed Violet.

Clint was a wonderful father. In all the ways that counted. Her son would be lucky to have him in his life. She would never do anything to jeopardize that.

She was definitely staying in Masterson County. Now she just had to work out the details.

"I think she's asleep now," he whispered.

Maggie nodded. Violet was a great sleeper, most nights. But traveling by air and being in what to her was an unfamiliar place could disrupt that.

Maggie was exhausted herself—and it wasn't quite nine.

She was used to staying up a lot later now—Mel had been a confirmed night owl, and as an official Mel's Minion, Maggie had gotten used to later nightlife than she had preferred when she'd been a ranch hand or housekeeper.

Once she settled in for a few days and went back to work—Mel had insisted she stay on the payroll and just work digitally; Mel wanted minions in various parts of the world to do Mel's nefarious bidding—she'd find her *own* routine.

One that worked for her.

Then, when the time came, she'd build a routine for herself and the baby.

Maggie suspected the older woman planned to expand Blessed Reunions when Mel's boss retired next year. Between Gretchen Reynolds's connections and Mel's unlimited funds and determination, Blessed Reunions could be huge.

Maggie was excited to be a part of it.

After her maternity leave was over. That was a good five or six months away. In the meantime, she'd just be doing preliminary computer work for BR.

There were a lot of other things she had to take care of first. Her brother Martin was the best contractor in the county. He'd recently purchased four houses in town to renovate. As future rentals.

Maggie was determined that one of those houses was going to be hers and the baby's, when the time came. They had two weeks to get it ready.

She'd have to talk to her brothers in a few days. Currently, the five doofuses were acting like she was going to stay right where she was—with the father of her baby. So Clint could protect and provide for her now, instead of them.

All tucked up and cozy.

They probably imagined she'd stay there, barefoot and pregnant, raising miniature Gundersons for the rest of her life. With them stopping by to visit the babies, bringing toys and treats.

Where she'd be all safe and secure and taken care of. Occupied.

They really did act like Masterson County was stuck in 1926 sometimes.

Her brothers probably expected she'd be marrying Clint as soon as possible and he'd be responsible for taking care of her forever. So they wouldn't have to any longer.

They weren't too thrilled with it being Clint, considering the bad blood between his stepfather and their family, but they'd probably overlook that if Clint was a good enough husband to her. If he earned it.

Grrr.

The idea of her being a single parent and happy about it most likely hadn't occurred to her traditionalist brothers.

They were wild hell-raisers, every one of them, but when it came down to it, they were rather archaic beasts.

Especially where Maggie was concerned.

Chauvinists, every one of them.

She loved each and every one of them. Tears hit her eyes as she remembered how homesick she'd been in the beginning. How she would have given anything to see just one of her brothers pop up in Finley Creek with her uncle.

In spite of the problems that would have inevitably caused.

When her uncle Phil had shown up at a dinner at Mel and Houghton's a month after she'd first arrived at what Mel called the Fortress of Ostentatiousness, Maggie had bawled like a baby, clinging to her uncle for close to an hour.

He had just walked in like he had been there a thousand times before. She hadn't believed her eyes for a minute.

It had been one of the best days of the past five months. She'd never know when he would be visiting, but he'd just pop in to check on her. She'd bawled every single time he'd left.

A huge part of that had most likely been pregnancy hormones—and lack of sleep; Violet had been teething like crazy—but most of it had been pure homesickness and fear.

Uncle Phil had just held her and rocked her, like he had after her parents' funeral.

Now she was home. She had her family again. And she had a purpose.

A plan. A genuine, authentic Maggie-Faces-the-World *plan.*

"I think I'm going to go to bed a little early tonight," she said as he backed out of Violet's room and pulled her door closed. "Travel zapped me."

He had the monitor in his hand. She almost took it from him—she'd been Violet's nanny for a reason, after all.

But she wasn't the nanny now. Violet wasn't *hers* to take care of. Not any longer. That was going to take some seriously getting used to. Clint wasn't getting up early to go in to the WHP post seventy miles away each day, either.

Not according to what he'd told her on the plane. Clint claimed he was just a rancher. He'd be a rancher and a landlord for the rest of his life. He'd almost promised her that.

"I was hoping we could talk for a bit."

Now nothing felt simple at all.

He'd painted the entire exterior. A pretty gray that paired well with the new red metal roof.

It had a white front porch now. With a swing.

Just like she'd suggested to him once during a casual conversation as they'd eaten dinner during the heat of a summer night. Spaghetti. It had been Violet's first exposure to pasta.

A soft smile touched her lips as she remembered laughing with him at the mess the baby had made.

The entire inside of the house had been updated, too. Changes he hadn't wanted to make because of the cost back then. There was a new dishwasher. New flooring throughout. Painted drywall instead of the outdated, horribly printed paneling from the 1980s that had smelled faintly of cigarette smoke when she'd gotten too close.

She was so glad that was gone. That dark paneling had made the house seem small and sad at times. Almost gloomy.

New furniture was everywhere—*wipeable* furniture. Very welcoming, and perfect for a family with small children.

It looked like an entirely different place. It was going to take her time to get used to it. It was beautiful and welcoming.

And completely foreign. Surreal.

"It looks nice in here. I thought you weren't going to do much inside? Not until the barns were finished." He'd had dreams of specialty cattle. He'd discussed it with her once.

"I didn't want you to come back to that run-down shack you left. You deserve a home you can be proud of. I...and this is better for the babies. A home where they can grow up safe."

"Clint, you do know that I'm not staying here permanently." It was best to go forth as she meant to go on. Get the confrontation out of the way now, so she could go forward tomorrow. "I need you to understand that."

It was better for expectations that way. Less likely to cause hurt.

To either of them.

"I'm going to do my damnedest to change your mind."

Then he was there. Right in front of her. His hands went to her once-waist, and he was pulling her into his arms. Holding her tight. Like he would never let her go.

Those strong arms of his wrapped around her like he meant it. Like she mattered.

Just like that.

Every feeling she'd had for the man came rushing right back. His scent surrounded her, she could feel his heart pounding against her, even with the baby bump between them. He felt perfect.

Terrifying.

She squeaked. "What are you doing?"

He had only touched her twice—before that Fateful

Night, as she'd thought about it privately—like this. Strong arms that she almost swore had gotten harder, stronger, tightened around her. "I'm so damned glad you're back."

To her surprise he buried his face in the hair she'd left down. His shoulders shuddered. Her hands went around those shoulders instinctively. "Clint?"

"I am not going to lose you now, Maggie. You might as well just get used to the idea. I was too stupid and too much of a coward to realize what I had before. But I've had five months to realize what a fool I've been. I've missed you every moment you've been gone. I'm not letting you go. I'll take your two weeks—and trade them for a lifetime. You'd better get ready."

He covered her lips with his own.

Maggie did the second-stupidest thing she'd ever done with this man.

She kissed him right back.

Because no matter what her New-Maggie plan said, being in his arms somehow felt *right*.

Like she was finally exactly where she belonged.

She was in serious trouble now.

## 9

THE FIVE MONTHS SHE'D BEEN IN TEXAS HAD CHANGED Maggie.

Made her see him for the jackass he was.

Clint knew that as he held her. Kissed her.

She was kissing him back, but the sweetly shy response she'd given him months ago had been replaced by something else. Something he couldn't put his finger on.

He pulled away as the dog pushed his way between them. The mutt adored Maggie. He'd grieved for weeks after she'd left.

So had Clint. The woman was the center of their world, after all.

"Mag...I...can't you give me a second chance?" There was nothing he wanted more in the world than the woman in front of him. He didn't have a clue how to convince her to fall in love with him again. "I...was stupid that next morning."

"The only thing that has truly changed between now and then is...this." Her hand went to her stomach. He felt the proof of their baby pressed against him for the first time. "Why lie about it? I know you down to your toes. You feel obligation and responsibility and like you're doing the right thing here. But I am not the same woman I was back then. I know myself better now than I ever did then. I had weekly counseling in Texas at a women's charity. It helped me deal with what happened with the shooting and some other things—and it helped me put what happened between us into perspective. Once upon a time, we would have automatically gotten married for the baby. Made the best of things. But we don't have to do that now. Contrary to what my brothers all think—it's not 1926 here."

"We wouldn't be marrying just for the baby. There wouldn't be a baby if there wasn't something between us." He had never been the kind of man to know what to say. Especially when it mattered the most. Nothing had mattered more than this moment. Damn it. Maggie was about to slip away. "You thought you were in love with me before."

"I did. But I didn't know what love really was back then. Not between a man and a woman, not really. I've seen it now. And I'm not settling for anything less."

She put one hand over his chest. Her fingers scorched him. His heart rate sped up and he knew she could feel it. Blue eyes stared into his. His were light blue, hers a darker blue—the baby would probably get those Tyler blue eyes, too.

"You don't love *me*, Clint. You just feel...responsible. Duty bound, or something archaic like that. And I...just can't settle for being an afterthought. We'll do what we have to for the baby, and we'll move on. I'm asking...for you to respect that. Just leave me alone."

She turned and walked past him, taking every bit of hope he had felt before with her.

Clint waited until the door shut behind her, then slammed his fist into the antique walnut that his great-grandfather had carved himself. Maggie didn't love him any longer.

And it was his own damned fault.

Those five months in Texas was one thing—they hadn't been in either of their control. Not truly. They both knew that.

It was the two months before that day Clint was paying for now.

## 10

Clive Gunderson looked absolutely horrible. Nothing Jasper Grady, mayor of the small town of Masterson, Wyoming, hadn't expected.

Clive had lost everything and would spend the rest of his life in prison—the worst in the state of Wyoming. Everyone said grief had made Clive do what he had done; Jasper didn't believe that.

There had always been something a bit broken in Clive. The loss of his younger son Jay had just enhanced that. Turned Clive into what he was now.

Broken, mean, and hateful.

It would resurface ever so often. Clive used to take it out on the deputies who'd worked for him. Jasper had been one of those deputies a lifetime ago. But he and Clive —they'd had loyalty between them back then.

It had been forged in the darkness one night, alongside a lonely highway. With a woman who'd had no business being out there that night.

Jasper would never forget what she'd looked like.

What had happened to her. What the photos had shown him all those years ago.

What he had seen. Done. Maybe his crime was one of silence, but it was still nothing he would ever be proud of.

"Jasper, what the hell you doing here?" Clive rasped. He had always smoked like a chimney, and the years were now showing that.

The years and the hell the man had gone through. Most of it at his own hands.

Karma had paid Clive back in spades. Jasper felt conflicted about that.

You reap what you sow—well, Jasper had sowed some foul seeds of his own. He was terrified those seeds would grow into poison that would ruin everything he had worked for since.

"I came to check on you." Jasper looked around the visitor's lobby. Looked at the difference between him and the men that populated the few tables. Scraggly, scruffy. Dead eyed and wasted lives.

He wore a suit that cost a cool four figures—on clearance.

He hadn't ever been able to bring himself to buy at full price. Leftovers from when he had grown up with plywood floors beneath his feet, and milk-crate furniture instead of tables.

But for his children—they had the best his money could provide. He'd given them the life they'd deserved.

He would always be proud of that. More, he would be proud that they'd taken what he'd given them and made something *more* of themselves. He'd taught them well.

His children had good lives. And he was so damned proud of that.

"What the hell for?" Clive shot him a look out of

watery, dead eyes. "Am I your latest charity case or something, Grady?"

Clive's hands shook; he had aged considerably since the last time Jasper had seen him. His hair hadn't been combed—probably in days. He looked...a mess.

Hardly capable of concocting a blackmail scheme like Jasper was facing. It wasn't Clive who had been tormenting Jasper for months. He would bet money on that now.

Disappointment and rage filled him. He'd been convinced it was Clive. Downright sure. All the evidence he'd amassed over the last two months had pointed straight to Clive.

That it wasn't...Jasper's gut clenched. He was back at almost square one.

Now...someone else was out there doing this to him. And Jasper had no clue who. He hated this, hated not being in control. No doubt, the bastard blackmailing him *knew* it, too. It was someone Jasper knew; he just hadn't figured out who it was yet. But he would.

"So why you here?"

"You look horrible."

"I look like shit. Say it. Or does that go against your wholesome church-going image now?"

"I'm trying to be polite, but if you want the honest truth, take better care of yourself in here. It'll only help your case." He knew what Clive had done—the slightly older man wasn't about to get out of prison.

He would get a good twenty years for nearly killing Phil Tyler's girl alongside Wreck Curve Road. The trial was over—Clive had done the sensible thing and pled guilty, finally—but as far as Jasper knew, they still had sentencing to be delivered.

"Nothing can help my case."

Jasper had to admit, Clive was right about that. What he had done to that Tyler girl was unforgivable. "The things you did to that girl—you had to know there would be consequences. Hell, if you had done that to one of my girls I'd have not even blinked before I killed you myself."

"Hell, I knew that. I just wanted to know what about her and her sister caught my son's attention so much. I needed the answers. I wasn't really thinking clearly at the time. My boy...he didn't deserve to go that way. My attorney says that might work in my favor, what happened to Jay, and all."

Jasper kept his thoughts on that to himself. He had seen the files himself—what the Tyler girl said Clive had done to her for years was beyond damning. He'd nearly killed Perci Tyler, alongside the same stretch of highway where the girl's own mother had died in a horrible accident. That had been particularly cruel.

People had been talking about *that* for weeks.

Clive's son Jay had died trying to kill the girl's twin sister.

Bad blood.

Everyone said the Gundersons were nothing but *bad blood* now.

Jasper didn't envy Clint Gunderson, the older boy, trying to build a life in Masterson County. If he was Clint, he would have already sold everything and moved far away from this little hellhole time had forgotten. For some reason, the boy had chosen to stay.

"We need to talk about that day, Clive. I need to know what you did with that box. The evidence box. You know the one I'm talking about." One box, eighteen inches by thirty. Thick cardboard.

Containing enough damning evidence to ruin everything Jasper Calloway Grady had worked for his entire life. To destroy everything.

"It's at my place. One of 'em, anyway. Always has been. Thought about burning it a thousand times. But just figured why go to the trouble? Ain't nobody cared about that truck stop ho anymore."

"Clint's girlfriend and the baby are back. Saw them drive through town last evening. They stopped at the gas station. Saw her in his truck myself."

"Where did they go? I didn't know he had a girlfriend." There was a spark of interest in Clive's eyes now. Finally. "How's my grandbaby? Who is the girlfriend? She from around here?"

"I haven't actually seen the baby. And the girlfriend is a Tyler girl. Martin Tyler's younger sister, from the looks of her."

"I've met that one, I think. Quiet girl. Pretty and sweet. Those brothers of hers are nothing but trouble, though. Bad seeds, the lot of them. Busted them all at one time or another. Troublemakers. Clint doesn't need that. He'd best be moving on to another girl."

Jasper did snort at that. He had met the Tyler brothers in question—and found nothing objectionable. Not that he'd want one of them for his own daughters, considering how hardheaded those boys could be, but they were hard workers, at least. Seemed intelligent enough, too. He'd hired the older one himself to do some repair work to the deck on the back of his house just this past summer. "I'm sure he'll do just fine. Where did you put that box?"

Jasper didn't have much time. This had to look like a casual visit. Nothing more.

He knew exactly how recognizable he was here now.

The mayor of Masterson would stand out.

"In the back office. I think. It might have been in that footlocker I buried a few years back. When I was drunk. Can't really remember. May have even been at my house in town. Last I heard Clint sold that house, and took all my shit to the barn at his place. I suppose it could be in there, too. Hell, that was what? Twenty, twenty-five years ago? How am I supposed to remember? Had the date on the box. That was it. And initials. Made it look like every other evidence box. Just like the others, so it would fit right in and be forgotten about."

Irritation set in. Jasper forced himself to sit back and look calm. He knew he was on camera right now—and knew he would be recognized. He had to behave himself now.

"Where exactly did you bury it? How did you bury it? Was it in something? If it is in the barn, what would it look like?"

Clive shot him a smile. "I didn't bury the damned evidence, not all of it. Not the damned scarf, anyway. Just the footlocker. Tried to tell you that last time. I wrapped that disk of photos in that bloody scarf and shoved it in the damned wall in the old ranch where the in-laws lived. Knew no one would check my old in-laws' place—they were already gone by then, and it was left to Clint, but he was living in Cheyenne at the time. What the hell is the boy doing now?"

"What wall?"

"In the study, I think. But might have been the dining room. Both had junk shoved in every corner and the same damned paneling. In-laws were damned hoarders. There was a hole behind a picture of Clint and Jay as babies.

Shoved everything right into the paneling. Probably turned into mouse bait by now."

Jasper didn't give a damn. All he wanted was to see it was fully destroyed. Otherwise, he'd spend the rest of his life wondering. Worrying.

He had to find them.

So he could live the rest of his life in peace.

And this damned blackmailer would move on and leave him alone.

Or…Jasper would find him and stop him the hard way.

He was prepared to do whatever was necessary. No one would threaten his children. No one.

He was a father first—and a father was supposed to protect his children. No matter what.

## 11

HIS HAND WAS BRUISED. CLINT STARED AT THE UGLY BLUE-
and-purple flesh over his knuckles two mornings after
he'd brought his family home as he boiled water on the
stove for Violet's oatmeal.

It felt both awkward and beautiful to have the opportunity to fix breakfast for his daughter again.

Maggie had been his housekeeper, but she'd always
gone back to her brothers' ranch on the weekends, leaving
him with his daughter. Maggie would retreat to her room
each weeknight at around eight, after she put Violet down
for the evening.

Especially after that night.

They'd taken turns getting up with the baby when
needed from that first night Maggie had worked for him.
Clint had always been careful not to overwhelm Maggie;
he hadn't wanted to lose her like he had the three house-
keepers he'd had before.

First, because he'd been desperate—he'd needed
someone he could trust to take care of Violet. After that, it

had been because he had cared about her. Been fascinated by her.

The last thing he had wanted to ever do was cause her to leave him.

Which was exactly what his stupidity had made happen. Well, Clint liked to think he learned from his own mistakes.

To his shame, he had seriously thought she'd just fall in line once he got her home. That it would be easy. Maggie was normally quiet and laid back and easygoing. Compliant.

He'd expected her to be compliant.

He should have known better. Clint was going to have to work for what he wanted. Needed.

He needed that woman like he needed breath.

That was something else he'd figured out along the way during those dark five months.

She'd spent most of the day before helping get Violet resettled into the ranch house, buying baby supplies online—and avoiding Clint whenever possible.

He knew what she was up to.

The sound of baby babbling came down the hall, along with the light footfalls of the woman he wanted.

Clint tensed.

Maggie was dressed in a pretty flower-printed maternity top and jeans. Her red-gold hair was pulled up in the ponytail he was used to seeing. But she wore makeup. Actual makeup. And she carried her bag. Panic threatened.

She only wore makeup when she was leaving the house. She could have changed her mind about staying. There was nothing he could do to stop her. "Where are you going?"

He had at least kept the panic out of his tone.

"I made an appointment at Dr. Kedrik's office today. She had a last minute cancellation. She's going to be my obstetrician." She shifted Violet to her left side awkwardly. His daughter babbled something incomprehensible and grinned. "If you're busy, Marin has offered to babysit Violet during my appointment. I haven't seen her yet since I got back, and we're going to do lunch before my appointment."

"Can I go with you?" The words slipped out before he thought them through. "To the appointment, I mean?"

Maggie hesitated.

"It's just an initial consult. To catch the doctor up on what has happened so far—and for me to see if I like her. We're not doing an exam today. Not really. No ultrasound, or anything like that."

He nodded. "Do you want me to go with you?"

She shook her head. "Not really. I'm used to going in alone. When there are ultrasounds scheduled, if they are, you're more than welcome to come. But...it's less awkward if I do it alone."

Because she had distanced herself from him since the kiss. It stung. But no less than what he'd expected.

Clint had stayed awake far into the night for the last two nights. Planning. Strategizing. It had been too soon to kiss her last night, but he couldn't regret it.

He wanted to kiss the woman in front of him again. And again.

He had never set out to convince a woman to love him before. It had just sort of happened for him with Miranda and with Amy. They'd grown together over time.

Well, he and Amy had. They'd been neighbors for

years. With Miranda, he would almost swear that woman had planned it—then seduced him.

With Amy and Miranda, it had just been simple. Easy.

It wasn't like that with Maggie. Far from it.

Maggie meant *fire*.

He'd burned for Maggie since the night he'd stumbled into her coming out of the bathroom after she'd worked for him about a month. She'd been in nothing more seductive than a tank top and flannel pants. That was all it had taken.

He must have seen her in the same thing four dozen times by then—but they'd bumped right against each other. Chest to chest. He'd wrapped his hands around the soft skin of her arms and just…held her. Wondered what she'd do if he leaned down and kissed her. If he pulled her close and just tasted the smile that seemed to always be on her lips.

Violet had only been four months old at the time.

Amy had been dead four months, and he'd been lusting after another woman.

He'd been so damned angry with himself, telling himself he'd acted as if Amy hadn't existed at all.

Clint had kept things professional between them after she'd first hired on, for that first month or so.

That was as long as he'd lasted. Everything she'd done had damned well fascinated him from that night forward. Every time she'd brushed against him in the hall or in the kitchen, his body would go on full alert. Every time he'd smell her damned shampoo in the only working bathroom in the house he'd turn into a horny idiot.

When she'd laugh at something his daughter had done, he'd want to scoop her into his arms and just taste that laughter because she made him feel again.

He'd wanted to *feel* so damned much after burying Amy.

He had adored how Maggie had cuddled Violet close, obvious love for his daughter in her eyes. Violet had been three months when Maggie first started working for him.

The way Maggie had fussed over Clint when he'd had a difficult day at work had made him feel like he mattered to someone again. That…he had needed that. He wasn't ashamed to admit it.

She had been soft perfection, right there in his world. Right there in front of him. Just down the hall. Tempting him.

Everything he had ever wanted.

She had terrified him. He'd known he wasn't good enough. He'd kept his distance for almost four long months.

But one night he'd been a fool…he'd been stupid.

Amy had always joked that she'd probably never see thirty. Said she was too reckless and crazy and too tragic of a figure—she'd always been melodramatic—to live a staid perfect small-town life.

She hadn't been joking when she'd been diagnosed. Far from it.

Amy had been terrified.

She'd made him promise to live the kind of life she wouldn't have. For her. For their daughter.

Amy had made him promise to keep on living without her. He hadn't known how.

That night he had been hurting. Grieving. Because Amy *hadn't* lived to see her thirtieth birthday.

Maggie had been there that night instead.

Maggie had been so damned alive in front of him. While Clint hadn't felt alive in eight months. Longer. He hadn't felt alive since the moment Amy had been diagnosed and they'd known she wouldn't survive to see their daughter. At the end...at the end they'd kept her alive on life support just for Violet's sake. To give *Violet* more of a chance at life.

He would never forget how that had felt.

"I...ok." Hell, he'd probably go into the doctor's office with Maggie and make a total fool of himself. Demanding answers to questions he couldn't even articulate yet. "Just...you're ok? Healthy? Nothing is going to happen to you?"

"I'm fine. This pregnancy is no riskier than any other pregnancy. Everything is going as it should. I promise."

He just nodded.

He knew the truth—the fear would never fully go away. Not until the baby was born and Maggie was fully recovered. Until he *knew* she would be safe. "That's good. Can...you text or call when you get there? When you're on your way home? I have some things to go over with the manager at Jay's ranch this afternoon. I can take Violet with me..."

"Have you considered doing the interviews for my replacement?" She looked at him directly. "For when I leave?"

Clint's blood ran cold. "I haven't thought about it."

Because if he had his way she was never leaving. But... she wouldn't want to be responsible for cleaning up after him now. Not anymore. She'd made it clear she wasn't his housekeeper any longer.

He had to respect that. Maggie wanted her career, too. That was going to have to be something he worked around. Respected. She deserved to have her own dreams, too.

He was never going to stand in the way of that.

But he wasn't going to lose her either.

"You probably should. We...you'll need time to train her before I leave. Need time for Violet to adjust."

She was so damned determine to leave. "You're just going to run. To not even try, aren't you?"

"I don't see it as running. I stuck for two months after that night. If you had truly wanted to change your mind, you would have long before you found out I was pregnant. We both know it's some archaic code of honor making you do this now, say you want more than what you insisted you ever could months ago. What am I supposed to think about that?"

Clint didn't have an answer for that. He just shook his head. He didn't have the words. He wasn't good at the words. "That maybe almost losing you and Violet made it damned clear where I stood. And what I really want. I can't lose you, Maggie. I won't."

"You never really had me. I was right here in front of you for two months after that night. Actually, it was eight weeks, and three days. You couldn't run away fast enough. Now, with hindsight, I'm glad we didn't do anything stupid. Anything *else* stupid, anyway. I will *never* regret that night. How can I? I love the baby so much. But if we had...if what had happened that day hadn't...I'm still figuring that out." She put Violet in her high chair and then turned. "Find another housekeeper, Clint. I'm not doing it any longer. I'm staying long enough to be certain Violet will be ok, and then I'm gone."

With that, and a kiss on Violet's blond head, she just... left. Walked out of the kitchen, greeted the dog on the porch, and kept going until she got to the small SUV waiting that he recognized as belonging to Miranda's younger sister.

Clint stood on his porch next to his big yellow dog and watched her ride away.

He didn't know what he was going to do now.

## 12

JASPER STEPPED INTO THE DINER, LOOKING FOR HIS FAVORITE Talley girl immediately. He was feeling good about things now, for the first time in months.

And he'd wanted to see *her* tonight before he went home to bed—where she'd probably star in his dreams again.

Marin did most every night, after all.

She was nowhere to be seen.

Maybe, when this was over, he'd ask Marin to dinner anywhere but the diner. Just as friends, of course. To begin with.

But one night wouldn't hurt. To celebrate ending that horrible chapter of his life. Just him and a beautiful woman, for one night.

Jasper wanted a few hours of Marin's attention just on him.

He was far too old for her, of course, but what would a harmless dinner hurt?

Marin's younger sister was the hostess today. He had always found her a sweet girl when their paths had crossed. She was nothing like her older sister; the confidence that characterized his Marin was just not there in the girl. He'd heard somewhere she had autism, but hadn't asked anything more.

Details of her life weren't a part of his business, after all.

He studied Meyra quietly while he waited for her to finish seating the couple in front of him. She looked more like her father than she did her mother, though the tall thin build was her mother all over again.

The quiet grace, as well. He'd always found that attractive when their paths crossed.

She shared that with her older sister. There was an even older sister somewhere in St. Louis, he believed. He knew of her, but hadn't interacted with her much in the last ten years or so. A redhead, as well, he thought.

Marin had a handful of cousins spread throughout the diner that he could see. Most of them were blond. Something they had gotten from their grandmother. Beautiful family of women.

He pondered them a while, wondering why neither of his sons had ever brought home a Talley girl. As far as he knew, Calloway and Cadell hadn't even dated a Talley. He didn't understand it. Unless it was the familiarity of it all. His kids had known the Talleys their entire lives.

As if he'd conjured him out of thin air, Cal walked into the diner at that exact moment. Jasper studied his oldest, a rush of pride filling him.

His boy was tall and strong and a damned fine businessman.

Cal had taken over his grandfather's ranch four miles south of Masterson and turned it into a damned fine business. Then he'd gotten his real estate license and gone on to build his own empire with a subdivision of all things.

His boy had done well for himself. As had his brother. Cadell was the best attorney in the county, handling just about everything. Of course, he was starting to run himself ragged at times. Boy needed to hire himself an assistant before he worked himself into a heart attack.

Jasper was going to have to say something to him again. Or see about hiring a competent assistant for Cadell himself. Surely someone in the county would work out. Or maybe the boys just needed women of their own. Women to make them see they couldn't work themselves to death like this.

He would like grandchildren someday soon, after all. Five kids, and not a one of them had married yet. A crying shame.

"Dad! Hey, great to see you."

"Just in time to buy your old man lunch."

"I can do that, but first…" The boy looked around. His eyes landed on the girl and lit. "I came to see Meyra. She owes me a date."

Well. Apparently, one of his son's wasn't blind, after all.

Jasper smiled at the girl as her older sister came out of the kitchen behind her. *Marin.*

His own heart started thudding.

There she was. Now his day had gotten a whole lot brighter. He was going to put Clive Gunderson out of his mind for the rest of his life now. And just enjoy the rest of his night.

# 13

---

Brandt Barratt, one of *the* Texas Barratts, studied the small Wyoming town with a critical eye. It was about like he'd expected. A typical western town, complete with cowboys and cowgirls everywhere he turned. Horse trailers were a dime a dozen on the small highway leading through the Main Street. He slowed near the vet's place, taking in a tall, dark-haired man and a small, beautiful redhead unloading a horse trailer.

The woman looked a bit like the woman Brandt was there to find.

He waved. The couple waved back.

He smiled at how simple life seemed here at first glance.

The main street was littered with the small mom-and-pop shops generic to every small town he'd ever been in.

He loved it.

His hotel was visible in the distance. The Talley Inn.

He'd heard all about Masterson, Wyoming. Good and bad.

It had piqued his interest. When a possible development in the area had been mentioned, he'd paid closer attention than he normally would have. He was a Barratt —Barratts meant Texas, not Wyoming.

Finley Creek and Barrattville, to be exact.

That's where all of his family had built their own legacies.

Brandt wanted more than Finley Creek, though. And wanted more than being a Barratt of Barratt County. He texted his twin sister Powell that he'd arrived. She was waiting for him to check in with an actual phone call, but Brandt wasn't stupid.

The last thing he wanted to do right now was listen to Powell as she went on about how crazy his idea was going to be. She had her own empire to build—and she was leaving him and the rest of their cousins in her dust— except for Houghton—and should understand why he wanted to do what he was planning.

Houghton was a tech billionaire who had only built up the wealth he had inherited from his father—who had built on his own inheritance. Houghton would always be the unicorn among their herd.

Brandt had a myriad of cousins and two brothers—and he was tired of living in their shadows. It was time to make his own way now.

Masterson was a good place to start.

He had one more message to send, and he did it quickly.

Maggie was his real reason for hopping a plane early this morning to Wyoming, so spur of the moment.

He'd learned about Masterson from a woman he'd fallen hard for—as a friend. Maggie Tyler understood him. On an intrinsic level. He wanted to let her know he was around. She had been going through a hard time over the last year or so. It was how they had met in the first place.

If it hadn't been for Maggie, he never would have considered Masterson. But this way, he got to build his own empire—and could check on Maggie in the process.

She was the closest friend he'd had in a long, long time —since he'd lost his childhood best friend in an auto accident ten years ago.

He would always love Maggie for that.

She replied back within minutes.

Giving him directions to the diner—where she was going to meet him for lunch. Introduce him to the locals, apparently. Her friends.

Brandt smiled, taking a deep breath of the cool Wyoming air. It felt different here, far different from his native north Texas.

He could get used to air like this.

He drove the rental SUV through the town, taking note of where the important buildings were.

He had a plan.

He needed ways to implement it.

The Masterson Diner was his first stop. When he walked in, he had to smile. It reminded him of a favorite spot in Texas. Mamaw's Place had the same dark-brown booth seats, and similar décor.

Maggie wasn't hard to spot. She and another woman, a beautiful blonde worth a second or third look, occupied a front booth. Brandt waved a brown-haired hostess away. He knew exactly where he was going.

Maggie saw him coming and shot him a beautiful smile. She slid out of the booth seat awkwardly. "Brandt!"

He wrapped his arms around her as best he could and

hugged her. "I think you have gotten more beautiful since I last saw you."

"Hardly. I've gotten bigger—in the handful of days since I've last seen you. Rounder, for sure." One hand dropped to her very obvious baby belly, ruefully. He found pregnant Maggie fascinating.

In a purely platonic, hypothetical way. Barratts were family men, after all.

"Every bit of you is beautiful." Brandt had been worried. Something about her made him care about her. It was a simple as that.

Plus, Powell had practically adopted Maggie as their little sister.

Brandt was terrified of his twin. It was best to go along with what Powell wanted.

Or so he let her think. "You doing ok? Mel told me about you leaving practically in a heartbeat. How's Rancher-cop Boy?"

Maggie had shared just about every detail of what had happened between her and some cowboy with him months ago. Brandt had his opinions.

But until he met this Clint in person, Brandt was keeping them to himself.

He wasn't stupid. Maggie had it bad for that cowboy. Brandt knew how to behave.

"I'm ok. Resolved. Brandt, I want you to meet a close friend of mine. Marin Talley. Her family owns the diner and the inn. Her sister Miranda is the woman who smuggled me and Violet to Mel in the first place."

He took a long look. Beautiful, in an ethereal way, with blond hair barely touched by gold red, if you looked close enough. The eyes were huge and blue and dominated her classically gorgeous face.

The woman held a thin hand out to him. He shook it and let it go. Fast.

"Yes. You will do, Mr. Barratt. Welcome to Masterson County. You'll find exactly what you're looking for here."

He shot her a look of surprise, then glanced at Maggie. "Excuse me?"

"Don't mind Marin. She reads auras."

"Yours is a beautiful jade, Mr. Barratt. It will match well... with who you will find here." The blonde stood, a mysterious smile on her lips. One that shouted happiness. What a strange duck, his grandmother would have said. "Maggie, sweetie, I'm going to tell you again. Stay right where you're at. It will benefit you all the most. Mr. Barratt, I'm going to head to the kitchen. Check on something with my baby sister. Welcome, and we'll have your room ready when you get to the inn."

With that, the odd blond walked away.

Leaving him looking at Maggie with utter confusion filling him. "What was that about? Auras?"

"I don't get it either, but she's an excellent judge of character and she seems to know who will...meld...as she calls it. A word of advice—if Marin ever tells you to duck, hit the ground, fast. She's never wrong. It's rather annoying, really."

"I see," Brandt said, watching the woman as she stopped to say hello to an older man with gilded blond hair and an expensive suit. She disappeared into the kitchen.

"So...why are you really here?" she asked as a woman called out from the kitchen.

The blonde reappeared, a younger brunette with hair just touched with red at her side. She was redheaded, but didn't resemble Maggie in the least. He'd gotten the impression just about every redhead in her county was a cousin or something. "Relative?"

"Not really. A few distant branches off the tree. That's Meyra, Marin's younger sister. She's very shy and quiet, so be nice."

"I see." Brandt studied the girl carefully. Beautiful, in that wholesome cowgirl kind of way. Her cheeks were milk pale. The eyes, were huge and innocent. So damned innocent the sweetness radiated from her. The exact opposite kind of woman he routinely engaged with.

That was one reason he was so fascinated by Maggie at times. She was real.

As real as his cousin Houghton's wife, Mel, his cousin Clay's wife, Bailey, and his cousin Turner's wife, Annie, now that they were around all the time. They were real, kind, snarky, intelligent, and fascinating. He envied his cousins a great deal. That didn't mean he was ready for a woman like them of his own. Not like Mel had been hinting. Said a woman would settle the restlessness in his soul, or something like that.

Mel was a real romantic at heart.

She'd tried to set him up with Maggie at least three times in the last five months. While he adored Maggie—he wanted nothing more than friendship.

Maggie felt the same. They'd had a lot of fun yanking Mel's chain, though, during those five months.

Brandt look at the blonde and her sister again; the redhead in the apron with the big green eyes and the hair in two thin braids...was gorgeous. Definitely worth a second or third look, too.

Too bad he wasn't in Masterson County looking for romance. Not that he would ever look in that direction—a woman like her shouted commitment. That wasn't Brandt's thing.

Yet.

It was in the plans, just several years down the road.

He was there to build an empire. Something his future family would be proud of. It was time he got started. "I'm looking for ranches to buy. Every single one that's out there and for sale that meets my standards; they're going to be mine."

Maggie gave a breathless squeal that had attention shifting their way for a moment. She practically clapped her hands. "You're really doing it? The *plan*?"

He and Maggie were both planners, at heart. She was the one person who knew exactly what he planned, and what motivated him. When he'd learned her rancher-cop had come for her yesterday, he'd decided there was no time like the present to start going after his own future.

That would let him keep an eye on Maggie right now, too.

"Yes. It's time to get started. I can't let Powell keep being the overachiever." He had two older brothers and a twin sister who had already made names for themselves in Finley Creek. He wasn't exactly the family screwup, but he'd been working for ten years to build his property management and construction companies into what they were today. But in Texas, *his* name blended in with all the other Barratts of Texas.

He wanted to see what he could make on his own. To see what he could do, without his name paving the way.

Now it was time to branch out.

Branching out meant anywhere other than Texas.

Masterson seemed like a good place to start.

"I'm so glad you're here. Talk to Flo, Marin's grand-mother. She'll know every ranch up for sale right now."

"I'll do that. Now...truth...how is the cowboy treating you?"

A confused look went through the blue eyes he loved so much.

Yep. Brandt had suspected all along, even with what she'd told him—Maggie had it bad for her cowboy. Still.

Head over heels and hiding it from herself.

Brandt was going to have to do his best to make sure the cowboy deserved her.

Good thing he wasn't going anywhere for a while.

## 14

VIOLET WAS NOT HAPPY. CLINT KNEW IT WITH ONE LOOK. SHE wanted something that he couldn't give her. He knew exactly who she wanted. He wanted the exact same woman.

"Mag-mag!" The big eyes were wet, and the little mouth trembled, absolutely destroying Clint.

"Maggie will be back in a little bit, honey. But Daddy's here." He lifted his daughter and carried her to the rocker in the living room. He'd rocked her there a hundred times before. It took little time to get her to sleep. He considered putting her in her crib, or at least the playpen nearby, but he'd missed five months with his daughter. He wanted to hold her as much as he could now.

Violet was happy, healthy, and utterly beautiful. But she was a lot of work. Maggie had taken care of her so well while they'd been apart. It was obvious she loved Violet.

He wanted nothing more than for Maggie to see that he and Violet loved her, too.

Fear of losing Maggie had him staring out the window while his daughter slept on his shoulder. He had just shifted her to her playpen when someone knocked on the door. Clint answered before the knocking and the dog barking woke his baby.

Rex stood on his porch, dressed in casual clothes for once. Clint opened the door and waved the other man in. Rex would stop by occasionally. He was about the only man who would.

Rex stopped by the playpen and watched Violet sleeping for a moment. "She's gotten even prettier. Prettiest baby I've seen in a while."

"I know."

"Odd, since she looks just like you."

"No kidding." There were tiny hints of Amy, but not many. Grief hit him. The knowledge that she'd never gotten to see the baby she had loved so much would always hurt. Always. "What are you doing here?"

"We have a problem."

"*You* have a problem. I'm not touching anything law enforcement related with a ten-foot pole." He'd made himself a vow the day he'd finished that last case. He wanted nothing more to do with the seedier side of life. He was going to surround himself with the land and the mountains and the animals—and try to forget the animal that was humanity. "I'm a rancher now. And that's it. I have other, more important things to worry about now."

"I know. Where is Maggie, by the way?"

"Doctor and lunch with a friend of hers." Maggie was eager to jump back into the life she'd left before—with everyone but him. He suspected she was going to find ways to spend as little time at the ranch with him as possible during those damned two weeks of hers. Clint was going to have to find a way around that. "What do you need?"

"Someone has been digging around in Clive's old files. Some boxes have gone missing. And I can't seem to locate some evidence reports. I was wondering if you had copies." Rex sent him a level look. "I know you've copied everything that man touched when he was the sheriff. I want to make certain you're not accused of tampering with anything. There are a few people who are still pissed at what happened. And I want to compare what you have versus what I've found for inconsistencies."

"They'll have to get over it. I've got copies of everything from when he was sheriff of Masterson County before Joel Masterson." Clint shot a level look at the other man. Rex was a force of nature. A master manipulator. If he wanted something from Clint, he could just about damned well get it. "You are welcome to copies of everything I have. That's it."

"I'd appreciate your help."

"I still have about a dozen of his case files to go over. Then you are on your own. I...need to forget Clive and what he's done to screw with my life. Need to move forward with Maggie and the kids."

Someone else would have to clean up after Clive. Clint had turned over everything he thought was important—to Rex and to Joel Masterson. Two of the only cops out there he trusted. He'd also sent copies to Miranda. Just to be on the safe side. Dated, time-stamped, official copies of everything—to cover his own ass. She was keeping them in her home office for him. And he'd sent copies to her official FBI: PAVAD email. And paper copies to her home.

Just in case someone *lied*.

Whatever happened next with it was up to them. "I have more important things to focus on. Like the fact that the woman having my baby in less than two months wants absolutely nothing to do with me. I have less than two weeks to change her mind."

Rex swore. "How are you going to do that?"

"I don't have a clue. She's agreed to stay here for a few weeks. I'm going to do my best to show her I'm not such a loser, after all."

"Good luck with that. How can any man ever know what a woman wants, anyway?"

"I have no clue." The dog barked from the porch. He always stayed there, watching over his kingdom. He'd shown up as a half-grown pup four years ago and stayed. Amy hadn't had the heart to get rid of him. Neither had Clint.

Now he adored the idiot. So did Maggie.

The dog was barking his excited, happy bark. Clint checked the window as Marin's little SUV bulleted up the drive. That woman…she was a traffic cop's dream—speed, speed, and more speed.

"Maggie's back."

"Then I guess you'd better get started convincing her to stay, then."

"No kidding."

## 15

"THANKS FOR THE RIDE," MAGGIE SAID AGAIN AS MARIN drove like a demon over the potholes in Clint's half-mile-long driveway. He'd somehow found time to clear the last of the melting snow and ice off the drive, but that didn't help. The holes were deep—and sloshy. "But can you try to avoid the potholes? Every time you hit one, I have to pee even more."

"I'd slow down—but then you may go tinkle in my passenger seat." Marin shot her a wicked smile. This was a familiar argument. Marin was terrifying behind the wheel. She hadn't gotten any less terrifying behind the wheel in the five months Maggie was gone. "So what will it be?"

"Whatever it is, I need a bathroom soon. Baby is jumping around in there today." She instinctively looked for Clint's new truck, but it must have been in the barn. The place looked deserted. He must have taken Violet in the truck with him to clear the long drive, then put the truck in the barn to remove the plow.

It looked abandoned now.

Scary.

Maggie pushed aside the memories. She wasn't about to let herself be afraid of *Clint's house*. No more.

The dog greeted them when they arrived, with a soft *woof* and ridiculous snuggles for affection. Maggie didn't stop to pat him on the head. It wouldn't matter—the dog was fully in love with Marin, anyway.

When Marin was around, no one else existed.

Maggie had one objective in mind: the bathroom at the end of the hall between her bedroom and Clint's.

She barely even registered the sight of two far-too-handsome men in the living room watching every move she made.

————

CLINT AND REX STARED AT THE REDHEADED WHIRLWIND AS she booked it as fast as she could down the hallway. Clint knew what that most likely meant, and he smiled. "It's a long drive from town."

"No kidding," a smooth female voice said from his front doorway. Marin stepped in. She'd been in and out of his place a hundred times when Maggie was his house-keeper. She and a few of her cousins were close friends of Maggie's. They'd always brought life and laughter with them when they'd come for Maggie. "I wasn't certain we weren't going to have to pull off alongside the driveway. Hiya, boys, you're both looking rather…healthy…today."

Rex practically growled.

She turned to the other man in the room. "Commander Weatherby, I almost didn't recognize you without the undertaker suit." Her expression told them both what she thought about Rexford Weatherby. And it wasn't favorable.

Rex practically growled.

She could be just as contrary as her older sister when it came to needling a man. Not many people even attempted to needle Rex Weatherby.

No *nice to see you* for Rex, apparently. They'd met before, on the case where Maggie had been targeted. Rex and Marin hadn't exactly clicked back then. No surprise there, by the book Rex and free spirit Marin were as opposite as two people could be.

"Hello, Madam Zelda, you predict the future any today?" Rex mocked.

"Of course. I just knew to wear my shit-kicking boots today." She shot him a beautiful smile as she slipped out of her coat. Marin was a gorgeous woman—Clint had seen grown men stutter when she smiled. Rex just scowled, apparently immune. "Bend over, Commander. It's time to get *kicked*."

Rex almost growled again. Those two were going to tear each other apart someday. Clint had to admit it would be entertaining to watch. On the sidelines, far from the fireworks. With flak jacket on.

"Hey, don't wake my kid, you two. Marin, thanks for giving Maggie a ride today." Clint stepped between the two, to play peacemaker.

"Anytime. Maggie's ordered a delivery from the diner —we do that now, by the way—for dinner. So I'm staying. I'm here to play with my little god-niece when she wakes. And we're going to look at furniture ideas for the house Maggie plans."

"Rex and I have some paperwork to go through in my office. You think you can keep to your corner if I keep him to his?" Clint shot a look at the other man.

He was glowering, straight at Marin. She wore a

flowing skirt with a silk scarf tied around her waist today. There was a matching scrap of silk tied around one thin wrist that fluttered as she moved. The collar of her sweater was cut low, to hint at what was beneath.

She looked good. And she knew it.

Rex's dark jeans and sweatshirt did nothing to disguise what a dangerous asshole he was.

The two were polar opposites—who he didn't fully trust to behave themselves if he left them alone. Neither one of them had what exactly could be called filters.

"I think I'll be fine. Maggie needs me tonight. She's a bit unsettled." She shot Clint a mild look. "Your doing, I believe, big guy."

He didn't say anything. Maggie was heading back down the hall, and Violet was fussing from her playpen.

Maggie stepped over to the baby. "Hi, baby. Did you have fun with Daddy today?"

"Mag-mag! Up!"

Maggie bent over and scooped his daughter into her arms. She turned toward him and smiled. A beautiful, perfect smile. For him. For a while there he'd thought he'd never see that smile again.

"Hi. Did she have a good day?"

Clint just nodded, unable to speak.

His whole world was right there, looking directly at him.

Marin laughed.

"The man has it bad for you, Mag. I see real drool now. And not from Vi," Marin said. "Give her over. I've spent five months not getting cuddles. It's time you shared."

Maggie handed the baby to her friend. "Be careful. She's soaked."

Marin was already grabbing for a dry blanket and

diaper from the stack nearby. "I'll change her, and then we'll sit in the living room and make jokes about Clint and his little buddy here while we wait for Meyra to deliver dinner. And you can tell me more about that hot rich guy who followed you back from Finley Creek. I was practically drooling eating lunch with him today. Talk about a beautiful, beautiful man. We rarely see them that tall and broad shouldered around here. Those eyes, and those shoulders...seriously yummy."

"What?" Clint couldn't help himself. It just slipped out. "Who?"

"A friend from Finley Creek is temporarily moving to Masterson. He's going to be buying some of the local ranches to start some sort of agribusiness industry up here or something. I'm not clear on what he does. But he's excited. It could bring good things here. He texted me this morning to let me know he's in town. He joined us for lunch today. He and his twin sister were some of my closest friends in Texas. I'm glad Brandt's here."

Clint just stared like an idiot.

He'd just known there would be a bunch of rich assholes sniffing around her, down there. Clint just hadn't expected one to follow her back to Masterson. Not so soon.

Marin shot Clint a wicked look as she carried the baby down the hall toward the nursery for her diaper change. "Don't worry, big guy. He's not for Maggie—he'll marry a Talley before too much longer. Not me, though. But that's our little secret."

"Seriously?" Rex rumbled next to Clint. "Now she match-makes, too?"

Marin didn't hear him; she was already well down the hall. Maggie headed down the hall to put her bag in her room.

Clint turned to Rex. He couldn't explain Marin, but he also couldn't discount what he had seen through the years. "I know you think it's bunk, but she's right far more than she's wrong. Just don't do anything to antagonize her. She's one of Maggie's closest friends. And I don't need Maggie telling me—or you—to take a hike right now."

"Let's just get the paperwork. And just pretend that woman doesn't exist."

Clint barely heard him; he was still focused on the idea that Finley Creek had followed Maggie to Masterson County.

What would it take for someone from Texas to convince her that her life was down there now—instead of up here with him and Violet?

He couldn't lose her now. Not to mention, he didn't want his son growing up with only occasional visits between them. No.

She couldn't go back to Texas.

Clint feared that was exactly what was going to happen. Unless he found some way to stop her.

## 16

MAGGIE ENJOYED THE EVENING WITH MARIN—MOST OF Marin's snark was directed at Clint's closest friend. Marin got under Commander Weatherby's skin.

And Marin enjoyed that.

Meyra arrived around six, a passenger side full of delivery meals from the diner. She stared at Clint and the commander, as if she hadn't expected to see them both there. Meyra was exceptionally shy, and it wasn't just because of the mild autism. She always had been, even when they were in school together. "Hello. I have a delivery from the diner. Marin's supposed to be here—and pay for this."

"I'm here. Come in, Mey, I ordered extra—and I'll settle up the tab in the morning. I have enough extra for two grown men—and one baby sister—to eat as well," Marin said from the dining room. "I'm going to leave my car here for Maggie to use until her brothers bring hers over. She'll need it. Meyra can take me home."

Meyra was hesitant to join them, but she usually did what one of her older sisters or cousins told her. Marin was always arranging ways for Meyra to get out of the diner and interact with other people outside their safe little world at the diner and the inn. "I wondered why you ordered extra."

"Just a feeling I had that I would need it." She shot a pointed look at the commander. "I hope you like meatloaf. You look like a simple meat-and-potatoes kind of man. Nothing too exotic for you."

Maggie missed what was said next. Clint had come up behind her, one hot hand draping over her shoulder. "What did the doctor say?"

"We're both fine. I really liked her. She reminds me of Dr. Kaur in Finley Creek."

"You liked it down there in Texas, didn't you?"

She nodded. "Not at first. At first, I was terrified. I had never been away from home for more than a weekend until I moved in here with you. I have only been out of the state twice when Dusty and Marin made me go to Billings with them one weekend. To be clear across the country, with a baby, with people I didn't know—it was terrifying. Then Mel took me under her wing—I started to find people who understood me. It was better. It wasn't home, but it was better."

"I'm glad. I hated the idea that you were off alone somewhere, you and Violet, and I couldn't get to you. No matter how I tried. I had nightmares about that almost every damned night." His arm slipped around her shoulders so casually as they stood in the kitchen and watched the three people in his dining room arranging the containers of takeout. This was the most people his place had had probably in a long while. It felt good; if he would take a chance, and let people in, he could have the support system he'd told her once he envied her.

She was a Tyler. She had family everywhere she turned. She'd always known that.

Clint had no one. Just Rex Weatherby and Marin's older sister, Miranda.

"Mags, I got the baby some mashed potatoes and peas, and chicken bites. I had Dixie make them plain," Marin said, moving around Rex like the other man didn't even exist.

"Thanks." Maggie didn't want to move away from where Clint held her. It felt good.

It felt right.

But she knew it was just a lie.

She deliberately stepped away. Before she curled up against his hard, perfect chest and just let him keep holding her forever.

## 17

CLINT FELT BEREFT THE INSTANT SHE MOVED. THE WOMAN just felt right when she was next to him. Those two months after they'd slept together had been the dumbest of his life.

He should have carried her off to a preacher first thing that next morning. The way a man would one hundred years ago. Just scooped her up and made her a promise that would last a lifetime.

Then spent their days building the life between them that she deserved. Only his cowardice had stopped that from happening.

Then again, if Maggie hadn't been avoiding him that day—she would have been right there in the front room of his house, possibly waiting for him, as he'd headed out there on his lunch break.

To check on her and the baby.

They would have been right in the path of the bullets. Fourteen. There had been twelve rounds shot into the front of his home. They'd gone through the front exterior wall and lodged in the living room drywall.

Two additional rounds had struck the nearest barn, probably from a final couple of wild shots.

Maggie and Violet wouldn't have stood a chance if they'd been in the house. Those first twelve bullets would have destroyed them.

The only reason they'd survived had been because Maggie had thought the shooter was *Clint*, and she'd wanted to avoid him. She'd slipped out the back door to take Violet to the barn nearby to see the horses.

Two bullets had struck that barn. One had caused a wooden beam to splinter. Shards of that wood had struck Maggie.

It had been that close.

He could have lost them both.

"Dinner is served," Marin said. "Come on, Mag, you barely ate anything at lunch."

A guilty look went over Maggie's face. "That's because I had oatmeal-cranberry cookies in my room this morning."

"Good one," Marin said.

Violet giggled from her high chair. She was hungry; her little mouth made smacking sounds and she babbled.

It seemed so normal. The two of them sitting down to eat with their friends and family around them.

Clint wanted that. He wanted a family, friends, a *life*.

Something different than the dark nightmare he'd grown up in. He wanted *light* for his children.

Both of them.

And any others that came along.

First, he had to convince the woman he wanted to have at his side that he wasn't the lost cause she thought he was.

He deliberately took the chair next to Maggie. Marin's sister settled down next to Maggie's other side.

Leaving the open chair next to Marin as all that was available for Rex. Clint smirked.

The guy couldn't escape—not without the paperwork he'd come for or without looking rude to the woman who had bought him dinner. Rex's mother had been a stickler for manners for her four sons. Rex knew how to behave. If he chose to.

Clint was enjoying seeing how Rex handled her. He hadn't forgotten Rex handcuffing him to a damned rail in the police precinct five months ago when Maggie had first disappeared with his baby.

To keep Clint from killing the man responsible.

Marin was exactly what Rex deserved.

If nothing else, Maggie was laughing with her friends. That was what mattered, after all.

Maggie was happy.

Clint didn't really want anything more than that.

---

## 18

CLIVE GUNDERSON'S STUPIDITY WAS GOING TO COST JASPER now. The other man had had his own secrets, too. Apparently, those secrets had erupted to destroy him.

Now Jasper had to clean up the mess. He hadn't stopped sweating since he'd gotten the latest message.

A secret was only a secret if one person knew it. He believed that even more than he had before. Now he had to clean up that mess—before it destroyed everything he'd worked for. His children...

He was a man in the public eye. He had done good things for the county. He would continue to do good things for the district. For the state.

Perhaps he'd one day step into the gubernatorial seat. Wyoming deserved a strong leader, one who cared about *families* more than business.

But first, he had to clean up the other men's messes.

He had done good things for his family, bringing them from a run-down two-bedroom bungalow in the worst part of Masterson when his oldest was a baby to the three-story home that was now far too quiet.

He had three daughters and two sons who were making their way in the world. Beautiful daughters and strong sons. Confident children he was so proud of he could burst. They were the best of him.

This...could destroy their worlds.

Jasper would do anything to keep that from happening.

That meant cleaning up this mess before it spilled over onto Jasper any more than it already had.

He was *so close* to having the answers he was looking for.

Jasper would clean this up, protect his children's well-being, and his own future.

Then he would move on.

It was going to be as simple as it sounded.

Jasper was almost there. Had almost found the person responsible.

An investigation of this scale was something he had done before. He could do this. It should be simple textbook.

He'd gotten his start as a stupid, wet-behind-the-ears sheriff's deputy when he'd been all of twenty-four years old. He'd worked for the Masterson County sheriff's department, for his second-cousin Clive, while taking night classes to get his law degree.

He'd spent six years being Clive's whipping boy.

Earning his stripes.

It had taken him almost all those six years to take the classes he needed and to pass the bar. Night school for law took a damned long time, especially when a man had a family to support and no real financial aid, and the college was more than four hours away. He'd drive up, take a few classes, then drive back in time to put in another eight to ten hours working for Clive.

It had been tough—on him, on his older kids, and on Jody. Maybe too hard. He'd always wondered if the strain of his education had contributed to her not being in the greatest of health after little Clancy had been born. Both she and the baby had taken a while to bounce back after Clancy's birth.

Jasper had managed. Triumphed. He'd wanted to do good things for his town. For his family.

A law degree had helped him support five children much better than a small-town deputy's salary ever could have. His children had had what they needed.

He'd do it all over again if he had to.

He couldn't let that all collapse now because night-mares had eaten away at Clive's sanity.

He had searched Clive's place before. Half-heartedly. But that was before someone had sent him that damned email two months ago—they knew what he'd done.

What he had watched happen, rather.

Jasper had never touched the people involved. He'd just been there *after*. For some, that was enough.

It would ruin his career. Embarrass his children. Bring them trouble none of them needed.

The blackmailer—there was no other real word for the person doing this—had mentioned details Jasper never wanted getting out.

They knew exactly how involved he'd been with Arthur Talley and his idiotic get-rich property scheme. And they knew about the *woman* who had blown the whistle all those years ago.

Jasper had thought he'd covered all his tracks. Years ago. He'd been tense for a year or two when Arthur had first hauled ass out of the county, taking his wife with him.

Hell, Arthur had even left his four kids behind he'd left so quickly.

Not Jasper. He'd stayed. Had a tightness in his gut for years, until enough time had passed that Arthur's little games had been almost forgotten. Until what had happened *after* was just a distant memory.

He would never have left his kids like that. Not like that. They'd needed him.

Arthur's kids had been lucky their grandmother was there to take them all four in. Flo Talley was a remarkable woman he'd thought of as a friend for years. He'd been friends with Flo's daughter, Jessica Lynn, as well.

Jasper and Arthur hadn't been friends. They hadn't even been colleagues.

Jasper had just seen something he shouldn't have.

It had almost destroyed Jasper's life. That was one of the worst years of his life—it had almost cost him everything he'd worked for and everyone he'd loved.

Jody had almost left him during that year, too. He'd been so tense and angry he had taken it out on her when he never should have.

Had they not had five children, she probably would have left him.

He would never forget that.

It was only after the five-year mark, and no sign that Clive was the least bit interested in digging into Arthur Talley, that Jasper had settled some.

Gotten on with his life. He had three daughters and two sons to raise, after all. By then he'd also had a very ill wife that he had greatly loved, that he lost a bit more every day.

Unlike Arthur, Jasper hadn't abandoned his five children like a coward.

He'd stayed and made damned sure he was a better parent after that. It was just a matter of time before his own sins rose to haunt him.

Someone knew. Someone was out there, ready to destroy everything he had ever worked for.

Jasper couldn't let that happen.

That proof of what he'd done had to be in Clive's old files. Somewhere.

Sources at the WHP had told him months ago that Clint had taken everything Clive had ever worked on, made copies, and left them at the WHP.

Clint had followed procedure.

Jasper hadn't. He'd removed all signs of his own involvement from the computer records years ago.

Except…the blackmailer had told him he'd missed something. There were more copies out there.

Clive had kept them for years.

Clint Gunderson had them now. Jasper just prayed the younger man didn't know it.

All of Clive's things were somewhere on his son's property. *Properties.* Clint had more than one, though they connected in a few places.

Jasper just had to find what he was looking for.

Hell, he couldn't seem to even get past the younger Gunderson's dog.

Jasper didn't want to hurt the goofy yellow lunkhead. He'd always had a thing for big stupid dogs. The last thing he wanted to do was betray the fact that he'd been inside Clint Gunderson's ranch.

He just wanted to get inside, find what he needed to

find, and live the rest of his life without this hanging over his head.

Without getting his ass caught in the process.

Somehow.

Jasper searched the immediate area. This was a risk, one he wasn't so certain he should be taking right now.

No one seemed to be around. That was good.

Jasper stepped onto the back porch. Reached for the door handle.

That was when Jasper saw the little SUV parked at an angle by the back porch. He had missed it; how could he have missed her, even in the dim light of twilight?

It was such a bright blue color, it stood out.

*Marin*. Sweat slicked his palms immediately, soaking into the black gloves Cloe had given him for Christmas.

That was Marin's car.

Damn it. He had been stupid. He should have checked the front of the house instead of assuming Gunderson was still out.

He wasn't alone, after all.

THEY WERE HALFWAY THROUGH THE DINNER WHEN AN ALARM sounded. Violet immediately started wailing. Rex and Clint both jumped from their seats. Clint swung the baby toward Maggie. She took the baby and held her close as she stood. "Stay inside."

Maggie gasped when Rex pulled a handgun from somewhere. She hadn't realized he'd been armed. Clint immediately silenced the alarm, then opened the gun cabinet in the corner. When he pulled out a rifle and loaded it before her very eyes, Maggie started shaking.

Marin's arms went around her.

Maggie's tightened on the baby. "What's happening?"

"Security system around the perimeter of the house. I didn't tell you because I didn't want you worried. And it was just as a precaution."

"It's probably a deer or the dog wandered too close to the back porch," Rex said. "But just in case"—he shot a significant look at Clint that Maggie didn't miss—"you three and the baby—stay inside. Stay away from the windows. Lock the doors behind us. All of the doors."

"Already done," Marin said quietly. "I locked the back door after I changed the baby earlier."

"Sure you did."

"Check for yourself if you don't believe me," Marin said with a frightened look at the door in question.

"No time. Keep yourselves inside."

"Be...careful...out there, Commander."

He grunted in response.

"Don't you think this is overreacting?" Maggie asked. There was more going on; she just knew it. Clint was hiding something from her. Her hands tightened on Violet. "Why would someone be out there now?"

"They shouldn't," Clint said bluntly. "Probably aren't. But I pissed off a lot of people in my time as a cop. I will never sit back and let a threat come toward my family again. I have an outer security system in place, but this one on the porches is new. I put it in last week. Haven't had time to figure out the kinks and adjust them. Kody might damned well be heavy enough to trip it."

"And I'm just a snarly bastard who's made a truck ton of enemies, honey," Rex added. He surprised Maggie by brushing a kiss over her forehead, then patting Violet on her back. "Who doesn't like my evening interrupted. It was most likely wildlife—security systems aren't fool-proof, especially new ones. You stay here with Madam Zelda and her sister, honey. I'll see to it that Clint is taken care of."

Then the two men were outside. Marin acted first—reaching out behind them and locking the door. "You two, take Violet into the hallway. Stay there. Just in case."

"What's out there?" She didn't believe in psychic visions or powers. Or even auras. But Marin did. And

Marin almost always seemed to know what she was talking about.

"Probably someone who will get what's coming to him eventually. A wolf in sheep's clothing, hiding who he really is." Marin stood in the only entrance to the hall—physically blocking Maggie, the baby, and her own little sister from the back door. "If someone comes through that door who shouldn't, you three go out the back window of the nursery. It's low enough to the ground for you, Mag. Keep going until you get to the far barn. I'm sure Clint and that buddy of his can find you there."

"And you?"

"I'll be bringing up the rear. Can't really run in these pretty shoes." Marin didn't seem worried. Not at all. Maggie wouldn't lie—that did help her relax. A little. "But it really won't be that necessary. Our heroes will be back in just a moment—angry and determined—but in one piece. Ready to devour the pies Grandma sent."

To put proof to Marin's words, the door pushed open. Rex came in first. Marin had shifted in front of Maggie. Maggie had to look around the taller woman's shoulder to see who it was. "What's happened? Where's Clint?"

"He's waiting for a deputy from Masterson, out on the porch."

"Why?" Maggie stepped around Marin. She didn't need her friend to protect her. Even almost eight months pregnant. "What was out there?"

"*Who,*" Rex said. "A prowler. Sped off in an old truck when we went outside. We both saw him."

"How do you know it wasn't someone coming to see Clint or Maggie that you frightened off?" Meyra asked quietly. Meyra had huddled next to the wall in the hallway, her arms around herself. "It could have been anyone."

"Someone just visiting would have said hello when Clint called out. Identified himself. But he's gone now, Meyra. I promise. You don't have to be afraid," Rex said as Clint came inside. "I'll see this is taken care."

There was such anger on Clint's face that Maggie's breath caught. Her arms tightened around Violet instinctively.

She hadn't forgotten what had happened five months ago. Not by a long shot. "I thought that case was over."

Even she heard the accusation in her words. Everyone paused to look at her. Maggie forced herself not to flip out. To breathe. She had dealt with that day, dealt with all of it. It was behind her. Five months of therapy at W4HAV—a women's charity Mel funded in Finley Creek—had made sure of that.

But back *here*…it was all rushing back. She should have expected that. Should have expected the memories to resurface.

It wasn't just the shooting—it was the two months of anxiety that had led up to it. She pulled in a deep breath as the baby kicked her again. She had to get her balance back. She was not going to freak out over this. She wasn't.

Maggie didn't freak over things. Ever. She never had, and she wasn't about to start now. She was a Tyler; she was tougher than that.

"It is. All of my cases are over. But Weatherby's aren't. He's here to get some of Clive's old cases. Someone's been screwing around in them. But other than that—I want no part of it. I'm finished with law enforcement, Maggie. I promise you that. I'm just a rancher now. Period."

## 20

CLINT SAW THE FEAR AND THE FURY IN TYLER BLUE EYES. HE stepped closer, wanting to touch her, just for a moment. He had made her a promise—he was going to keep that. "I'm done with law enforcement, sweetheart. You can count on that."

"I just…are we safe here?" Maggie held his daughter close, one feminine hand covering the little blond head as she soothed her. Violet was calm now, but her eyes were still wet. Clint would never get enough of looking at Maggie right now—especially when she held Violet.

His world was right there.

That someone had threatened them tonight burned him to his soul.

"As safe as I can make you."

"And it wasn't someone visiting, or lost, or from the census bureau or something? How do you know?" She rocked awkwardly until his daughter drifted off in her arms.

He just did. But he wouldn't lie. "In order to trip that particular alarm, he had to be screwing around near the back door. Been up on the back porch. If it hadn't been locked, he would have found his way in. The alarm had a delay that I need to fix."

He'd have come in the back door while they'd been eating.

Where Maggie was. Violet. Their friends. He looked at the three women; they wouldn't have posed much of a problem for a determined intruder. Especially if an intruder was armed.

"Marin locked it earlier."

Clint shot the older woman a look. She nodded. "I had a feeling it would be necessary."

Clint ignored Rex's snort of derision.

"Thanks."

It took another half an hour before an SUV with *Masterson County Sheriff's Department* emblazoned on the side pulled in. The sheriff himself stepped out.

Clint automatically tensed.

Things would never be that easy between him and the Masterson brothers. Not after what Clive and Jay had done to two of the brothers' wives. The sheriff, Joel Masterson, had nearly lost two sisters-in-law and his own brother because of Clint's family.

Neither man was ever going to be able to forget that.

"Gunderson? What's happened?"

"A prowler tripped the rear security alarm," Clint said. "We wanted it on record that we called it in."

"Anyone get a good look at the guy? We've had reports of petty burglaries in this area. Quick pawn items are being stolen and hocked. If one of you got a good look, that would go a long way."

Clint shook his head. "Too dark." He'd be doubling the number of security lights at the back of the house, first thing in the morning. Money wasn't as tight as it had been —not since he'd sold the two-story house in town Clive had signed over to Violet after his arrest. That money had gone to repairing the house they lived in—the rest had been put into a savings account for Violet, for when she was older.

He had boxes full of Clive's junk still to go through. He'd just dumped it all into the barn at one of the other ranch houses. He was going to have to make time to go through them for good. "Guy jumped into an older-model truck—full cab, extended bed, toolbox on the back. Dark red or orange in the security light a hundred feet up the driveway. But with the snow flurries, I couldn't see much more than that."

"Any idea who it was?" Joel asked, giving Maggie a quick one-armed hug.

Clint shook his head, resisting the urge to pull Maggie into his own arms, and away from her cousin by marriage. "Guy was hard to see. Had a hat on, low. Coat with the collar turned up. Wore gloves. Didn't carry himself like he was a young guy, but was reasonably fit."

"What in the hell was he looking for?" Joel asked.

"That's the million-dollar question, isn't it?" Rex finally holstered his weapon and grabbed his coat. Anger practically vibrated off him. "Guess we'll just have to answer it. But first…pie."

## 21

"DAD?" CLOE LEANED FORWARD, ACROSS THE TABLE. SHE loved the diner, and not just because she was good friends with one of the Talley girls. It was the food—she said it reminded her of her mother. Jody had always made a point of taking each of the children to eat dinner with her by themselves once a month. So they knew that even though they were one of five children, they were special and loved. It had taken him a few years to revive that tradition after he'd lost his wife. Now he was glad he had.

This girl of his was absolutely beautiful. Smart as a whip, too. A nurse…like her mother. Yes, Cloe was the most like Jody. A part of his wife lived on in each of his children. He would never truly lose her fully. Not with his children so much like her. "Yes, baby?"

"What's bothering you? I can tell something has been lately."

"Just some things at work. That's all. Nothing for you to worry about." Two days. He'd been a mess for two days since Clint Gunderson and Bob Weatherby's boy had almost caught him out there.

"You sure?"

"I'm sure. So...what's been happening lately?" he asked, anything to distract her. Cloe could be a bit tenacious when she was worried about something.

"Great, actually. I may be taking a supervisor position next month. If it comes available."

"Good. I'm proud of you, kiddo. In case I haven't said it lately."

"I know. Listen, why don't you come over to my place for dinner this weekend. I have a friend from work I'd like you to meet. She's a nice lady a few years younger than you. Her husband was killed in Afghanistan several years ago. She has three teenagers who are starting to drive her insane. I told her you might have some pointers."

His daughter, the perpetual matchmaker. Well...maybe it was time. "I'll do that. But no promises. I'm not interested in a long-term relationship with anyone just yet. I have a few things to take care of, first."

"Good. So...now..."—her expression turned serious—"the real reason I asked you here..."

"Oh?"

"Someone called the hospital for me today. I didn't recognize the voice—but they...the caller told me to ask you what you did to Janice Johnson twenty-two years ago. And if I knew where you'd helped bury her body. Dad? What's going on?"

Jasper swore. No. The bastard had gone too far. "That damned prank caller."

"So you know about this?"

"Janice Johnson moved to Billings seventeen years ago, honey. She had three kids, had just divorced, and never came back to Wyoming. She would call your mother occasionally. Someone has been prank calling and harassing my office for the past two months. Just being idiots, using a toy to distort their voice. I've reported it to the proper people. But he isn't the first prank caller or harasser I've dealt with in my position. It's rather par for the course. I'm just sorry you were brought into the middle of it. I'll take care of it."

He was good at deflection, at lies. Janice Johnson had moved to Billings seventeen years ago. But she wasn't the only Janice Johnson to have ever lived in this county. There had been Janice, the wife of Bill Johnson, before that. It had been her...

There was still worry in his daughter's eyes. Fear for him.

Well, Jasper was afraid, too. Because they had just stepped up the game between them. More than just the photos he'd been sent.

There was nothing he wouldn't do to protect his daughters.

Someone bringing Cloe into this...well, it had just changed everything.

Jasper was going hunting.

As soon as he dropped Cloe off at the hospital before her lunch hour ended. He had to—there was no other choice now.

## 22

AFTER CLINT AND VIOLET TOOK OFF IN HIS TRUCK TO HIT THE hardware store and run errands, Maggie spent a few minutes reevaluating her plans. She spoke with Mel for around an hour about what her work would look like now that she was in Masterson, spoke with Marin briefly about Clint, and spoke with her brother Chandler about meeting him and Martin in town sometime in the next few days to talk about the houses Martin was almost ready to rent out.

She winced.

Chandler—her most easygoing brother—hadn't been too happy to hear that she wasn't staying exactly where she was—like her brothers had all expected.

He'd demanded to know what Clint had done to chase her off and if the bastard—the father of her child, for Pete's sake—had done anything to hurt her. Wanted to know if Chandler—and probably the rest of them—needed to come get her immediately.

Chandler hadn't liked it when she'd told him it wasn't any of his business, but she just wasn't ready to stay tucked away on Clint's ranch washing his undershorts and warming his sheets. That what had happened between them had been a one-night stand with consequences. Consequences they were figuring out how to handle—together. That was it.

Her brothers always had flipped whenever Maggie spoke about sex.

Maggie needed to take control and stop being so ridiculous.

In everything.

She wasn't going to keep hiding herself *inside* the house, either.

It was time to claim her freedom back.

The ranch...she'd been back long enough and hadn't ventured out of the immediate yard surrounding the house, other than her trip to the doctor and the diner.

In the two days since the prowler, she hadn't stepped foot outside at all.

Because of fear.

Well, Joel Masterson had called. He'd caught a twenty-two-year-old guy from the south part of the county who'd driven an old red truck—and had stolen goods in the back. The kid had confessed to seven different burglaries.

They had the prowler now. She was safe.

Safe. She couldn't hide in the house forever.

She hadn't even gone to the barn where the horses waited. Clint had four horses. She'd loved every one of them.

The last time she'd seen those horses, she could have died. That had affected her more deeply than she realized.

Panic attacks when she thought about the barn weren't a good thing—and weren't realistic in a ranch town like Masterson.

Maggie hated feeling like a coward.

Well. It was time to stop being a coward. If she couldn't even face her fear of the barn, how could she face the rest of life?

Control—it was time she took control back. Along the way, she'd use the cool March air to get her stupid libido back in check. No more lusting after Clint Gunderson, even subconsciously.

How could she move forward with her plans when she was stuck in the past?

She couldn't.

Maggie grabbed Clint's spare jacket off the hook by the back door.

Horses first.

Clint later.

Her brothers...never.

It sounded like a plan.

---

## 23

Maggie followed the dog to the barn, carefully. It was still muddy and slushy and not all of the snow had melted yet. The last thing she needed was to fall.

Kody barked at her once, then took off up the hill after a hare. He loved to hunt—but as far as she knew, he was rather pathetic at it. She laughed at his antics.

She'd missed him, too. Missed life here in Masterson County.

It felt right to be home now. The doubts that had plagued her about returning to Masterson County when she'd been in Finley Creek were starting to fade away.

In one week, she would be moving to town. Building a life for herself and the baby. Maggie had spent a few hours that morning planning, anticipating what that would mean for her, for the baby, for Violet and Clint.

She hoped he'd let her have Violet sometimes. Hoped she'd be able to preserve her relationship with the little girl she loved so much.

Violet would be just fine where she was. She had already rebuilt the bond she'd had with her father before.

She adored Clint and felt safe with him. Maggie knew that to the bottom of her soul—Violet would be ok. It was time to focus on *her* plans and needs now.

Without Clint nearby to cloud her head. She couldn't let him keep unsettling her.

She was moving to town. It was time she got started on making that happen. T

here were houses available soon, plus, her cousin Nikki had a small apartment above the bookstore Maggie's aunt had once run. It was only eight hundred square feet, and a single bedroom, but it would work if nothing else was available right away. Or if her brothers proved uncoop-erative.

She just didn't like the idea of all of those stairs at Nikki's place.

Hopefully, there would be a house somewhere in town. Especially if her brothers turned…difficult. They could—if they thought they were doing what was *best* for her. Buttheads. They were all five total buttheads. No doubt about that.

Independence had been her dream, her goal, for at least the last three months, but now that she was back in Masterson, she wasn't sure that was what she wanted at all.

It seemed too easy here. Fitting her life to Clint's again.

Maybe because her life had just paused five months ago—when it had already been melded so tightly with his.

All the emotions and jumbled needs between them aside, she'd woke each morning all those months ago knowing she would see him.

Went to sleep every night going over what tiny bit of

contact they'd had during the day. Analyzing it for hidden meanings or anything like that.

Now, she realized that had been no way to live.

It hadn't been fair to either one of them.

She should have confronted him that day, the morning after.

Instead of letting this whatever it was between them build and build until it had almost destroyed them. Mel had pointed out once that if Maggie hadn't been avoiding Clint the day of the shooting, she and Violet might very well have been killed.

It was rather hard to forget that.

They'd had guardian angels watching over them that day. She could never regret that.

What had happened between her and Clint those two months had been for a reason.

It was time she accepted that.

Maybe those two months had been for her to grow in.

To grow up.

She'd always had her brothers to run to if the problem got to be too big. And she'd done just that time and time again, because if they could fix it, they could control it. She wouldn't have to risk doing something to lose them. Or be taken from them.

Maggie was far too risk averse when it boiled right down to it. She was a bona fide wimp.

She'd learned that that was a habit she'd developed and fell back on every time something happened.

She couldn't keep living like that.

She couldn't keep using the house in town as a way to avoid Clint now either.

There was stuff between them they had to work out.

Really work out. No holds barred. No more skirting the issues.

Maggie would take the first step.

Tonight, she and Clint would talk. Determine what they were going to do for real now. The least they could do was decide on a name for their baby. They hadn't even discussed it.

It was time.

Time she acknowledged the real way her future was headed.

Time to stop running.

Maggie was starting to suspect she'd deluded herself a bit in Texas. There, without him right in front of her, she'd convinced herself she hadn't loved Clint after all.

Well, now...she just wasn't so sure.

First, she was going to conquer the horse barn.

Then...she was going to conquer the man.

One way or another.

It was time Maggie stopped running from life.

Darby, Clint's horse, was a big, dark-brown guy with soulful eyes and a gentle way about him in spite of his massive size. Except when he was working the small herd of cattle Clint was growing.

Clint planned to diversify his properties someday. He wanted the cattle, specialty horses, and wanted to rent out the four houses on the other two ranches—there were two foreman's houses on Clint's properties, too. But they needed a lot of work and updating. Once the money was actually there to do it.

Four rental properties, plus income from the ranch. He'd told her all about how he intended to support Violet and the new baby on the way back from Texas. He'd been almost excited about his plans. About how different things were going to be going forward.

She knew what he'd been hinting.

He had been telling her in his own way that he had a plan for how to take care of her, too.

Darby whickered softly in greeting. She had been standing by Darby when the bullets had struck the barn. Struck the support beam right there.

It had splintered, sending shards shooting toward her and the horse. She'd instinctively wrapped herself around Violet to protect her, at the last moment, then fallen to the ground. Darby had almost stomped on the both of them that day.

Darby had taken the worst of the shrapnel.

But they were safe now. Even Darby. She spent a few moments talking to him, rubbing his nose lightly.

Crying.

She must have cried for fifteen minutes before the urge to go to the restroom again hit her.

She gave a watery laugh when the baby kicked her, reminding her that he was awake, and his afternoon gymnastics session was about to begin.

Clint's baby was definitely going to be very, very active. Hell on wheels—like his father and his five uncles.

Maggie headed inside, taking the shortcut to the rear of the house.

She had to figure out what it was she wanted, first. For real. Without the lies she'd told herself in Finley Creek.

Then…then she'd take that next step.

Whatever that step happened to be.

## 24

Jasper had one chance to get this right. The blackmailer, or whatever he wanted to call him, had gotten so close to Jasper's little Clancy—his baby—that Jasper could see the birthstone necklace Jody had given the girl for her birthday when Clancy had been fourteen in perfect detail. Right there.

The blackmailer had to have been within six feet of his baby girl to take that photo. Right there next to his baby girl.

Coupled with the call Cloe had reported, it told him one thing.

It was time Jasper acted. Did what he had to do.

This was more than just calling Cloe at the hospital. It was simple to figure out where Cloe worked—there was only the one hospital in Masterson County, after all, and a handful of medical offices and clinics. He could count them on one hand. But to be that close to one of his daughters...

Rage boiled.

And impotence.

His hands were tied. Jasper knew that.

He had to find the incriminating evidence. Destroy it.

That was the first step. The second was eliminating the blackmailer and anyone else who had seen that evidence so that they couldn't come back to haunt Jasper's children later.

He'd searched Clive's old place in town first, but there was a young woman living in that house who seemed to only leave for work and an occasional trip to the diner now and then.

Jasper had had to be a bit cleverer in getting into that place.

The young woman had moved into Clive's place from somewhere in the next county over. He'd met her before, a reserved social worker who truly thought she was helping the kids. A pretty woman around Claudia's age named Judith, with pale flawless skin, long dark hair, and big green eyes behind plastic-rimmed glasses.

She'd reminded him of Jody when he'd first met her. That sweet, loving air and quiet vulnerability about her was quite captivating. Brought back those memories.

Poor thing would be disillusioned along with the rest of the social workers eventually. Jasper had seen it happen before.

There had been nothing of Clive's left anywhere on the property. Jasper had gotten in and out of the woman's house just the night before while she was working late. She worked late far too often. It just wasn't safe for a woman out there in the more deserted parts of the county, not that late at night.

Anything could happen to her out there all alone.

Her bedroom had smelled feminine and sexy, and he'd

wanted to linger. To figure out that beautiful woman's secrets.

He found her almost as fascinating as he did Marin Talley. They were close to the same age, he thought. Beautiful, sexy—fascinating.

It had been a long while since he'd spent time surrounded by the scent of a beautiful woman. He'd never admit it to anyone, but he'd checked her underwear drawer. Searched it. Just to be thorough.

The social worker preferred serviceable cotton and lace over silk.

Pity. He had been imagining that under her staid business suits she always wore hid racy silk in bold, sexy colors. But her bedsheets had been silk. He'd run his hand over her pillow just to feel the soft against his skin. Imagined her in that bed at night.

Imagined himself next to her.

Nothing had been where Clive had said it would be. Damn him.

Either Clive was seriously confused, or he was jerking Jasper around.

The next logical place was this. Jasper had seen Clint and Bob Weatherby's oldest son cleaning out Clive's house himself that day right before the social worker had bought it.

Carrying old boxes he would bet his entire bank account on had contained case files. They'd loaded Weatherby's truck up, and then Clint's. And taken off.

If he was Clint, he'd want those old case files someplace close. To protect them, if needed. Yes. This made the most sense.

They had to be around Clint's place somewhere.

Maybe…maybe Jasper was starting to get a bit desperate. He'd have to be careful; not make stupid mistakes.

He had to slow himself down. Calm down. Before he did something that destroyed everything he had worked for.

He could have been caught so easily at Clive's old place. The entire town would have been screaming about how he'd been digging through that woman's underwear drawer. Stalking her or something. It would have scared the shit out of her.

Mayor Jasper Grady—nothing but a sick, sexual pervert.

He wasn't that. Not at all.

To his shame, he had almost sort of enjoyed the excitement of it. Watching Judith for two days, making certain she wouldn't be home when he was there.

It had reminded him of how he'd felt following Jody around town back when they first met.

How he'd wanted her. How she hadn't wanted him.

Jasper had eventually changed her mind.

He wasn't stupid. He knew how small towns operated. He'd seen it before—whenever something happened and someone in Masterson got arrested. The entire town would be talking about it. And the person's family would be affected.

He worried most for his Claudia if he was ever caught. She was just getting started in the WHP. She had a long way to go; she was only twenty-six and had been on the job less than two years. He'd wanted her to have a four-year degree first and had pushed for it.

She'd listened.

He was so proud of her, but she was a woman in law

enforcement, with the mayor for her father. She would always have to overcome that, as it was.

Add in him being arrested and going to prison for his part in a murder when she was just in elementary school—that could destroy her career before it even got started.

He couldn't do that to his girl, not as hard as she'd worked to get to where she was. He just couldn't.

He had a signal jammer. It hadn't been too hard to order it off the internet once he knew where to look. He'd had it for a while. A few weeks; since the blackmailer had gotten more insistent. He'd bought it the same time he'd bought the wig on the seat next to him.

Jasper couldn't be stupid. And he couldn't get caught.

No. That would destroy everything.

He jammed the signal, ensuring that whatever security system Clint had had in place the last time Jasper had been out there couldn't stop him this time. Everyone was using the Wi-Fi security systems these days, and why not? Jammers were illegal in the United States.

A random punk burglar wasn't going to be able to get their hands on one. Not that easily, not in Masterson. Jasper had had to call on some old…friends…to have one appearing on his doorstep.

Jasper slipped out of his truck and to the back door.

It was time.

He couldn't stay there forever. Clint was going to return eventually.

He'd passed the younger man on the main highway an hour ago, just before the man turned into the drive of the old Carson place.

If he was visiting Mrs. Carson, Clint would be a long while. That woman loved to talk.

Jasper tried the door handle. He had a set of lock picks,

and he had known how to use them for years. He might be a bit rusty, but he knew what he could do. They'd gotten him into the social worker's place, after all. Judith.

He'd have to make a point of catching her in the diner for lunch one day, pay for her meal. Silently make it up to her what he had done.

Get those green eyes turned in his direction for a little while.

Gunderson's back door was unlocked.

That surprised Jasper, considering what he knew about Clive's son. What he knew had happened out here. If it had been him, Jasper would have had the place locked up like a fortress.

Most people in Masterson County did leave their doors unlocked, but that a former WHP IA detective would? Well, that defied all logic.

He waited a moment, listening for the dog.

That dog could be a real problem.

He didn't want to have to hurt him, but Jasper would if it became necessary. Maybe.

Maybe he'd just slip the dog something to make him sleep a while, instead.

He waited for the barking to start.

Nothing. The dog hadn't heard him, then.

Jasper stepped inside.

## 25

She'd cried over what had happened, cried for dreams she'd made when she'd been stupid and foolish. Now... Maggie was going to put what had happened behind her.

Deal with Clint, the man he was now, and quit wrapping him up in the memories of what had happened before.

What had happened five and a half months ago had changed her. It had changed them both.

They were different people than they had been then. It was time they learned how to accept that about one another. Maybe it was time she learned to accept that about herself.

She didn't know if she loved him. But she had time to figure it out.

It might be the return to Masterson County throwing her off. The readjustment to the world she had just abruptly had to leave behind.

Maggie didn't know.

Seems like whenever Clint got near, everything she *did* know went straight out the window.

The man sure knew how to do two things—confuse her and send her hormones into overdrive.

Her boots crunched on the melting snow as she made her way to the side door off the kitchen.

She slipped her boots off in the mudroom and hit the powder room as quickly as she could. At least, the powder room was strategically placed for a busy ranch.

Small blessings.

She'd pull on some thick socks—thankfully, she could still reach her feet even with the baby—and settle herself down in the kitchen.

Maggie wanted cookies.

Clint had kept her mother's recipe box; it had been right where she'd left it. But the rest of the kitchen had been remodeled. Perfectly.

Maggie had been dying to check out the new, six-burner, double-oven gas stove for days. She loved to cook —and hadn't gotten much opportunity in the last six months. Not with Houghton's personal chefs on duty twenty-four hours a day.

Maggie wanted cookies. And she had Flo Talley's cranberry oatmeal cookie recipe right there.

She could have cookies waiting when Clint and Violet made it back from the store.

Just like she used to.

It was time to take Maggie back.

She could do it.

Maggie had just come out of the powder room and rounded the corner to the back hallway to grab warm socks when a sound had her stopping.

"Kody? Come here, baby. Is that you?" He had a doggy door on the utility room entrance that Clint left unlocked during the day when someone was around the ranch. He went in and out all day long. Usually loudly.

He was a bit of a klutz.

She looked up as she rounded the hall corner.

A man stood in the hallway.

And it definitely wasn't Clint.

## 26

SHE WASN'T SUPPOSED TO BE THERE.

Jasper bit back a curse when he rounded the corner of the hallway and came face to face with a heavily pregnant redheaded woman he recognized. She was no older than his Cloe.

The woman's gorgeous blue eyes widened. She took a few steps back.

Jasper resisted the urge to adjust the wig he wore and the fake beard he'd glued on as a precaution.

Hell, she was just a kid. He'd attended her graduation the same time as his middle girl's. Cloe and Maggie had been friends for years.

Her abdomen was swollen unmistakably, surprising him.

Never would he have guessed this girl would be wandering around Clint Gunderson's place in her bare feet, her stomach swollen with some man's baby.

She wasn't married. She had no business having some man's baby until she had a husband to help her.

Clint's. It had to be Clint Gunderson's. It made the most sense.

He wondered if Clive knew he was getting another grandchild soon.

He hadn't realized one of the other Tyler girls was pregnant. Well, two or three of Phil Tyler's girls were all pregnant, he thought. Hard to keep up with the Tylers sometimes. They all looked alike, were all around the same ages, and were just about everywhere a man turned—every last one of them redheaded and blue-eyed, as far as he knew.

He knew the girls a bit better than the boys.

This wasn't one of Phil's. He was certain of it.

Just how vulnerable she was to him hadn't been lost—on either one of them.

There was no way in hell he'd ever be able to hurt this young woman. He'd known her since she was just a girl herself.

It took him a moment to place her exactly, but she didn't have thick glasses—or a Masterson brother next to her. Had to be...

"I'm not here to hurt you, Maggie. I'm just looking for something."

"Wh-what?"

"I'm not going to hurt you." He tucked the gun back in the holster he carried. Then put his hands where she could see them. "I'm just here looking for something of Clive's. That's all."

"Then why didn't you come to the front door? Knock?" She was inching her way to the rear door of the kitchen. He wasn't about to let her run out into the cold and wet barefooted. "I-I'd have given it to you."

Jasper shook his head at her. He reached out and encircled her wrist. He'd have to do something with her, to buy himself time to get out of here. "I don't think it would have been that simple."

He tried to disguise his voice just in case she recognized him. It was possible. She'd spent the night in his damned house at least a dozen times he could remember off the top of his head.

The last thing he wanted to do was frighten one of his children's old playmates. He wasn't that kind of monster.

Maggie was just a girl. From the size of her baby belly, she was about to be a mother any day. She didn't need him scaring her like this.

"Clint is more than willing to get rid of anything to do with Clive. Take what you want and go."

She yanked against him. He pulled her closer with one hand. Those big blue eyes of hers—every Tyler he knew had eyes near that shade—were terrified.

Jasper was a father to three daughters. He had always hated it when they were afraid. Poor kid. This was the last thing this girl needed. She looked ready to deliver that baby at any time.

"It Gunderson's? The baby?"

She nodded, almost frantically.

Clint never should have left her alone. Anything could happen to a lone pregnant woman this far from town.

Clint should have known that by now.

Of course, Jasper had left Jody home by herself thousands of times. He wasn't a sexist. Far from it. But *this* pregnant?

No. Maggie should never have been left here alone like this.

"Hold still. I am not here to hurt anyone. But I need

you to cooperate. Don't make me get the gun out. I do know how to use it."

"What are you looking for? Maybe I can help you find it?" There was so much hope, so much fear in her words… it hurt him to hear it. Poor, sweet kid.

He always had loved pregnant women. There was something so…special…about them.

"It's a box and an old case file. A very specific one. From years ago. Probably in a plastic bin somewhere." Clint Gunderson and that Weatherby boy had been carrying clear plastic bins out of Clive's old place. Jasper was almost certain of it.

"Clint has case files in the rear office. And out in the small barn. Just behind the kitchen door. You are welcome to go in there and look. I think some of them may be his stepfather's."

"Stepfather?"

"Clive isn't his real father."

"I didn't know that." He was just going to keep her talking. She was still shaking. Terrified. He hadn't wanted that. He cupped one gloved hand on the back of her head before he even thought about it. Just to comfort. It was hard to put the father in him aside long enough to terrify. "How far along are you?"

"Eight months now. It's a boy." Her eyes were trained on the gun still resting in the holster on his shoulder. Jasper thought about moving it, tucking it in the small of his back. Just so she couldn't see it. Wouldn't be so frightened of it. "We…we're still deciding on names."

"That's always a fun time. My wife and I took forever. I thought our oldest son was going to be out of the hospital before we named him." Thirty-two years ago. He remembered. He thought this was Maggie's first; Clive's son was a widower, he believed. And had already had a daughter. Well, Maggie was going to be a busy girl soon. Things changed when you added that second one. Third, fourth, and fifth, too.

"Why don't you just leave? I...nothing has happened here. You haven't hurt me. I think it would be best if you just go." She was shaking against him. All big-eyed and afraid.

He felt lower than a garden slug.

He thought about it. And it made the most sense. He had his hat pulled down over his head, and the wig was well fitted. The fake beard was an entirely different color than his natural blond-and-gray hair. The scarf was still around his face. He was fortunate it was damned cold in Masterson County right now. He'd bundled himself up as best as possible to avoid the security cameras, if they weren't the new Wi-Fi ones.

Not that that mattered. She hadn't looked away from the gun even once.

He hadn't touched her or anything without gloves. DNA would be hard to come by. He nodded.

To his shock, she grabbed the lamp from the hall table. She heaved it at him. Jasper swore, instinctively reaching out to catch it before it caught him in the head.

Maggie ran right past him.

Straight toward the front door he hadn't remembered to close behind himself.

Jasper reacted instinctively to what his subconscious recognized as a threat.

He grabbed for her.

The girl slipped on the laminate flooring and went down. In the snow melt from his own damned boots.

He caught her, fear for her and her baby rising up to overtake all sense of self-preservation.

She struggled. He tried to get her back to her feet, but had to let her go, she was wiggling too hard.

Jasper tried to keep her from hitting the floor, but the fool girl twisted. He was half a second too late.

To his horror, his elbow caught her in the face.

Maggie kept going. Down.

Her head struck the door handle to the study with an audible crack. Jasper caught her right before she landed on her baby, heart pounding at what could have happened. He pulled her close for a minute too long.

He knew exactly how dangerous a fall could be to a pregnant woman. Jody had fallen almost twenty-seven years ago—the baby, his little Claudia, almost hadn't survived. She'd come ten weeks early at a whopping three pounds. Claudia had always been his little fighter.

Jasper pulled the Tyler girl to her feet. He put his hands on her cheeks, seeing the terror, pain, and panic on her face. "Shhh. You're ok. You're ok, honey. Just a bruise or two, nothing more. Baby's fine, Maggie. Nod if you understand me."

Maggie nodded. "Just go."

He was close enough to feel her baby kicking against him. Poor girl. He had no right to do this to her. "Ok, catch your breath. You're ok. Nod if you understand me, Maggie."

It took a moment. Then she nodded, sending red-gold hair brushing against his cheek.

Jasper stepped back. "I want you to listen to me."

"Just...leave me alone. I—"

"Don't panic. I'm *not* going to hurt you. I really am just

here to get something old of Clive's that would be embarrassing if it got out."

An understatement, but he needed to calm her down. He couldn't just leave her like this.

"Just go."

She twisted in his hands. She'd start fighting him again at any moment. Stubborn, those Tylers were all so damned stubborn.

She was a spirited girl; she wouldn't be cooperative for very much longer. Right now, he had her terrified and in shock. Soon, she was going to think she had to fight her way free. The longer he lingered, the worse it would get. For the both of them.

Her eye was swelling. She'd have a shiner, where his elbow had struck her. She needed to put ice on it. Take time to calm herself down a little before her man got home.

It was time for him to go.

Jasper thought for a moment.

He'd been in this house before, years ago. He remembered it well enough.

"I'm going to do that. I want you to go down the hall, to the last bedroom at the end of the hall. Go in and close the door. Don't come out until you've counted to two hundred. And, Maggie—don't do anything stupid. I know who you are. I know where you live. I even knew your uncle Ben well before he died. I know all your brothers and your cousins, too, including Augusta and her sweet little sisters. Nice girls, all three of them alone out there at that place of theirs. Hate for something to happen to them. It would take forever for help to get to them. Wouldn't it? You don't want to do anything to make me angry. Can you do that?"

She nodded. Her arms tightened around her abdomen. Protectively. "I promise. Just go. I won't stop you. Leave my family alone."

Jasper—the monster in a pregnant woman's nightmares. It would take him a while to forgive himself that.

"Good. You're a smart girl. You always were, I think. If it's you I'm remembering and not one of your cousins. Nikki, perhaps. You do resemble her, and Phil's youngest girl rather closely. I've always struggled to tell the three of you apart. I think it's the gold red hair." He deliberately ran one gloved finger through that silky hair. It was very pretty.

His daughters all had hair as rich chocolate as their mother's had always been. Other than the hair, she reminded him of his girls. Probably because they'd all grown up together. Played together. He felt like a real rank bastard for what he was doing to her.

But...he had to do it.

She paled even more. Maggie understood what he was implying. She didn't recognize him, and that was terrifying her. "I'll do what you said."

"Good. Go. Rather...count to three hundred. Just to be extra safe. That's five minutes. You stay in there for five full minutes like a good girl."

He watched her hurry down the hall as fast as a heavily pregnant woman could.

Once she was in the rear bedroom, he took the kitchen chair he'd grabbed and jammed it up under the door. She'd be able to get out through the window, if she absolutely had to. She shouldn't hurt herself too badly doing that. The window was only a few feet from the ground and nice and wide. Gunderson would need to make certain his daughter didn't sneak out of it when she was a teenager.

Jasper could give the younger man pointers on wild teenaged daughters.

He smirked at the memories that brought.

Jasper's eldest girl had had a wild streak when she'd been in her mid-teens. He'd ended up with alarms on all of Claudia's windows. It had taken her two years to figure out how to reprogram them. But she had, and then all three of the girls had taken advantage of it.

His girls were smart, smart girls, after all. With a love of adventure.

Locking Maggie in would buy him even more time.

Time that would be needed. He needed a minute or two to get to his truck.

This had been one of the stupidest things he had ever done. Had it been Gunderson, he'd probably already be dead. Jasper had gotten lucky today and he knew it.

He had to be more careful next time.

Because he knew the truth: he couldn't quit. He had his own family to protect, after all.

## 27

MAGGIE CAUGHT HER BREATH AS SHE PULLED HERSELF BACK
to her feet six minutes after she'd heard the intruder jam
something under the door handle. She'd landed hard on
her hands and her knees in the snow and mud outside
Violet's bedroom window.

Her left hand went to her stomach. The baby was kicking. He was fine, for now. But every inch of her own body
hurt like the blazes.

She rounded the house and hurried back inside—
though going back *in* was the last thing she wanted to do.

Maggie needed her bag, her keys. Her phone.

Her boots.

Her way out of this place. Thanks to Marin, she had a
car. A way off of the property.

Her friend had said she'd need the car—Maggie
wished Marin had bothered to tell her why.

She'd watched the man's truck pull away before she'd
ever contemplated climbing out the window. Maggie
knew she couldn't get away from him if he came for her
again, not in the condition she was in.

She'd had no choice but to stay where she was until Maggie knew it was absolutely safe.

The last thing she could do was stay at the ranch now. He could decide she wasn't any real threat and come back. Or he could decide she knew too much. And come back.

To do whatever he wanted.

It just wasn't safe there.

Her head hurt, her face hurt. The baby was moving like crazy; no doubt, he felt her stress.

She needed to know he was ok. She had to get out of there.

She stumbled toward the table where she'd left her phone and keys. She thought about calling for help, but they were forty miles north of town.

That could be just too long.

Her cousin Derrick's ranch was four miles up the road. Someone would be there, one of her cousins or the few hands that they employed. If not, she'd let herself in and use their phone to call Joel. Or she'd drive herself to town. Not her first choice, but…it was anywhere but *here*.

She wasn't staying here.

Not after this.

She held herself together the best she could, fear for her baby eclipsing everything.

She wasn't hurt, nothing more than bruises and a headache. He'd hit her cheek hard enough to give her a black eye—she was almost certain of that. Bumps, bruises —she'd survive.

But she was going to get to the hospital. Have the baby checked.

Somehow, she made it to Derrick's. It was just past lunch, but her cousin was on the porch, lumber surrounding him and half the flooring ripped out, wearing nothing but a Masterson Mavericks sweatshirt and ripped and faded jeans. "Derrick...Derrick..."

She almost burst into tears seeing him there, strong and sure and safe.

He came off the porch like he had wings, tossing the hammer aside quickly. "Mags, what's wrong?"

"Someone was in the house. He knocked me down, hit me in the face, locked me in. I couldn't stay there. I couldn't. I need to go to the hospital...I'm pre—"

He scooped her close, just rocking her slightly. "No need to say anything more—and the baby's rather hard to miss, kiddo. Let's get you to my truck. I'll drive you in to see Perci at the hospital myself."

Exactly what she'd been counting on. He practically carried her with an arm around her once-waist until he got her to the old truck he'd had for years. Within moments he had the engine started, a blanket wrapped around her shoulders and the heat vents pointed right at her.

"I'm going to assume that there is a Mr. Maggie's Baby Daddy floating around somewhere in this county that I need to get ahold of?" He shot her a glance, looking so much like her brother Michael she couldn't help but start to calm a bit.

He was a Tyler, after all. Tylers took care of Tylers out here.

"Clint. He...someone will need to find him. He's got Violet in town somewhere. I...someone needs to find him."

"*Gunderson*?" Derrick frowned. "Hell, Maggie, he's way too damned old for you. He's older than I am."

"Only by about two or three years or so. There are eleven years between Clint and me."

"And about a century of experience. What's his intentions toward you and that baby?"

"Are you serious?" Maggie gripped the door handle. "This isn't 1926, Der."

"This is Masterson County, and you are my baby cousin. It's my Tyler-duty to make sure some guy doesn't take advantage of you. Or any of the rest of the girl-pack. So do I need to go kick his ass or not?"

"My brothers already threatened to. So I think that's covered." The baby gave a hard kick. Hard enough to reassure her a little. Her head still hurt. Her left eye watered and throbbed and burned.

As if he'd read her mind, Derrick flipped down the visor. "There should be tissues or something in the glove box. You've got blood under that eye."

She held the tissue to her eye the rest of the drive into town.

Maggie just leaned back against the seat. Her cousin wrapped his strong hand around hers and squeezed reassuringly.

She pulled in a breath as a sob threatened to escape. As what had happened started to sink in.

By the time Derrick pulled into the hospital parking lot, she was crying quietly.

All she'd seemed to do since getting pregnant with Clint Gunderson's baby was *cry*. Damn it.

Maggie was stronger than this.

Derrick was close to panicking. He never had been able to handle female tears. Her cousin Perci would make herself cry on purpose when they'd been in junior high, just to make the older Derrick twig out.

Perci had been a bit of a brat back then.

He scooped her up in his strong arms before she could

stop him. Maggie just wrapped her arm around his shoulders and clung. He'd probably be calling every brother she had within the next fifteen minutes. And then all the cousins. Maybe even the second cousins that populated this side of the state.

Maggie knew how Tylers worked, after all.

Tylers tended to stick together when something went wrong.

Her cousin Perci was standing by the ER intake desk when Derrick carried her in past three nurses she recognized, including the mayor's daughter.

Everyone in town was going to hear about this.

Perci's own stomach jutted out in front of her, just as much as Maggie's. "What's happened? Mag—"

Derrick put her back on her feet, and Maggie turned toward one of her closest friends, as well as family. "I... there was someone in the house. I was knocked down when I tried to get away. I struck my head. I made it to Derrick—"

"Ok, let's get you into an exam room. I'll get Dr. Paterson. Or Nate. Whoever is free." Perci had an orderly grab a wheelchair. Before Maggie could protest, she was being wheeled toward an exam room near the rear of the ER. "Anyone I need to have Tiff call for you?"

"You mean the father?" Maggie asked drily. She was starting to calm, though her head still felt like it was going to explode. "Perci...there is something I need to tell you. About the father..."

"Don't worry," Perci said firmly. "I know you were living with Clint Gunderson before you left. I'm not naive —nor am I blind. You got that hot cowboy cop's clothes off and had some fun at least once, didn't you?"

Well, that was one way to put it. But there was no

anger, no judgment or censure like Maggie had half feared there would be.

Clive had almost killed Perci, after all. It had taken her cousin months to recover.

"I was afraid you'd hate me." Clint's brother had almost killed Perci and Pip, and Perci's brother-in-law, Matt.

There was no love lost between Gundersons and Tylers. Some of her more vocal cousins had a lot to say on Clint's antecedents. No one had wanted to listen to her when she'd said Clint was different.

That was one of the reasons Clint had given for them not being able to even try a relationship seven months ago. Because of her family. Like they were a doomed Romeo and Juliet of Masterson or something. She never had bought into that.

"It wasn't you out there on the road that day, Mag. Nor was it Clint. I've made my peace with him. I never had a war with him, to begin with. My main concern is how well he treats you. I didn't even know you were together."

"We...weren't, aren't...maybe. I'm not sure exactly what we are right now," Maggie said as Perci took her blood pressure and oxygen stats. As she started to feel a bit calmer. "We...did something stupid. Two months later, I took Violet and left because of the shooting. I feel...like everything was on pause for five months. Now...I was confused by him then—and I'm even more confused by him now. I thought...I knew what I wanted before I returned to Masterson County, but...he..."

Perci hugged her. Maggie resisted the urge to cling. Her cousins were the closest things to sisters she'd ever had, and she loved every one of them. "You'll figure things out. Hot Masterson County men are extremely difficult to figure out, but I have full faith you'll succeed."

"I had a plan. Get back to Masterson, find me a house, work remotely for the woman in Finley Creek. Build a life independent of my brothers—and of Clint. I thought he wouldn't want more than that one night. He'd said as much the morning after we...made the baby. I was good with that."

"He what?" Perci helped her into the hospital gown. "Maybe he's dumber than I thought. Guess not every man can have both looks and brains like Nate and his brothers."

"Clint told me almost eight months ago that there wasn't room in his life for a relationship. The morning after. It was just one night. Now that I'm back and halfway to being as big as a whale, he says I'm all he's ever wanted. That he's wanted me all along." And there was no way under the blue moon that Maggie would ever believe it was *her* he wanted. No matter what he said to the contrary. "And the way he looks at me..."

"You're not as big as a whale," Perci said, then patted her own stomach. "I am. Now, tell me about how he looks at you. Inquiring minds want to know if it's anything like how Nate looks at me. He gets this expression...wow."

"He wants the baby. He thinks that telling me he wants me will get him that. His sense of honor or something. He's obsessive when it comes to doing the responsible thing. So that he doesn't look like Clive." Maggie had always been close to Perci and her twin, and Perci's two sisters. Their babies would grow up playmates with Maggie's. She was looking forward to that. "I've given him two weeks. He has...a little over one week left. I want my house in town by then. But...I want my house in town."

Maybe. What she really wanted was Clint right now. In that exact moment, Clint was all she wanted.

She would have said more but Perci's husband knocked on the exam room door. After a few questions about what happened, he inspected Maggie quickly. "When are you due?"

She told him the date. "The baby's a boy. Everything has been going well. I just want to have him checked out. Make sure that man didn't hurt him."

She shuddered. Nate patted her on the shoulder, then cupped her injured cheek gently in his big hand.

She would have to deal with the knowledge that someone had been in the house when she'd been there alone later.

Right now...right now, she just needed to know that her baby was ok.

## 28

CLINT STOOD IN THE MIDDLE OF THE HARDWARE STORE TRYING to juggle getting everything he needed and keeping Violet from throwing a massive fit. He fought panic; twenty pounds of girl human shouldn't be this terrifying. But she was.

Big blue eyes blinked at him.

She was getting droopy. He made the quick decision to spread his coat over the bottom of the cart and let her snuggle down in the warm denim. He had just gotten her situated when her big blue eyes closed, and she snuffled her way to sleep—calling for her "Mag-Mag."

It just about broke his heart.

He had no idea how Maggie managed to get anything accomplished while also taking care of Violet. Add in the pregnancy and her job…

She had to be a miracle worker.

It was no wonder Maggie kept falling asleep around nine each night. She had to be exhausted.

Clint wished he had the resources to hire her some help. But that wasn't in the budget. Not for a long, long time. Unless her salary from her online job would be enough to help them manage to pay for additional childcare.

At least part-time each week. He could manage a few hours each day in between running the ranch, if needed.

Worry for how they were going to manage with a second baby while she worked and he was working the ranch had him distracted as he moved his way through the next aisle.

It was there that Rex found him. The other man's body language had Clint tensing automatically.

"I've been searching for you all over town. Try answering your cell once in a while, damn it."

"Couldn't. Violet was throwing a fit. What's happened?" *Maggie*. His first thought would always be Maggie. And their baby. Always. He pushed the panic away.

"Leave your cart. I'll have Officer Grady get it." Rex jerked his head to the young WHP deputy who had trailed after him, a slightly awed expression on her pretty face. Clint vaguely recognized her as the mayor's daughter. "Someone broke into your ranch."

Ice shot down his spine. "Where's Maggie?"

"She's at the hospital, just getting checked out. The intruder knocked her down in the hallway. She's bruised, but was able to drive herself to her cousin's place up the road. The Tylers are looking for you now. I don't know what they intend, but I've had your back this long. Figured I'd see this through. Come on."

Clint was already moving.

Clint scooped Violet up, coat and all. Fear had his chest tight. "Is she ok? Tell me the truth."

"She seems to be, from what I heard when I talked to

Joel Masterson. But I knew you'd want to be there. Everyone's talking about the fact that she's back. And very pregnant. They've put one and one together. Well, they are assuming you and Maggie put one and one together. Congratulations, by the way. I guess we can finally say that out loud now."

They'd kept all mention of Maggie and Violet as quiet as possible while she'd been gone. To keep someone after Clint from learning of Maggie's importance to him. Most of the town hadn't even realized she'd been working as his housekeeper for months before the shooting.

Probably her brothers' doing.

She hadn't exactly advertised that she'd been living in his home all those weeks ago. He'd understood it then— and was doubly glad of it now.

"Who the hell was in my damned house?" Fury coated his words. "Thought Masterson said they'd caught a kid from the southern part of the county breaking into places?"

"Apparently, it wasn't this guy. You just got lucky with someone else."

No shit.

"I never would have left her there if I hadn't thought they'd caught the guy." He never should have left her alone.

## 29

Maggie heard Violet crying as Nate wheeled her out of the exam room. She could have walked, but she appreciated the ride.

Nate was probably being overly cautious. She'd seen the way he was hovering over his own pregnant wife. She'd had a hard time not envying Perci that, even if it was driving Perci crazy.

She and Clint…they hadn't had that. Even if Maggie had stayed five months ago, there was nothing that said they would have ended up like Perci and Nate. Far from it.

More likely, they would have argued constantly over what was best for the baby until they couldn't stand each other, and she would have quit her job and moved back home to her brothers. Where she'd probably still be now.

Maggie wanted nothing more in the world than to throw herself into his arms right now and let him hide her from the world, just for a little while.

To her surprise, Nate wheeled her straight into the waiting room, where Clint was pacing, holding an agitated Violet, a panicked look on his face. Violet was red-faced, and overtired. Maggie knew it with one look. That was something she could fix, at least.

"Hey." She reached for Violet instinctively. The baby came right to her, and Maggie snuggled her close. Violet was rebonding with her father, but there was no denying that in the little girl's mind, Maggie was her sense of security. "You didn't have to bring her here; Derrick waited for me. He could have driven me home."

Not that she trusted her cousin would have. He had been making noises earlier about just hauling her back to his ranch where he and his brothers could take care of her. Protect her themselves. Under lock and key.

She'd pointed out that that was kidnapping. Derrick had just kept grumbling.

He'd also muttered about driving her to Martin's and letting her own brothers be responsible for her. Even though they obviously hadn't been doing too great of a job lately. He had plenty to say about that, too.

Coming home to Masterson, she'd stepped right back into 1953.

Heaven help her.

Worse; heaven help the women her cousins finally married. Maggie hoped they were ready for a step back in time.

Clint dropped down in front of the wheelchair. His left hand wrapped around hers, his right hand covered the baby. Her arms tightened gently around Violet. "You ok, Mags?"

She nodded. There were people staring at them. This… this was the first time anyone had ever looked at them, seeing them as a couple.

Together.

Hard not to freak about that.

"I will be. I'm tired, though. I need to..." Well, she didn't know what she needed to do. "I just..."

He straightened and turned to the man behind him. Rex was asking questions of the sheriff's deputy Derrick had called.

He was probably the only friend Clint really had.

Rex was a beautiful man. He was easily as big as Perci's husband, but not quite as muscled. Lean and strong. He had a dangerous, terrifying look about him.

Violet settled into her lap and started chewing on her shoulder. Baby drool soaked into her blouse. She hated feeling unsettled like this. Awkward.

Everyone was staring at her. Nate and Perci excused themselves, leaving her with Derrick and Clint and the commander.

Maggie took the easy way out—she focused on taking care of Violet.

Until Clint scooped his daughter off Maggie's lap and plopped Violet into his friend's arms. "You can carry Violet, Weatherby. I'm going to get Maggie settled in the truck. Time I took my family home."

Derrick stepped up, a glare on his handsome face. "I called your brothers, Maggie. They're on their way. They had to take the backroads in. The creek flooded out their road again. They want to check on you for themselves."

She winced. The last thing she needed was those five baboons showing up here demanding she be taken somewhere they could protect her.

Although...it was almost a tempting thought. Just let them take her home and tuck her into her childhood room and stay there forever.

No. She wasn't running away any longer.

Six months ago, that was exactly what Maggie would

have done. *Ran*. But she was the new Maggie now. She'd given Clint her word; and she wasn't ready to leave Violet yet. Not yet. "Thanks, Derrick. For everything."

Derrick leaned down and kissed her cheek. "Anytime. I'm not going anywhere. Not unless you tell me to."

She nodded. Tyler men had a habit of being way too overprotective. Especially of Tyler women. She'd missed them all so much. "I'm ok. I'm safe with Clint. I promise. Call my brothers. Let them know where I'm going and that I'm fine. I'll call them tonight."

Almost. She hadn't forgotten what Clint wanted, after all.

Clint waited almost impatiently. When Derrick was gone, Clint looked back at Maggie. "You ready?"

She'd already taken care of the rest of the paperwork. Derrick had handled what he could. Mel ensured all her Minions had excellent insurance, and Maggie had the card in her wallet.

It was almost anticlimactic.

But...she hadn't forgotten what had happened. She would have to face it eventually. "I'm ready."

"Let's get you home," Rex said, perfectly comfortable holding Violet—who was having fun poking him in the ears and eyes. "You can tell me what happened whenever you're ready. I'll take your statement personally."

She just nodded.

The last thing she wanted to do was go back to Clint's place right now.

But that was exactly what she was going to do.

## 30

*Brrr.* Masterson County was far colder in March than Texas. Brandt would have to get used to it.

He would also have to get used to driving in it. He was going to need a sturdier truck, for one thing. This rental was great, but if he was going to make Masterson his home base—and he had decided that was exactly what he was going to do—he was going to have to get better transportation. One that didn't dwarf him, for one thing. He was six foot six, after all.

That was the first thing he took care of that morning. By the time lunch rolled around, he was the proud owner of a Ford F-150 Limited. He liked a big truck.

He'd eventually have to find a house of his own. Brandt was a man who liked his creature comforts. He'd have to talk to Maggie; see if she knew of anything that would meet his needs. He'd want close to town, he thought. Easier to access food that way.

Mostly, he just wanted to check on Maggie. He hadn't seen her in a few days and was concerned.

Like Powell had reminded him on the phone earlier—

Maggie needed them to watch out for her. Especially with that cowboy of hers. Maggie was definitely naive where men were concerned, after all.

Brandt hadn't met the cowboy yet. It was about time he did.

See what the guy was really like.

He had his suspicions—if Clint Gunderson was a good man, he wouldn't have laid his hands on Maggie to begin with. Not without some seriously strong emotions behind it. Not every man was just after a good time with a woman.

Brandt certainly wasn't, even though he enjoyed the female species very, very much.

He was building his empire now so that when he found the woman he was meant to find, he would be ready. To give her the world.

Her and any little Brandts that came along after. Barratts were family men, after all. It was a matter of Barratt pride. It was just a matter of time before he found the woman he wanted that with.

The diner beckoned. He turned his collar up against the snow and headed in that direction. A Talley granddaughter met him at the door. "Hello, Mr. Barratt, welcome back to Masterson County."

He checked the name tag discretely. The Talley women strongly resembled one another. "Thank you, Dusty. Does this snow ever end?"

She gave him a smile identical to the little waif cousin of hers. She was definitely a beautiful woman, too. "Eventually."

"I'm starving. What's on the menu?" He looked around the diner, checking the occupants out of habit.

"Grandmother's specialty, chicken cordon bleu sandwiches, and potato wedges. I cut them myself this morning."

"Great." Home-cooked food, beautiful women, beautiful countryside. He could see making Masterson County his home.

"I'm back, Dusty," a quiet voice said behind her.

Brandt turned. There she was. The little waif.

He'd made a habit of looking for her whenever he stepped into the diner. Just because she intrigued him. He'd seen her a few times at the inn, but she seemed to prefer the diner over the inn. The kitchen, mostly. She scurried around the place like a little mouse.

He didn't know why he was keeping track of her. He just was.

Tonight, though...the little waif had no business being dressed in a dress like that. It was green, like her eyes. And cut far too low. Revealed too much. Was far too old for her, though it was sedate compared to the dresses he'd seen women in his sphere wear. Mel had dresses that made this one look like a granny dress; she wore them just to make Houghton drool.

Lots of men drooled over Mel with Houghton.

But on the waif...no. The waif shouldn't look like *that*. He fought the instant lust by reminding himself she was far too young for him.

"Great. Run home and get changed. You can tell me about your date later. I have half an hour before I'm supposed to meet Matt at Michael Tyler's ranch to help inoculate the cattle. I'll fix you a plate."

"Thanks, but I'll just have dessert." Her cheeks pinkened beautifully. "Calloway ended up buying me dinner at R.J.'s already."

Her cousin gave a wicked laugh. "Oh, so things went

well, then. Mr. Barratt, if you'll follow me. Meyra, I'll see you when you get back."

Brandt dutifully followed her, mind running over the implications of what the waif had said.

He'd seen R.J.'s Tavern. It had had a For Sale sign in the window, and he'd taken a look at the building. It was a place that served drinks; you had to be twenty-one to enter. Maybe the waif wasn't a teenager after all?

If she wasn't, she wasn't much older than that.

Brandt was sitting there trying to figure the little waif out when Marin slipped into the booth across from him. She seemed to have attached herself to him, he thought. Probably for Maggie's sake.

He didn't think she had a bit of a romantic attraction toward him. Brandt knew when a woman was interested in him, after all. "Marin...answer me something. You Talleys...how old and who are who."

"A bit of a strange question."

"Just humor me. I'm starting to get a bit confused." He suspected she'd answer him honestly. "You are the eldest, right?"

She shook her head. "Not even close. My sister Miranda is thirty now. She lives in St. Louis—"

"And works for the FBI. I met her once when she was checking on Maggie."

Marin nodded. "Then Darcey. She's the eldest of my cousins. She's going to be twenty-nine soon. Dixie and I are within three months of each other. We're twenty-seven. She's older."

"You don't look it." He had guessed she was around twenty-two or twenty-three. Apparently, he'd been wrong. He had met Darcey, too. He thought. "Darcey is the radio..."

"Personality," she said, laughing. "People love her voice, but Darcey is a bit shy. She'd rather be working at the inn, but does the radio because she interned there in high school and they asked her to fill in one night. She got a lot of viewers then. They offered her a job after she graduated college. After us, we have a cousin who actually lives in your neck of the woods. Miranda was probably there visiting Charlotte when she stopped by to see Maggie. Charlotte lives in Value and works with the Finley Creek TSP as part of the mobile forensics unit."

Well. He hadn't known that. Small world. "I know the supervisor of that unit. She's married to my cousin Clay."

"Interesting. Charlotte looks a bit like my sister Meyra, just shorter, with darker hair."

Brandt thought for a moment. He'd met Bailey's friends at the wedding. There had been a green-eyed woman with dark reddish-brown hair, he thought. She'd had a man's name and a wicked smile…

"Chuckie?"

Marin laughed, beautifully, drawing attention her way easily. She…was a powerful woman. Terrifying, really. "She hates that name, but it's stuck down there at the TSP. Her father calls her that. He is the reason she moved down that way. He lives in Value, I believe."

"Go on. I know there are more of you."

"There are three more: Dusty, your hostess this evening. She works for the vet here in town, part-time. She and Maggie were good friends in school and were in the same class. Her sister Daisy is less than a year younger, at twenty-three. You'll find her mostly in the kitchens at the inn and at the diner when she's not teaching at the elementary school. As for the one you are really asking about— Meyra is the youngest. She's twenty-three, a few months younger than Daisy. Plenty old enough to drink, if that's what you were trying to figure out. She's not a kid, Mr. Barratt. Just quiet and very shy. Growing up in the center of town like we did has been difficult for her. Well, Meyra and Daisy, and to some extend Darcey. But...we stick together."

He nodded, feeling heat his cheeks for the first time in a while. He had wanted to know about her sister.

He'd thought she was just a kid, no more than nineteen or so. So he'd dismissed her from his mind.

Mostly.

She hadn't looked like a kid today. He'd turned thirty, two months ago. He had a good seven years on her; it made a difference.

Marin laughed at him again. Brandt had the feeling she knew exactly what was going through his mind now.

Dangerous.

The women of Masterson County were downright dangerous. Each and every one of them.

He'd have to keep that in mind.

## 31

CLINT WAS GOING TO HOVER WORSE THAN ALL FIVE OF HER brothers combined. And that was saying a lot. Her brothers had taken a shortcut that bypassed the rear side of the hospital and led right to Clint's properties.

They had been waiting for her long before Clint turned in the drive. Maggie knew what happened next wasn't going to be pretty. "Clint...just let me handle them."

"You think they'll cause a problem?"

"Once they realize I am fine, they'll go away." She hoped. Michael was standing on Clint's porch with that beyond determined look he got when he was furious. Michael could be harder to deal with than Martin at times, when it came down to it. "Maybe."

"They are just concerned," Clint said. "I am half tempted to send you and Violet off with them, anyway. Until we figure out who this guy is."

Maggie had told Clint and Rex exactly what had happened in the hospital parking lot. Rex had recorded her statement on his phone. Then the two men had discussed what of Clive's it could possibly be that the man was looking for.

And they had called Joel again. Rex had had a frank discussion about what Maggie had told him with the local sheriff—Joel covered the county, but Rex was the WHP commander of the region. They worked together as a courtesy occasionally. Maggie had just rested her head—still aching—against the back of the seat and tried to rest. At least a little.

She refused to let herself be afraid of Clint's ranch. Not any longer. It was just a place. Even if some bad things had happened there, it was just a place.

There was worry in his blue eyes when he looked at her. Because he cared. He parked the truck, leaving Violet sleeping in her car seat for the moment.

Then Clint came around to her side of the truck and opened her door. Warm hands went around her almost waist, and she let him lower her to the ground. Let him steady her.

And then…she was getting exactly what she wanted. Clint's arms wrapped around her so tightly she could barely breathe. The baby went crazy, kicking against his father as if he *knew* who it was holding her. "I'm so sorry I left you alone."

Maggie's arms went around his waist. Her fingers fisted on the soft flannel of his shirt. "I'm ok, Clint. I promise. He just…scared me mostly. He didn't hurt us. Not really. We're ok. We're ok."

The man was shaking against her. She could feel the tremors running through him. "I can't lose you, Mags. I lost Amy, and I can't lose you, too. You just mean too much to me. I can't even stand the thought."

Maggie pulled back slightly, then stretched up on her toes. She ignored how awkward it felt. Her arms slipped around his neck, and she pressed her lips to his.

In that moment, she never wanted to leave Clint again.

## 32

Rex heard her laugh the instant he stepped into the diner. He scowled, even as he immediately sought out Madam Zelda.

There she was—with a guy as big as Rex was himself, who had a ridiculously sophisticated and polished *aura* about him.

His scowl deepened.

She was laughing, happy with the man. Looking far too beautiful for Rex's peace of mind.

Flirting? He couldn't tell from where he was. It wouldn't surprise him at all. She liked to get men all tangled up in her.

"Hello, Commander Weatherby," a quiet voice said behind him. He turned. The lunatic's younger sister stood there, looking beautiful and alluring in her own particular way.

Talley women were far too beautiful for a single man's sanity. He wasn't about to admit that, though. "Hello, Meyra, I thought I'd grab some dinner before I head back out to my own place." He had forty-two acres just fifteen miles northeast of Clint's main place. He'd bought those forty-two acres because sometimes a man needed a peaceful place to think.

After the things Rex had seen on the job, he needed that peace. He wasn't going to ever do anything with that land, but it was his. His peace.

As far from downtown Masterson—such that it was—as it could get.

"Meatloaf is the special tonight, too."

"Good. That was the best meatloaf I've ever had," he gave her a genuine smile. He had liked her a great deal when he'd been at Clint's the last time. She wasn't as awkward as people thought. Just quiet. Peaceful. In ways her older sister often overshadowed.

He was half convinced Madam Zelda did it purpose-fully, drawing attention to herself—to protect. He had to admire that, at least.

He had three younger brothers of his own, after all.

Meyra led him to a table right next to her damned sister.

Marin turned and looked at him, watched every move he made. "Well, Commander Weatherby, fancy meeting you here. This is my turf, you know. Didn't think you'd be brave enough to step inside. Since I'm so terrifying."

"Too damned bad. You'll just have to learn to share." The woman was enough to have him swallowing his tongue. That blouse she wore—it was cut far too low. No doubt the playboy she was with was enjoying it. "Who's your friend?"

He wasn't local to the county. Rex was sure of it. A guy like this…would stand out.

"Commander Rex Weatherby, meet Mr. Brandt Barratt, of the Texas Barratts. He's here looking at ranches to build an agribusiness of his own. I'm keeping him company."

"Nice to meet you," the younger man said smoothly.

Rex didn't like him. On principle alone. He knew about the Barratts, and he knew that was where Maggie had been hidden all this time.

And this guy had followed her home.

Loyalty to his closest friend had him hating the guy, too.

"Relax, Commander, Brandt and Maggie are just good friends. He's not here to step on Clint's toes."

"Marin, Daisy wants you in the kitchen to help her lift the potatoes when you get a chance," Meyra said.

"I'll be in in a moment. And, Mey, I want to know all about Calloway Grady and what happened today. Going to go out with him again?" The lunatic sent a smirk at her companion that Rex didn't understand.

Meyra gave a smile she definitely shouldn't have ever possessed. "I just might."

Dangerous. Talley women were definitely dangerous creatures.

As Barratt excused himself to hit the restroom, Marin turned to Rex.

"Ok. What's eating at you? Something's happened, hasn't it? To Maggie and Clint and the babies. Tell me."

"How in the three hells did you know?"

"Easy. There's a black spot in your aura. Right there." She brushed one hand against his left shoulder. The touch practically burned. "It got worse when Maggie was mentioned. Believe it or not—just is she going to be ok?"

"She'll be just fine."

Trouble had a way of finding Maggie now, though.

Real trouble. Rex had to stop it. Before Clint lost what mattered most.

## 33

BRANDT STEPPED ONTO THE PORCH OF THE GUNDERSON
ranch, taking in the operation with a single glance. He
liked what he saw. Someone was putting some serious
effort into the place. It was decent. If it was for sale, he'd
offer top dollar. But Maggie had told him the place had
been in her cowboy's family for generations. Gunderson
probably wouldn't ever sell it, unless it started being a loss
overall. Brandt doubted it was.

But he wasn't there on business, so he just had to turn
that part of his brain off.

He wanted to check on Maggie. Brandt knocked on the
door.

A dark redheaded man with fire in his blue eyes
answered. "Who the hell are you?"

"You Clint?"

"Michael Tyler. You?"

"Brandt Barratt." Brandt was used to tense situations.
The guy wanted to punch someone. Brandt doubted it
would be him—most men hesitated when faced with a six-

foot-six, three-hundred-twenty pound man like Brandt. Of course, this guy wasn't that much smaller. Three inches and fifty pounds, maybe. "I'm a good friend of Maggie's from Texas. I am here to check on her."

"She's inside." The man moved out of Brandt's way. "I'm her brother."

"Of course. She's mentioned all of you several times. You're the one who runs the family ranch?" Brandt held out his hand. The other man shook it, but it was obvious he was upset about something.

Brandt had a feeling he knew what it was. If someone had broken in and knocked his pregnant sister down when she had been all alone, he would be beyond furious. He'd be flat out pissed.

And ready to go hunting.

Maggie was in the kitchen, with four other men who all resembled her and Michael in some way. Brandt crossed the kitchen to her quickly. Violet was in her high chair and started yelling when she saw him. "Ban-Ban!"

"Hi, Baby Vi." He kissed the baby's little forehead like he always did when he first saw her. But Maggie was his focus. "Hey, kid. I heard what happened. Decided to come see you for myself. See if you need a ride right back to Texas. If so, I'll call Houghton and get the jet here within a few hours."

"Like I was telling my brothers...I am just fine. And I'm not going anywhere. I'm tired of always running away. It's time I faced my demons right here. Clint and I...we have some things to work out between us. I can't do that if I run away again."

Brandt wanted to protest, but there was a determined look in her eyes. One he'd seen before. If Maggie wanted to stay—well, Brandt was there to see that was what happened.

But Gunderson needed to do a better job of keeping her safe. Brandt saw the black eye for himself.

And he hadn't missed the patrol car parked at the end of the drive.

## 34

Maggie was still trying to figure out how she felt about Clint two days after the intruder had knocked her down.

Brandt had distracted her from what had happened—and had acted as a good buffer between her and Clint. Rex had come back after dinner, with a crime scene tech. Even though everyone knew the possibility of getting an ID through DNA was very slim. Rex had still promised to try.

The attacker had worn gloves. She doubted his DNA had gotten anywhere. Rex had overseen the entire process while glaring at Brandt.

Marin had shown up two hours into the process, just adding to the fray.

Rex was hard at work tracking Maggie's attacker.

He hadn't found anything in the two days since the attack.

Clint was staying armed.

Rex and Joel had both doubled patrols in their area, though it was still an hour or two between passes by.

It was as good as it was going to get until they had the man in custody.

She wasn't going to let herself live afraid. Nor was she going to let herself *run*.

Even though that was exactly what Clint wanted her to do. He hadn't come out and said it.

Clint had warmed up to Brandt, once he realized the other man was serious about building his empire.

Brandt had helped Clint run her brothers off. That had probably bought him Clint's loyalty forever. Her brothers were definitely not happy with her choices now.

Whereas Maggie had found *New Maggie* in Finley Creek, Brandt was looking for himself in Masterson. Funny how it had worked that way.

She was thinking about the other man when she slipped into Clint's room, the half-full laundry basket balanced awkwardly at her side. Marin had come back around long enough to do all the laundry and load the dishwasher and sweep and mop the floors.

Marin had sung horribly off-key while she'd done it. Maggie suspected she'd done so simply to get beneath the ever-glowering Rex's skin.

Marin was a highly gifted singer, like the rest of the Talleys. Marin's aunt had been the choir director at the high school for years before she'd passed away.

Marin apparently loved tormenting Rex whenever she could.

Maggie hadn't been able to just *sit* around the house while Clint was out doing what it was he did, so Maggie had helped when Marin would allow it.

Maggie refused to act as his housekeeper, either. But she'd had to do something.

She'd give him his laundry and hightail it back to her

room. See if Mel was online and talk to the other woman about hot, confusing men to see if Mel had any insight into how to deal with Clint.

Any insight would come in handy right now.

A sound behind her had her whipping around.

Just as Clint stepped into his room, hands working on his shirt buttons.

Maggie stared at the strong, broad chest as it was revealed one button at a time. Oh my. Beautiful.

Clint had always seemed like the most beautiful man in the world to her. She'd certainly seen more handsome men—Finley Creek had introduced her to a lot of sophisticated, successful, beyond hot men—but Clint had always been the one to catch her attention. To make her heart pound and sweat slick her hands. To make every sense and nerve she had go on full alert. "What...what are you doing? I—"

Clint had one of the most perfect male chests she'd ever been privileged to see. And she'd seen a fair few— even Hunter Louis Clark, up close and personal, currently considered the sexiest man in Hollywood. But Clint...

She wanted to touch.

Every bit of her was tuned to him like a magnet. Eight months pregnant or not. A curl of heat went through her. She fumbled the basket stupidly.

Maggie wanted to touch. That hadn't changed in eight months. If she hadn't found him physically attractive all those months ago, this kid wouldn't be kicking her right now.

She wasn't exactly super experienced—Masterson was a small county, and it seemed like she was related to half the eligible guys—but she hadn't found her way into Clint's bed a virgin.

What she was supposed to do *now* wasn't exactly all that clear, either.

For a moment, she wished Violet would wake. Call out for her.

Anything to get Maggie's feet to move before her hands did something stupid.

"I need to take a shower. I'm not in your way, am I?"

Maggie just shook her head.

In her way? No. Distracting her—that was more accurate. By far. "I'm...I'm ok. I was just...looking for..."

"Something in the bathroom?" He shot her a mild look. His hand was still unbuttoning. As if it didn't bother him that she was there at all. As if him getting naked in front of her was perfectly normal...

Hell, the top button of his jeans were undone.

She almost swore he was taunting her on purpose. Like he was planning something now.

Maggie forced herself to look into his blue eyes. "I was just—your laundry got put in with mine. I think Marin got a bit confused. I wanted to bring it to you before I head to bed."

"Thanks." He took the basket from her hands. "I don't want you to think you have to clean up after me, though. I know...that's not what you want to do any longer. And you should still be resting."

"I'm fine now. It isn't what I want to do. I...am not made to be a housekeeper permanently. I learned that in Texas. I'm good at what I do for Mel. I want to keep doing it. Keep helping people." Now it was just her babbling. Trying to distract herself from the naked chest in front of her. Damn him. He was doing this on purpose. "I'm not cleaning up after you. Just...helping out. I know you've been busy."

Sequestered in his home office with Rex, talking about things Maggie just didn't want to know about. Trying to determine what from Clive's files would have resurfaced to cause problems now.

Maggie just wanted to pretend that what had happened had been a fluke.

She knew better than that.

The intruder had known her name, known which cousins resembled her the most, and known that Augie, Junie, and Em were alone out there clear at the bottom of the county. He'd made certain to point that out.

She'd gotten the message. She did anything stupid and he would go after her family. Her cousins—who were the most vulnerable.

One good thing had happened from Perci and Derrick knowing what had happened to her—every Tyler in the county was now on the alert.

And everyone was looking for an older man in a dark-orange truck.

She fought a shiver. She would never forget how she had felt, knowing she knew the man—but not being able to say his name.

The baby gave a big kick—big enough to have her saying, "Oh!"

Clint immediately stepped toward her, his hands out. "You ok? The baby?"

"Is fine. Just woke up and is moving a lot." She pressed her hand to her left side, where the kicking was still going on. On impulse, she grabbed Clint's hand and pressed it to the spot where their son was awake. "He…he is a bit of a night owl. Loves to keep me awake later in the evening. That's when he's most active."

He shot her a look of confusion. "He does?"

Maggie nodded. "He has a pattern. Dr. Kaur—in Finley Creek—said that was normal. He just likes to sleep during the earlier part of the day."

"I...didn't get to see or know all this with Violet. Amy was already sick, and we were so focused on that and on what the pregnancy was doing to hinder her recovery... hell, Maggie, all I really remember about then was *fear*."

"I know." Miranda had told her what it had been like for Clint. Compassion and hurt for him had her stepping closer. "But this pregnancy—it's healthy, Clint. Our baby is perfectly ok. I promise."

"I...worried every night for five months that you were ok. You. Not just the babies. I hated not knowing where you were, and whether or not you needed me. It was a living nightmare. It turns out that you didn't need me. And I'm so damned grateful for that, grateful you and Violet and our son were safe when I couldn't be there to protect you, with people who cared about you; but...I want you to need me now."

Maggie just gawked at him. She didn't know what to do here...not at all. The emotion in his blue eyes was reaching out and crushing her heart. "I'm ok. I was home-sick at first. But I had Violet to take care of. I am so sorry I just took her and disappeared. I never..."

Hard hands went around her—so gently she almost cried. Clint was a strong man, but he had never been rough with her in any way. He'd touched her like she was made of glass that night they'd spent together. Like she was fragile and beautiful and so damned precious to him.

She hadn't known it had been his late wife's thirtieth birthday. Or she would never have let it go past that first kiss.

He *had* needed her that night. Just not in the way she had needed in return.

Life lesson number 387 learned, apparently. Be careful what you wish for.

By the time she'd figure out how she felt about that night, she'd been starting to realize that she had bigger problems to worry about.

Like the baby they'd created.

Maggie had come to terms with that months ago. Five months away hadn't changed anything between them.

Except that his archaic sense of honor was probably screaming at him to do the right thing.

"I know you didn't. And you did the right thing. You got my baby, and yourself, out of here. Where you could be safe. I…if I lost you, or Violet, or this baby…I don't think I'd be able to go on. Not even for a moment. I failed you all. And for that, I can never apologize enough."

Oh, the big male idiot. He truly thought he was to blame for what had happened that day. He'd had almost six months to convince himself of that, too. To dwell on some perceived failing. Of course he had.

What had happened the day she had left Masterson County had happened because a bad man made an even worse decision. Period.

The big dork.

"I…you're a good father, Clint."

"Am I? I almost got her killed. Almost got you and our baby killed. I could have lost everything that day. I'm damned lucky that I didn't." His hands rose to cup her cheeks. "I am so damned lucky to have you in front of me right now. You are my world, Maggie Tyler. You and the babies we both love. Nothing is going to change that."

"Clint…" She wasn't stupid. She knew what he was

implying, what was in his face. His tone. "I...we'll figure out what to do about the baby between us. Then...once Violet is settled in, I'm leaving. I'm not...staying."

She didn't sound the least bit convincing now.

Now...all she felt was confused.

If someone had asked her if she was in love with Clint Darrin Gunderson she would have said without hesitation that she loved him fully. But eight months was a long time to spend thinking and alone.

He'd wanted her. But that wasn't the same.

"I'm going to change your mind. You belong here with me, with Violet. You and the baby. We...we can build a good life together. A decent life. And I'll love you. Each and every day of my life, I will love you."

She wanted a man to look at her the way Houghton looked at Mel.

Like the world couldn't turn without Mel there to guide the sun.

She didn't know if Clint could do that. "I...don't think we should do anything to confuse the issue, do you? I'm going. I can't stay here."

"I don't understand why you want to go," he said bluntly. His hands dropped to rest on her waist—or what remained of it. His fingers spread, sending heat shooting through her everywhere. Heaven help her, Maggie wanted Clint to keep touching her forever. That was seriously dangerous thinking. "We've made a baby. Don't we owe it to the kid to do what we can to form a family for him— and for Violet? You're the only real mother she's ever known."

"I know. And I hope...that once I'm settled in at my place in town, you'll let her visit with me. Or let me babysit sometimes." The pang of grief was real. She loved

Violet so much—and to be with her, Maggie could almost see giving in to what Clint was saying. Just to get to be with the baby she loved so much.

But it wasn't fair to pin a relationship between her and Clint on the baby and Violet's tiny shoulders. She wouldn't do that to them.

"I don't want to lose you. You, Mags. I've thought about you every night and every day and everything in between for five months. Hell, longer. I was obsessed with you. For weeks before that night, I swear I breathed you."

"I thought about you, too. About what happened between us." She'd been almost inconsolable at first, but too afraid to let it show. "And...I came to the realization that what had happened had been a big mistake. One that I don't want to repeat." As she said it, she saw him flinch. As if she'd struck him. "We...do what's best for the baby. And go from there. I'm not the same girl I was when I left here. Or when I slept—had sex with you that night. Far from it." Maggie tilted her head back. She was five five.

Clint was a good nine or ten inches taller than she was.

She'd loved that about him before. How strong and sure he'd seemed.

She'd been fooling herself. Thinking that she could build a life with him and Violet on his ranch. A nice, sweet, steady life. That he was a reserved, taciturn man who had just needed *love* to break through the hurt. Her naivete had cost her. Had changed everything. But it had also given her the baby.

Maggie would never discount that.

Clint was still a man worth loving—if she would let herself be weak, she'd be throwing herself against his chest and doing just that.

But she'd finally realized something she hadn't ever before—Maggie was worth loving, *too*.

All the way. The whole deal. The stuff books were written about.

Real love. Not just something comfortable and easy Clint fell into.

She wanted him to love her like that. It sank in that she wanted *him* to love *her* like that, too.

She couldn't settle for less than that. She just…couldn't. It had to be the real deal, or nothing at all.

Nothing steady and calm about that. Just familiar and easy. Right there for when Clint needed her, and nothing more. She couldn't be an afterthought now.

That was exactly what he'd made her feel like for weeks after they'd made the baby.

No more.

"I know. I know exactly what my stupidity did to you. I just hope, with time, you'll forgive me." He still cupped her cheeks. Maggie was almost afraid to move. Afraid of what he—or she—would do next. "And I find you more than fascinating now. Just like I did then. No, more. Because I know how it can be between us, now."

A hot rush of sudden anger went through her. She'd not thought he would do this, would try to manipulate her. Not like this. She would have given anything to hear these words once. Now…

"Don't lie to me. I know you don't…want…me. You're trying to take a complicated situation and make the best of it. I won't be your lemonade. Or your consolation prize."

He stepped back, a puzzled expression in the blue eyes just like those Violet had inherited. "What in the blazes are you talking about?"

"I know that night didn't actually mean anything

significant. You made that abundantly clear. I don't appreciate you lying to me now, just so that I'll give in and stay. To just make everything easier. No work involved, no stopping to think about what I need, just 'Hey, here's this woman, we made a baby, and hell, might as well make the best of it—since she's already right here in front of me.' I can't do that. I just can't. More—I won't."

There was more fire and bite in her tone than she had ever directed at him before.

## 35

*HERE THERE BE SERPENTS.*

Clint knew he was treading on dangerous ground here. She had a look of heat and fire and fury all rolled into one in her Tyler blue eyes.

Fire that told him he was about to royally screw up.

She'd had months to convince herself that that was what he wanted. She thought Clint just saw her as convenient.

*Convenient?* That was the last thing he believed. "It meant something. That night meant something to me. Hell, it meant everything to me. That's why I panicked. I didn't realize just how much until you were gone."

"After you learned about the baby." She shot him a level look. "You told me word for word: it meant nothing. You don't remember? Now that I'm pregnant you're trying to make the best of things. Trying to convince both of us that...that night was more than what it was."

It wasn't a question. Maggie really believed it.

Hell, the woman probably thought the only reason he wanted her at all now was because of the baby. Damn it.

It had never occurred to him that she'd feel that way. To his shame, he'd thought that since she'd had feelings for him before—he doubted she'd have ended up in his bed to begin with if she hadn't—that it would be easy for him to convince her to just...go along with what he was planning. He really was an idiot at times. "No. It wasn't like that. It wasn't. I touched you that night because I was hurting too much to be able to stop myself. Because I had been wanting you all along. Weeks, months—every move you made, practically every breath you took drew me. Pulled me. Terrified me."

"After that night?" Skepticism was written all over her face.

Clint took a step toward her, and then another.

"Hell, no. *Before.* Before I ever touched you. No. I'm talking about before you left—but were right down the hall. It felt like you were a million miles away. And I knew it was my own damned fault. I didn't mean what I said that morning. About..."

"Using me? You didn't put it into those exact words, but I figured it out pretty quick." Pride had her chin rising. Her eyes burning with blue flame when she stared at him.

She was the most beautiful woman in the world.

He wasn't going to lose her. He'd stopped being a coward the day she'd almost been taken from him. He was going to fight for the woman he loved.

Even if it meant fighting the fears she'd had—fears he'd caused.

*Never* would she have said these things before Finley Creek. Clint knew that. She would have blushed and evaded and been afraid of the confrontation.

Maggie had changed.

"The last thing I wanted to do was hurt you." Never had he spoken truer words. "Ever."

"You did. But it was half my fault. I'd built up foolish dreams myself. But…we just have to focus on the baby. Babies. We have to do what is best for them first—and then focus on what we need to do for us. Separately."

Maggie stepped out of his arms. Deliberately.

Clint had never felt so cold. He wanted to wrap himself around her, just hold her where she couldn't leave him again. "What if what's best for all of us is for you and me to be together? Because I've thought of nothing else since the week you moved in. It took me a damned long time to get past the guilt. My wife had only been dead three months—and I was wanting you in my bed. Desperately. Dreaming about you instead of her. Tell me: What kind of man does that make me? I lasted another four months. That was it. I can't give you up, Maggie. I just…can't. I want you too damned much."

## 36

JASPER STAYED IN THE BARN SHIVERING LIKE A FOOL FOR hours, two days after he'd tried to search Clint Gunderson's place before.

This was the stupidest thing he had ever done. It was risky and dangerous and someone could get seriously hurt.

But…that last photo was seared into his mind. Jasper didn't need to pull it up on his phone. He knew exactly where it had been taken. At the church where Cloe volunteered every Wednesday running a donation room for children in the foster system. It was a project that had been her heart for more than three years now.

She had been smiling at the camera. She'd known the photographer well enough to be smiling. With a slightly flirtatious look in his most impish daughter's eyes.

He hadn't been smiling when he'd read the attached message. Far from it.

*"Get me what I want, or else you'll never see your beautiful daughter again. I'll do to Cloe what they did to Janice."*

Rather hard for Jasper to misunderstand. It was a clear threat to his daughter.

He still hadn't been able to figure out who was targeting him. He'd been searching for weeks—for both that single box of damning evidence and the one responsible for stalking his daughters.

But he was close. He had to be getting close.

Jasper wasn't stupid, nor inexperienced. He knew how these things tended to turn out.

Usually nothing came of blackmail—except exposure. Embarrassment. Arrest, if there was something illegal involved.

There was.

His was a crime of omission. He'd known—and done nothing.

He had never regretted anything more. He should have said something, done something years ago.

If what he had done ever became common knowledge his children would despise him.

He couldn't do that to them.

He just couldn't.

Jasper had to do something before this son of a bitch made good on his threats. Go after one of his three girls.

Jasper would fight to see that never happened.

Would do whatever he had to.

Including search every inch of Clint Gunderson's ranches over and over again until he had the answers.

Jasper stayed where he was—and planned.

## 37

CLINT ROLLED OVER AND CHECKED THE CLOCK. THE IDIOT dog was barking like a lunatic.

Three a.m.

He'd be getting up in ninety minutes to get the day started, as it was. He'd stayed up late thinking about what had happened between him and Maggie—if he'd gotten two hours of sleep, it would shock the hell out of him.

The woman had somehow managed to avoid him for another two full days after the intruder. Even when she'd be right there in front of him. She'd had friends and family in and out of his house, using them as a shield against him. Looking at him with big blue eyes that were both confused—and determined. Resolved.

Clint was starting to get desperate.

He had to come up with a plan to show that woman just how much she mattered. Before it was too late.

He was never going to give up. Not on Maggie.

Kody was going crazy. The dog was usually a lazy lump this time of night, sneaking into Clint's bed—or Maggie's—to snuggle under the blankets. Whichever of them was the biggest softie usually let him in their bed at night.

There was a doggie door in the mudroom.

The dog could get himself in and out, if needed.

But this…Kody didn't act like this.

Clint grabbed his gun, years of law enforcement making that instinctive.

Kody wouldn't be acting stupid without a reason. The dog was too smart for that. Clumsy as hell, but smart.

Clint grabbed his phone and slipped it into his pocket. He'd check on Maggie and Violet—then shut the dog up before he woke them.

But first, he had the security cameras connected to an app on his phone. It wouldn't hurt to take a look.

Not after what had happened to Maggie. He wasn't going to be stupid, or careless again.

He'd made certain the cameras were activated before he and Maggie had tucked Violet in her bed last night.

If something was going on, he'd be able to see it.

The dog barked again.

That's when Clint smelled the smoke.

## 38

Harsh hands shook her awake. Maggie could hear Violet crying, could hear Kody barking.

Could hear Clint calling her name. Cursing at her.

Telling her to wake up. That he couldn't carry both her and Violet.

Maggie sat up as quickly as she could. "Clint? What's going on?"

"Fire. We need to get outside now." He pulled her to her feet. With one hand. "Take her."

Maggie took the baby.

"Shoes. I'll need my shoes. And my bag." She had her bag right there in the armchair. It was easier to go on autopilot.

Terror robbed her of the ability to think beyond the moment. She slipped her feet into the shoes he grabbed for her, her arms tight on Violet. "It's ok, baby. It's ok."

"Come on. We're going out the back."

She just nodded and stood. His hand was warm on her back, reassuring.

There was smoke in the hall. Coming from the front of

the ranch house. Where the family room and the study were.

She could see the flames. See them devouring everything Clint had done while she and Violet had been gone.

Destroying everything.

Tears ran down her cheeks unchecked, and not just from the smoke.

Her arms tightened around the baby girl she held as Violet screamed in terror.

Clint got her and Violet to the back door, then called for the dog.

Kody didn't come.

For a moment, Maggie was certain Clint was going to go back. To get to the dog.

Kody had been Amy's dog. Clint loved that dog so much, too.

"Kody, baby, come!" She yelled, terrified the dog would ignore the command.

They couldn't let him burn up in the fire. They couldn't.

But she didn't want Clint to go back into the flames. Kody was in the hall, barking at the flames.

"Get out. Take Violet up the drive." Clint shoved his phone into her pants, the front of her underwear. "Go. I'll get him out. Call 911."

Her terror increased tenfold.

Clint couldn't go close to the flames. He couldn't.

Clint jerked open the back door and yelled again.

This time...Kody ran toward them both, barking the entire way. Clint grabbed his collar before he darted outside into the night.

Maggie stumbled out onto the porch. It was burning

too. Hardly anything was left of the right side of the house.

Their bedrooms were all at the left of the house.

She could hear the horses in the barn. Could hear them reacting to the smoke blowing in that direction.

Thankfully, it was cold and wet out. The larger, newer, horse barn was saturated with melting snow, and was farther from the house.

The four horses would be safe.

But the side barn, the one closest to the house, was fully engulfed. No livestock was kept in there. Just junk. It was just junk in there. But the house…

The dog pressed against her side, Violet was awake and crying. Maggie pressed Clint's phone back into his hand. She just rocked the baby and rocked her.

As the flames burned.

Just kept burning and burning. Destroying everything.

## 39

CLINT PULLED THEM TOWARD THE FAR BARN. AWAY FROM THE house, away from the smaller barn that was fully engulfed.

It stood fifteen feet from his back door and had been built by his great-grandfather to house his horse years ago. His grandfather hadn't wanted to trek across the yard to get to the horse at night—he'd been a bit on the lazy side.

The small barn had been built too close. When the ranch had been expanded in the fifties or sixties that barn...had just been too close. Especially with the cluster of trees Clint had been meaning to cut down when he had time.

Two of the trees were already engulfed.

Clint had been meaning to tear that shed down for months, but hadn't had the time. He'd been so focused on getting the house ready for Maggie and the babies...

It had been far too close to the house.

It had been burning for a long while.

There were burning branches from the trees on the porch of his house. The old wooden roof he had meant to replace was engulfing before their eyes.

A large burning branch had fallen onto the boards he and Rex had unloaded just the day before. Clint had been meaning to redo the entire back end of the porch to make it safe for Violet to have a place to play while Maggie swung in the porch swing.

Tinder. He'd provided the damned tinder.

That was all it had taken. The boards had just laid there and burned.

Burning for hours.

If the dog hadn't barked…

Movement to his left caught his attention.

That's when he saw it pulling out from behind the tree line—that same dark orange truck he'd seen the night of the prowler.

Every instinct he had flared, told him to get in his own truck and chase the son of a bitch down. To beat the answers out of him.

What was that son of a bitch hoping to accomplish setting a house on fire where a pregnant woman and a baby had been inside?

Rage unlike any he'd ever felt flooded him.

Now he understood how a good man could be driven to kill.

The only thing stopping him from doing just that, chasing that bastard down, was the woman crying in his arms. The baby terrified, held between them.

His family needed him now. But he was going to find that bastard and make him pay for this.

First chance he got.

## 40

MAGGIE STOOD IN THE COLD AS THE LIGHTS OF RED AND BLUE shot everywhere around her, reflecting off the light snow falling around them. As the sounds and yells flooded her ears.

The scent of smoke flooded her lungs.

Fire.

Almost everything Clint had was in that house.

A strong arm went around her. Violet was terrified; Clint held the baby tightly. His other arm was curved around her once-waist. His fingers were splayed over their son. Holding them all close.

He'd found rope in the back of his truck bed and looped it through Kody's collar. Holding the dog close, too. She hadn't even realized he'd done that.

She curled into him as the volunteer firefighters— including two of her own brothers—worked to keep the blaze contained to just the house. Clint lived too far away from town for the fire department to have ever had a chance of getting there in time to save the house.

That house had been in Clint's family for more than one hundred and forty years.

Now they just fought to save the rest of the barns. So that it didn't destroy anything else.

Someone had done this. Deliberately.

With her, Clint, and the baby inside. She shivered and shook, fighting the urge to vomit. They hadn't cared.

The man she knew—but couldn't identify.

Whoever had done this hadn't cared that there had been human beings inside. An innocent little girl.

It was as simple as that.

Just like the man before who had nearly killed her and sent her running to Texas. Whoever could start a fire in a house with a baby—they did not care who they hurt.

For a moment, she wished she was back down in Finley Creek now. Wished she was so far away that this couldn't have happened to her. To Violet.

Tears covered her cheeks.

The house was gone. Clint had lost everything in that house. All the memories of Violet as a newborn. All the memories he had of Amy. Everything he'd saved of Amy's for Violet.

That little baby hadn't deserved to lose the last connection to the mother she'd never know. Violet had already lost so much. Maggie turned toward Violet, reaching again. "Give her to me. Right now. Please. I need to hold her, Clint."

She just needed to hold Violet, to know she was safe. Just for a moment.

Maggie didn't know if he'd heard her. It was so loud, the sounds of men fighting the fire.

Her hands reached.

He passed her the baby without hesitation.

Then his strong arms were around them both, and he was holding her as tightly as possible.

Maggie buried her face in his strong chest and just tried to forget what was going on around her.

To forget the nightmares again.

---

## 41

THIS WASN'T WHAT JASPER HAD INTENDED TO DO. BUT HE'D gotten into those boxes and found dozens, *hundreds*, of case files. Disks and flash drives had abounded. Jasper had found three bloodied scarves, just in photographs alone. He had quietly and carefully tried searching all of the boxes in the shed after using the signal jammer again. Just to be safe. The photos he needed had to be there somewhere.

He'd cut the telephone wire and internet cable, too. Just in case there was a landline, still.

It had been horrible. There had been far too much to ever have hoped to find what he was looking for. Even if he'd had hours to search.

Clive had been leading him on a merry little game, telling him to search here. No doubt the other man had gotten a laugh at Jasper's expense.

It would be something Clive would enjoy doing. Especially if he was bored and it gave him a bit of a power trip.

Jasper hadn't had any other option.

There was no way he'd have been able to find what he

was looking for in there. He'd had no choice but to destroy it all, in hopes that what he was after would be caught in the blaze.

He'd torched the shed easily enough, with fuel he'd found in a lawn mower out back. Just that easy, after he'd put a cinderblock against the dog door around back. Just to keep the big dog inside.

The last thing he had ever expected to happen was the roof of Clint's actual house catching fire after the trees. The barn was old; it had been saturated from a Wyoming winter, even though the sun had been out for a few days now. The house...had just been too close. He hadn't been able to stop it from happening.

Not really.

There had been nothing he could do to stop it. Once he'd realized it was igniting, he had known...There had been nothing to be done.

Jasper couldn't just take off, not without knowing Gunderson and his family had made it safely outside.

He might have been a real bastard, but he wasn't a murderer. Especially of a pregnant woman and a toddler. He'd known Maggie since she'd been in preschool. He couldn't let her burn like that.

All he could think to do was throw a damned land-scaping brick through the window to get Gunderson's dog going.

He'd stuck around long enough to make sure Clive's son had gotten her out.

If Clint tracked down who owned this old truck, Jasper would be in a heap of trouble.

It was still registered to Jasper's father-in-law, after all.

But it had been dark, he'd been too far from the house for easy visibility, and he'd obscured the license plate with electrician's tape to alter the number. It was as good as he was going to get.

He'd hide the truck on the old place and make certain he was seen in town in his own newer SUV.

Jasper still wore the fake facial hair and wig. Had still worn gloves.

He was safe.

For now.

And hopefully…hopefully, the evidence was destroyed now. That was one part of his problem eliminated.

Now he had to move on. Find out who was stalking his daughters. Stalking him.

He consoled himself on the drive home with the fact that Clint Gunderson had two or three more properties to choose from. All were reasonably livable.

The boy and his family would have a roof over their heads within hours.

They wouldn't be out in the streets, even if the Tylers would have ever let that happen.

No. Jasper hadn't done that much harm at all.

Especially if it meant keeping his children safe.

Everything came at a cost, after all.

One just had to be prepared to pay it.

## 42

REX CURSED AS HE CAME UP ON THE DESTRUCTION. THIS...SON of a bitch...this hadn't been necessary. He ignored the rescue and fire and WHP personnel on scene and kept looking until he found the people he wanted to see.

There they were.

All three of them.

Rex jogged up to Clint's side. The other man jerked a nod at him. Maggie was crying in his arms, the baby held tightly between them. Violet was wailing, too.

Rex's anger boiled. This family hadn't deserved this.

The radio had been abuzz—an arson fire.

*Arson*, at Clint Gunderson's ranch.

Rex looked at the flames as they destroyed what his friend had been working to build for years. What had been in Clint's family for a century and a half.

He knew the other man's dreams for the place. They'd discussed them before. Clint had wanted to build a place his children could be proud of. Rex understood that.

He flinched. Rex had hung drywall in that house himself. Had painted until sweat was rolling down his back and he was vowing never to agree to help Clint again. But he would have; all the other man would have had to do was ask.

The house was destroyed. There would be nothing left of it but ash.

Maggie was safe. Violet was safe. The baby they were expecting was safe. Even the damned dog was pressed against Clint's leg, terrified of the chaos, but safe.

Rex saw some of his own people working the perimeter. He jerked his head at Melvin Scanlon, one of the supervisors under him.

Rex trusted the guy to know what he was doing. "What's the situation?"

"Just getting started. Gunderson reports the dog started barking, and it woke him. He realized what was going on, and the smoke alarms started going off—he was able to get his wife and baby outside. In time to see an orange truck pulling out of his drive. Fire started in the nearest barn, as far as we can tell. No signs of what started it yet, but we figure it jumped to the wooden boards on the back porch from the trees, there. Gunderson had the boards drying out under the awning for repairs next week. Or so he says."

Rex didn't correct him on Maggie's status. As far as he was concerned, she was as good as Clint's wife already. "He did. I helped him unload the damned things a day ago. It was my idea to put them there. Everything filters through me."

## 43

Her brothers Chandler and Reese were two of the volunteers. The MCVFD did what they could, but Clint knew the truth. His house was gone. Everything in it would be nothing more than ash.

He had digital photos of Amy, saved in the cloud. Digital photos of Violet as a baby, with both him and Maggie. He'd even scanned some of his mother's family and his birth father's, and important documents.

He hadn't lost every tie to the past.

But that wasn't important to him now.

What was important was the woman and two kids he loved with every breath he took.

Maggie was shivering, snow falling all around her. Someone—he suspected it was Rex—had found her a blanket somewhere and had wrapped her in it.

Clint swore.

He wanted to stay, see this through. But his family had to take priority. He looked at Rex. "She's freezing out here. They both are."

He'd only grabbed the baby the one blanket Violet had already been wrapped in.

"Put your family in my SUV, Clint. I'll take you into town."

Clint nodded. He should drive his truck. He looked for it.

A fire engine blocked him in. "The inn. We'll stay there for a few days. Until I can regroup."

"We can talk there."

Maggie let him lead her docilely away. She hadn't said anything since she'd wanted to hold Violet.

She'd turned in on herself, was consumed with the baby. Protecting Violet from the trauma of the night.

He was going to do no less with her. "Help me get her somewhere safe, Rex. Help me protect them. That's all I ask."

"I'll do that."

"Nothing else here matters. Not really. I say let it burn. All I care about is her and our children. I just need to get her out of here."

"I understand. Let's do just that."

Clint looked around.

Maggie's borrowed SUV was the closest, but it was blocked by patrol cars. "There will be a spare diaper bag in Marin's SUV. It'll be unlocked. The locks are broken on it. Grab it, will you? I'm getting my family out of here."

## 44

Madam Zelda was waiting on the porch steps when Rex pulled to a stop in front of the hotel over two hours later.

Of course. It was going to be that woman everywhere he turned. Just his luck.

She was dressed in daring purple silk pajamas that looked like they came straight from the 1920s, and were practically cut to her navel. Hints of feminine flesh taunted him.

If he hadn't been so damned tired, he'd have looked. Rex would admit that.

She seemed to favor that era in her odd-ball clothing choices. Probably spent hours online shopping for them—or hitting thrift stores. Looking for just the right cut and material to make a man's hands itch to touch. To see if she was as soft as that silk looked.

Damn the witch.

Maggie had fallen asleep ten minutes into the drive. Clint handed Rex the diaper bag that had been in the back of Marin's SUV, along with the car seat that Rex had moved over to his own SUV himself, then swung the baby out into Rex's arms.

She snuffled and put her tiny head on his shoulder. She hadn't lasted half as long as Maggie. He patted the little back until she fell asleep again.

Rex met the crazy woman on the inn's large front porch. "Who called you?"

The last thing Clint needed was this going around like crazy already. The man couldn't catch a break lately.

Hell, if he was Clint, he'd say screw it, pack his woman and baby up, grab the damned dog, sell what properties he owned, and take her somewhere else to live.

Put Masterson County behind them.

But her being a Tyler—that wasn't likely to happen. Not as attached to each other those Tylers were.

It was up to Rex to help his friend make it as safe a place for her as he possibly could.

"No one called me, Commander." The witch took the diaper bag from him quietly. Her cheeks were pale in the porch light. There was worry—and fear—in the big blue eyes. "I woke a few minutes ago and knew someone would be needed. We have a night clerk, but I'm going to take them in through the family entrance. I'm not registering them in. As far as our records will show, they were never here."

"How in the hell did you know something was happening?" The woman had to have spies everywhere. That was the only explanation he could find.

"Don't worry, commander, you don't have a leak in your precious department. I just woke up and knew someone would need me tonight. Would need a place to stay. It was just a feeling. That's all it ever is."

There was a look in her eyes that told him one thing— she was lying to him right now.

"That's bullshit, and we both know it." He didn't believe in that, and he never would.

"Is it? You're standing right here now, aren't you?" She shot him a pointed look out of those damned blue eyes of hers.

Rex would admit it: the woman got under his skin. Fast.

If she wasn't as kooky as a cuckoo clock, he'd think she was one of the hottest women he'd ever seen. But he'd never thought bat-shit crazy was a turn on.

Rex just grunted at her.

He carried the baby inside as Clint led a drowsy Maggie up the back walkway.

Madam Zelda went to her friend's side and hugged her quickly. She was older than Maggie, he thought, by a few years. Very protective.

Loyal. He had to give her that, she was extremely loyal.

Right before his eyes she efficiently got them up the back stairs and into a room in the family wing. He hadn't even realized there was a "family" wing in the place.

Rex just followed, listening as she talked. "It's Miranda's suite. She's not going to be back in town for a few months. There's a private bath there through that door. If she won't let you in the bed with her yet, Clint, that sofa pulls out into a sleeper. Extra blankets are in the far closet. I'll bring breakfast up later, whenever you are ready. I know you'll want to avoid people for a few hours. Until you get your bearings."

Clint just nodded. Maggie had already sank into the bed, still dressed in her smoke-scented clothes.

Hell, they were probably all the poor woman had.

Clint wouldn't have had any more than that, either.

Nor would the baby. Shit. Everyone knew babies needed *things*. Things Rex couldn't even begin to think about. They'd lost everything for Violet, and had another baby coming—they'd need supplies. Fast.

"Hell, Gunderson. I'm going to run to the damned store. Grab you all something to wear tomorrow." He'd never bought maternity clothes before. He had no idea. "Get some diapers and things, too."

"I'll go with you," Madam Zelda said so firmly he didn't argue. "You'll need help getting everything they'll need. Clint, Dusty is the only one who knows you three are here, other than me. If you need anything, hit number seven on that phone. It'll dial her phone directly."

The last thing Rex wanted was to spend even one more minute with the woman, but Clint had his hands full. The man was rocking his daughter while standing over his pregnant woman. After losing his damned home because of arson. The man had taken enough abuse for one night.

Anger was just below the surface. Rex clamped it down. Now wasn't the time.

He'd put a car out in Masterson tonight. Of deputies he somewhat trusted. Other than standing guard over them himself, there was nothing else he could do. Except help them get started on tomorrow. "Come on, then. Let's get going. It's an hour drive."

He was going to be stuck with the woman for another three hours minimum. And it was almost six a.m. now.

"I'll change and join you in a moment." Marin hugged Clint quickly. "You'll be ok here. Just rest. I have a bag of things you might be able to wear. Agent Knight left his bag the day Miranda was attacked. He told me to send it with Miranda next time she's here. He won't mind lending them to you for the night. There are some sweats in it that should fit you, if you want to shower. It's in Miranda's closet. She's got pajamas that'll fit Maggie in that drawer. They're elastic waist and button top."

"Thanks again, Marin. We really appreciate it."

Just like that, she handled everything. Rex just stood there and watched.

Madam Zelda just somehow seemed to make things happen.

## 45

CLINT SHOWERED. HE WAS TOO DAMNED TIRED TO THINK, AND too keyed up to sleep. Maggie was fitful on the bed. He'd wanted to take her to get checked out at the ER, but she'd refused. She'd just wanted to get Violet someplace safe. First responders had cleared Maggie and Violet and Clint—and even the dog—at the scene.

He'd gotten them all out in time.

If they needed anything, Marin's cousin Dixie was an ER nurse, and Clint thought one of the doctors she worked with lived across the street. And Rhea Masterson, the woman who'd founded the hospital to begin with, lived a block from the hotel now. Help would be close.

The fear in Maggie's eyes was something he would never forget. He spent the next several hours trying to figure out who could be responsible for this.

Violet fussed, looking at him with her big blue eyes. He lifted her quickly. She needed a bath; he handled that as quickly and quietly as he could, then redressed her in the pajamas that had been in the diaper bag in the rear of the

SUV. Maggie had always carried a spare diaper bag, and they didn't smell too heavily of smoke, thankfully.

By the time he was finished, Marin and Rex were back. They had bags of stuff for him and Maggie and the baby, and even a bag of dog food for the dog. Kody hadn't come out from beneath the desk in the corner since he'd darted under there hours ago. Even the dog was traumatized.

Clint didn't say anything, as overwhelmed as he was.

Marin set her bags on the couch quietly, then reached for Violet, who was reaching for her. "I can take her back to my room, Clint. Keep her there today. Let you and Maggie rest."

Clint nodded. Violet had already fussed a few times, and he wanted Maggie to sleep. Violet was familiar with Marin again. She'd be ok. Just down the hall. "Thanks."

"No problem. Between us Talleys, she'll be well taken care of." With that, she took his daughter, a bag of diapers and wipes, then glared at Rex until the other man got the idea and marched out of the room with a huff.

Just like that he was left in Miranda's bedroom while Maggie slept right next to him. Clint climbed on the bed and leaned back against the pillow. There was no way he could sleep now.

Hell, it was almost eleven a.m. Nothing *night* about it.

He still hadn't processed how he felt about the destruction of the home he'd been remodeling for his family.

That ranch had been in Gunderson hands since the day it had been built back in 1877. Losing it was more of a blow than he would have expected.

Clive hadn't been his real father—but Clive's younger brother had been. He'd taken off before Clint was born.

He'd never known the man who'd abandoned him, but he had known his grandparents. And his great-grandfather. That man had been one of the only ones to ever give a damn about Clint.

He had never forgotten that.

He'd spent the last five months fixing the problems within the house itself, reprioritizing the work on the ranch to focus funds on the house. When not searching for the bastards responsible for his family's absence in the first place, he'd been fixing that house.

For her.

He'd wanted a house Maggie could be proud of, a house where his two children could grow up comfortably. Safely. A place they'd be proud to invite their friends to play.

Happily.

He'd never be rich, but he would be able to provide whatever his family needed.

Now all that hard work was gone. He couldn't even begin to process what that would mean for them.

He still had two other houses he'd inherited, close enough to the one that had burned. There were two smaller houses even further out, where ranch hands had lived.

With a few days' work, he could provide adequate shelter, at least. He had money to get Maggie and Violet a room here at the inn while he did that, too. Or she could take Violet back to her brothers' place for a while. There would be room for them there.

She and Violet would be well guarded, too.

But the modern updates he knew she would want— they would have to wait a while.

Until he could get them for her. He would. Clint made her a silent promise. Maggie would have everything he could give her.

As Maggie shifted on the bed next to him, he reaffirmed to himself the real truth.

That house wasn't what was important. To either of them.

He had what was important. *Who* was important. If Maggie, Violet, and the baby were safe—he had everything he could ever want.

Maggie shifted again. Her blue eyes slowly blinked open. She looked around, her confusion on her face. "Clint?"

"Hey, honey. It's ok. We're safe here."

"I smell like smoke." Confusion cleared. Tears came next. "The fire…the ranch. Where's Violet? Where is she?"

She sat up, fear on her face, looking around for his daughter.

"We're at the inn. This is Miranda's room, remember?"

Maggie nodded, pulling in a calming breath. "Violet?"

"Marin has Violet today. So you and I can rest, and talk. Plan."

Maggie pulled herself up into a seated position. "I need a long shower first—and clothes."

"Marin and Rex took care of that. There are clothes for you there. I don't know if they are maternity clothes, but they're clean and dry."

Thirty minutes later, she emerged from the bathroom, clean and dressed in a baggy sweatshirt and pull-on pants, a broken look on her face.

Clint stood. He opened his arms. He just needed to hold her for a moment or two. If she'd let him.

Kody snuggled up to her side. Maggie knelt down awkwardly and hugged him. Buried her face in his fur. The dog stood patiently until she was finished, pressing himself close to her side. Damn doofus was scared, too.

Clint just waited.

Then she almost jumped to her feet and practically threw herself into Clint's arms. He tightened his hold around her. "It's ok, honey. It's ok. We're both ok, Violet's ok, and the baby is just fine. We're all just fine. Even the dog. We're all ok."

"Where are we going to live?"

We. He tried not to focus on that one small word. But... it felt right. He would fight to keep it.

"Hey, don't worry about that now. I have two other houses, remember? They need a little more work than the ranch house did, but they're both bigger than the one that burned. Plenty of room."

It was true. They were bigger. Almost as old, but...they were bigger. That might come in handy if she wanted another kid or two after this one came.

They were places he'd vowed never to live again—one had been Jay's, inherited from their grandmother, a foul woman Clint had never liked. The other had been the ranch where he'd grown up himself. Clint had far too many nightmares to go there. Jay...before he'd died, he'd spent some time and money fixing the place from their grandmother up quite a bit. It would do for Clint's family now. "And I have land left for Violet from her mother's family. We can always build a house out there with insurance money. We'll find the right answer when we need to."

He'd have to pick one of the houses—probably the one in the best condition. Then he'd have to make certain it was safe for Maggie and the babies.

He wouldn't have much time for that, but if he had to,

she had brothers who were building a contracting business.

Maybe they'd be willing to help him. At least give him the family rate.

If it was meant for her, they'd probably jump at the chance. And Rex. Rex had three brothers who had offered to help him out, if needed, too.

He'd make her a home. No matter what.

But first…he and Rex had an arsonist to catch. No one was going to threaten Clint's family ever again. "I want you to take Violet back to your brothers' place, first thing this afternoon."

"Why? What are you going to do?" Maggie settled on the corner of Miranda's bed. "Clint? What are you planning?"

"Rex and I need to find the son of a bitch who did this. I need to know that my family is safe. I'd be happier if you took Violet back down to your friends in Texas, if you want. I have enough money in the bank to get you and Violet a flight this afternoon. See if that Barratt guy can go with you, take you back down there." Not his first option, but the other man could keep her safe.

"You want me to take her away again?" Maggie just stared at him like he was crazy.

Hell, yes. He wanted her to take Violet and run. What man wouldn't? "I want the three of you as safe as I can possibly make you. That means either you go to your brothers' place and they guard you, or you get out of the damned state. I can't lose you, Maggie. I just…can't. I can't survive that. I know I can't. I love you too damned much to lose you, too."

Everything he felt was in those words. He just hoped she understood how much he meant it.

## 46

MAGGIE SAW THE FEAR IN HIS EYES. HER BREATH STARTED. She finally knew what she wanted to do. She wanted to press against him and just hold him—have him hold her. She didn't want to leave him.

Ever.

That he could have been killed tonight was starting to sink in. It terrified her. That man could have shot them right where they'd stood, watching their home burn. Done anything to them.

The baby kicked, reminding her that what she wanted didn't matter all that much now. What mattered was her keeping the babies safe. "I'll go to my brothers', but I want you to come with me."

"I can't do that."

"Why?" Stubborn male pride, most likely.

"Because if this guy is after me, I don't want them anywhere near you or Violet." Clint's hands rose to cup her cheeks. "I don't want the two of you ever hurt because of me. I love you, Maggie Tyler. Whether you believe that or not, it's the truth. *I love you.* And I can't lose you again. I won't. No matter what monsters I have to fight. No matter what it takes. I *love* you, more than I have ever loved a woman before. And that was what terrified me eight months ago. My feelings. And that's why I closed myself off then. I couldn't stand the thought of the hurt of losing you now. And then my damned nightmare came true because of that son of a bitch. I...have been living that nightmare every day for months. Until I found you again. I can't go through that again."

Maggie almost fell over. There was no doubt in her mind now—Clint meant the words he'd just said. It was right there in his eyes. In the way his hands were clinging to her.

He was shaking against her. A strong man brought weak.

It was more than just the baby between them.

Maybe after everything that had happened made it impossible for her to think. She just stretched up as best as she could, until she could press her lips against his.

She just wanted him to hold her now. They'd figure everything else out later.

Right now, she just needed him to hold her. And she needed to hold him, too.

*That* was what she was going to do.

———

CLINT FOUGHT NOT TO JUST GRAB HER AND CARRY HER TO THE bed behind them. He held her like she was glass, so afraid he'd hurt her. "Mag—"

"Just hold me." Her arms tightened around his waist. He felt their baby pressed between them. "I don't want to go away again."

"I don't want you to go, either. But I can't stand the thought of something happening to you or Violet. Even if there was no baby between us, I would still feel that way. I was frozen until that night. Dying inside. Hell, I could barely function with Violet. She needed more than I was then. All I could think about was work—because I could control it. Didn't have to feel. Until you."

"What are we supposed to do now?" Maggie asked. Clint just held her.

"I don't know."

Somehow he guided her back to the bed. "We talk. Decide what it is we both want. No more avoiding the hard conversations."

"I...have a plan. I want...my own life. My own career. I feel good about what I have planned. You can change everything about my plans, and that scares me. "

Because she didn't trust him, or didn't trust how she felt? Clint didn't know, but they would find out.

"I know. I'll support you however I can. But don't ask me to give you up. We can work everything else out, but that. I won't let you go, Mag. I just...can't. I don't think that is something I can do." Clint dropped another kiss on her lips. He just waited for her to pull away.

But she didn't.

One small hand rose to clench his borrowed T-shirt. Clint tangled one hand in still wet red hair. He held her close, grateful that he still could.

## 47

---

HE SMELLED LIKE SOAP AND MAN. *CLINT.* MAGGIE JUST wanted to press her face into his chest and let him hold her. Let him help her forget the events of the night before.

She hated herself for being such a wimp. She should be stronger than this. But she wasn't.

Maybe she wasn't like Mel.

Maybe she was still mousy, practically invisible Maggie. Nothing but a ball of hormones and fear. She told herself to toughen up, that she had to stick to her guns.

She couldn't let Clint change her mind. She had a *plan.* One she had been determined to stick to.

Stick to the plan. Clint was not the plan.

But his arms were warm and strong around her. And heaven help her, despite what she'd been telling herself for five and a half months, plus one week, his arms around her felt *right.* Perfect.

As if she'd returned to right where she belonged.

He was clutching her like he never wanted to let her go. Maggie rested her head against him. "What are we supposed to do now?"

"I don't know. You and Violet will go to your brothers' in a few hours. I'll have to deal with the WHP and Joel Masterson. I'm sure they'll have questions for the both of us. Hell, I'm probably a suspect."

"But you were with me."

"Because of our romantic involvement, we'll be doubted on that, too. Especially if someone wants to make trouble."

She shivered. "Why would someone still be after you?"

"Hell, I don't know. I've wrapped up every case I was involved in. But Rex and I will be finding out. I'll keep you safe, Maggie. You have my vow."

"Maybe you need to leave, too? Sell everything and just get out of the state forever? What do you really have here now? Besides me and the baby?"

"You, Violet, and the baby. My home. My family history. Violet's heritage."

"I just don't know if that is worth it. I…can't stand the thought of someone hurting you." Her hands tightened on him.

Clint couldn't be hurt. He just couldn't.

"I know. That's exactly how I feel about you, Maggie. The five months you were gone I couldn't breathe. I'm not sure how I made it through. Knowing you were out there and I couldn't get to you…couldn't touch you, couldn't hold Violet…that is my worst nightmare. It will always be. You are my home. Not some sticks-and-bricks in Masterson County."

"Come to Texas with me. Let Rex find who did this." Even as she said it, she knew the truth. Clint would never hide himself away behind stone walls. Not him.

"I can't run. I need to finish this. It may have something to do with Clive, or it may have something to do with my own cases. But I can't leave it unfinished. If I do, I'll always have the fear that it *wasn't* finished. That someone slipped through the cracks. That we won't ever be safe. We can't live watching over our shoulders all the time. That's no kind of life for you and the kids."

His hand dropped to cover where their son rested.

She just nodded. She understood. None of the men she knew would just run away, either. No. They'd stand against any threat. No matter how afraid they were.

Clint would be no different. No matter how terrified it made her. "Just be careful. I...*we*...need you."

"I promise you, Maggie Tyler, no matter what: I am going to be there for you every minute of every day. Until the day they put me in the ground sixty, seventy years from now. I will be *yours*. Forever."

## 48

BRANDT HAD SPENT THE LAST TWO DAYS BOUNCING AROUND the state, checking out old ranches and foreclosures wherever he could find them. He'd found six that would meet his original plans. He'd called it a hunt well done.

Like all Barratt men who had come before him, he was a hunter at heart.

His first stop back in Masterson was the diner. He was starving.

Brandt had never eaten better food than he'd found at the Masterson Diner. Even the best chefs Houghton could hire couldn't compete with that woman and her bevy of gorgeous granddaughters.

He was one of the first ones through the doors. Breakfast smells assaulted him. Brandt was led by his stomach more times than not in these kinds of situations. And he was starved.

The hostess on duty was none other than his favorite little waif.

She was as sweet as cotton candy, and Brandt wouldn't

deny it—he found her fascinating. Even more than her far more outgoing sister and cousins.

It wasn't anything he could explain.

He...couldn't stay away. He also couldn't help but wonder what the little waif would do if he just scooped her up some day and carried her away. He contemplated it for a moment.

It was rather a Barratt family tradition. Find the woman that fascinated them—and just carry her away.

Not that he was going to do anything like that. He was a civilized man.

He had far more control than Houghton, after all.

She had a worried look in her big green eyes that struck Brandt hard. "Hello, little one. What's wrong?"

She just looked at him, then glanced at her sister beside her. Marin had on clothing far more casual and sedate than he was used to seeing her in, in just the week he'd been around. The same worry was in Marin's blue eyes as was in her sister's green.

Marin had a familiar baby strapped to her chest, watching the crowd around them all.

Violet.

The baby recognized him. "Ban-Ban!"

Marin slipped her out of the carrier and passed him his favorite girl of all time. Brandt cuddled her close. "What's going on? Maggie ok?"

Marin was the one who answered. "Clint and Maggie's home caught fire and burned last night. Maggie's still sleeping at the inn. Violet is staying with me today."

Brandt's arms tightened around the little girl he adored. "What happened?"

Marin shot him a level look. "It was arson, Mr. Barratt.

Someone burned down their home deliberately. Clint is trying to figure out who now."

Brandt made a decision. He was going to find Maggie and convince her to come back to Texas with him as soon as he could get Houghton's private jet to Masterson County.

He wasn't about to let anything happen to Violet or Maggie. Not if he could stop it.

Sometimes…a hunter had to turn into a protector. It was just the way it was.

## 49

THEY'D JUST HELD EACH OTHER FOR A FEW HOURS. NEITHER one of them was going to get more sleep. Not considering what had happened. Maggie rested on his lap, her lips swollen from his kisses. She'd needed his touch—and had needed to touch him. So much. She was going to go back to her brothers' place. She hadn't wanted to, but he was right.

It was safest for Violet there. In the meantime, she was going to make a list of everything she and Clint and the two babies would need to make the house he'd inherited from his brother their home.

And it was going to be *theirs*. She was staying with Clint. No matter what. She'd made her decision watching the ranch house burn. No more doubting.

She belonged with this man. No matter what came their way.

"I'm only staying for two days. That's about all I will be able to handle of my brothers. It takes a far stronger woman than I am to deal with the five of them in one place. In two days, we're moving into Jay's house. *All* of us. It will be ours from here on out." It was a bold state-ment, but it was the truth. "I have some cash saved up. I didn't just play around with Mel while I was in Texas. I worked."

"I have some money in savings, too. From selling Clive's house. I was intending it for Violet's college. But we can dip into it, if we have to. To make the house safe and livable. I'll get contractors out there as soon as I can. It'll be a good place for us." His fingers spread over their son. The baby kicked against them.

"We can make this work." Maggie said it out loud for the first time. "We can do this. Together. Equal say. Part-ners. Real partners. From this moment on."

"Always." Clint hugged her close. "I want nothing more than to be with you, and the kids. I actually wouldn't mind five or six, if you are up for it."

"Only if you carry half." She grinned at him, fighting tears again. "Because this one is sitting on my bladder."

They were joking around now, but both knew that they were just delaying the inevitable. They had to face the world soon. Face the fire.

It was just a matter of time. There would be witness statements to give, people would be showing up with donated clothes and food and full of questions. Everyone would want to know what happened.

And Rex and Clint had to catch the man responsible. She knew they would. She had complete faith in Clint to do just that.

Worry for him threatened to overwhelm her. "I knew him, Clint. I just can't figure out who he is. He knew *me*. Knew enough to tell me that he'd always confused me and Pan and Nikki. He had to be close to us, right?"

"Not really. Masterson is a small town. Anyone seeing your cousins and you together and learning your names could have said the same thing. He won't get close to you again, honey. I can promise that."

"No one can make those kinds of promises."

His arms tightened around her. "No. I suppose I can't. But I'm going to do my damnedest."

"In the meantime, we have things to do. I need to check on Violet. And we need to get moving."

The world outside the windows waited. They couldn't hide forever.

Nor could she run away.

Maggie wasn't going to run away from life ever again.

## 50

"I want to take Maggie back to Texas with me," Brandt said to the woman walking next to him.

"I don't think you'll be going to Texas anytime soon."

He liked Marin Talley a great deal. And while she was one of the sexiest women to have ever walked the planet, he felt almost brotherly to her. He was as comfortable with her as he was Maggie. Although…Maggie made a man want to protect more than Marin.

Marin was the kind of woman who would stand at a man's back, her own sword drawn, ready to fight her own dragons.

"Why is that?"

She shot him a mysterious smile. "You'll find more in Masterson County than you could have ever hoped to find. If you stick around long enough. You've buzzed in and out of town since you first arrived. How can you find what you need when you don't stand still long enough to look around you?"

Maybe the woman was crazy, but he liked her.

"Let's just find Maggie."

"I know exactly where she's at. Question is…is she ready to be found?" She led him into the private wing of the inn. "This is where our family lives. Who wants to be wrapped up in the inn 24/7? Not us. Grandma—and our father when he was visiting—wanted to give us as normal a life as possible. We each have a small suite in the hotel somewhere—a few of us are on the first floor, off the kitchen—but we have a large family room on this floor. And a real kitchen. But only Meyra hangs out there, now. She's the real miracle behind the food you love so much. She's taken our family recipes next level." She unlocked a door using the keypad next to it. Brandt followed her into the hall, which led to a reasonably sized family room. An old dog was sprawled out on a low couch in front of a window that overlooked a garden. It felt like a home. If he hadn't been seeing it with his eyes, he would never have expected it.

"If so, she's magnificent."

"I'm glad you think so. Most people overlook my sister. She's the quietest of us all. We had this part of the inn remodeled when I was twelve, taking out some of the smaller single rooms and turning this into the family wing."

"Nothing wrong with being quiet."

"No. There isn't. Here. Maggie and Clint are in Miranda's room. It's the last on this floor." She stopped at a wooden door and knocked smartly.

Maggie's cowboy swung the door open.

"Da-da!"

Clint reached for his daughter.

"Hey, cowboy. We're here to keep Maggie company

while you go do what you got to do," Marin said, pushing her way in.

Brandt dutifully followed.

## 51

JASPER COULDN'T KEEP USING HIS FATHER-IN-LAW'S TRUCK, eventually someone was going to see it and put two and two together. He wasn't ready for that. But he was feeling hopeful, even after the fire.

When he had returned home, there had been one more message on his answering machine. This time, the voice wasn't as distorted as it had been before.

He had gotten sixteen texts, fourteen emails, and twenty-two threatening phone calls since this all began. The harassment had continued for well over two months now. Someone wanted that evidence badly.

It was far more likely that they just wanted Jasper on a string. They were enjoying toying with him.

There was only two people that it could be.

Clive Gunderson and Arthur Talley.

Clive was in jail, and he was certain it wasn't him doing this shit. So it had to be Arthur Talley. Greedy bastard always was trouble.

The one thing Jasper could do was protect himself.

To do that, he had to act on the plan he had come up

with earlier. The first thing he did was hit the smallest house Gunderson owned.

It was barely locked. Jasper had little trouble getting inside. He searched every room, for any possible boxes. It wasn't hard to do; there was almost nothing kept in the house at all. Just a bunch of drywall stacked up in one room.

Jasper paid careful attention to what he suspected was the dining room and the home office areas. But there was no paneling in the place like Clive had indicated there would be.

No, it was plaster, the old kind from at least one hundred and fifty years ago. The old plaster was often made with horsehair and lime. There were no holes behind pictures of Gunderson's children anywhere. No. There weren't even pictures of Gunderson's children.

This place was a dead end.

Unless he was searching in vain. What most likely had happened was that every evidence box had burned in that shed. It made the most sense.

Clive was lazy—he wouldn't have separated out that one particular box of evidence, not considering all of the other foul things Clive had probably been involved in.

If what Jasper had been looking for had been in that storage shed, it was gone now.

But he had to make sure.

Clint's other place was going to prove riskier. For one thing, it was in better shape. Clint would most likely choose it for his family sometime soon. Jasper would. The place was big enough for a good half-dozen kids or so, after all.

But Jasper would do what he had to do.

## 52

Jay's house was actually a beautiful place—under the age. Maggie tried to study it objectively. To remove the knowledge of what Clint's brother had had planned for Pip.

There had been some work done on it. By Jay. He'd been cleaning it up while he had been stalking her cousin Pip.

Guess he had to have something to do in his nonstalking time.

She shivered.

She was determined to move past that. This was the best place for Violet now, and for the baby when he got there. It was in the best condition, had barns big enough for all the horses to move into, and was even closer to town. And it was larger.

It just needed a *bit* more work.

They could do this.

It connected to Clint's larger property along the rear acreage and had once been a part of the original

Gunderson settlement. Gunderson, Wyoming had had its own post office ninety years ago.

With only nine houses, all belonging to members of the original Gunderson family and their ranch hands, the post office had dwindled, and the hopes of a small town in that area had been erased. All that remained of those houses was this overly large but slightly rundown ranch house, the two houses that had belonged to the hands, and one place that was uninhabitable, the roof had caved in long ago.

Most of Clint's ancestors had died young, several being lost in the wars, or had moved out of state to disappear forever more than sixty years ago.

Now there was just Clint. And Violet. And the baby Maggie carried. They were literally all that was left of Gunderson, Wyoming.

Maybe she and Clint could do their part to fix that eventually.

"It doesn't look like much now," Clint said. "But the inside of the house is sound. Safe. It still needs a lot of work."

"I heard he was redecorating it and remodeling it for Pip."

Clint just nodded. "Is that going to bother you? I mean, after what happened to your cousin?"

Maggie just shook her head. Bad things happened. She couldn't let herself dwell on them. She had more important things to worry about, like having a roof over Violet's head.

That was the most important thing now. Taking care of Violet, and the baby. She could do that.

And Clint.

That moment in the fire, she'd faced the truth. If he had turned back and been lost to her in the flames, it would have destroyed her. Because she loved this man. Loved him just as deeply as Mel loved Houghton. She would never deny that now. "It'll be fine, Clint. It just needs a little work. But I can see the children playing here. Being safe here. I can see where it would be a beautiful home eventually. The babies need a home. We have one right here, just waiting for us now."

The house had been built in the craftsman style, and was large, larger than the house that had burned. The siding was faded. The paint needing scraped. It looked like the entire siding needed replaced. The porch boards were worn, and it looked like there were some holes in a few places. Those would have to be fixed soon.

There was character. Charm. It just needed cleaned up. The yard was a little grown over and muddy from the melting snow, but she could see places where roses had probably once grown. Probably planted by his great-grandparents years ago. She'd have to see if she could rescue those roses somehow. Revive them.

There was an old hand pump well right there, too. She wondered if it still worked. It would be wonderful in the summer if it did.

"This was my grandparents' place. They left it to my mother, who left it to Jay, with the majority of the acreage, and left me a small part of the land behind the house here, since it was assumed I'd inherit everything else someday. They wanted Jay to be set, too."

He had let it slip before how his father's parents had favored Jay over him. Clive had also favored Jay. Probably because Clint was a stepson, and for some people, some horrible people, there was a difference.

She reached for the baby in Clint's arms. Violet came to her immediately, and Maggie settled her on her hip.

She didn't understand that at all. When you loved a child, it shouldn't matter who had created them.

A familiar F150 was coming up the drive. They'd left Marin and Brandt back in town, but apparently, they'd found them again.

Clint looked at her. "Seems your friends have found us."

"One thing I can say about Brandt Barratt, he goes after what he wants intensely. Drives his sister insane. But…he has a lot to prove to his older brothers and sister. I can understand that. I think that's why we clicked."

"And there's nothing more between you than friend-ship? He seems like a good man."

She saw it. The insecurity in his blue eyes.

That was probably something he would always battle, because of the way Clive had treated him and Jay.

Clint would always feel like he was second best. Lacking.

Like…like *she* had felt she was just convenient to him, he felt he wasn't good enough for her.

That was why he had been so focused on telling her he could provide for her and their children. Because he wanted her to think he would be good enough for her.

Now she understood.

Everyone had their fears, after all. Their insecurities.

Their own battles.

Maggie stretched up on her toes, and pressed her lips to his first. Violet giggled between them. "Da-da, Mag-Mag!"

Her arms tightened around Violet. "It's not like that between Brandt and me. We connected, yes, I won't deny that, but it's different...like, we understand each other on a soul-deep level because maybe we were siblings in another life. You don't have to worry about my feelings for Brandt. I promise. He's not *you*."

Marin called out a greeting.

"Marin says he's destined to be her brother-in-law, too. Hard to look past that."

"Like I can see that happening. A Barratt, with Meyra? She'd run and hide just at the mention of it. And as for Miranda...well, that woman would make mincemeat out of your pal. I think he might be too *nice* for her."

"No kidding. We're just friends, Clint. I promise. I only have room for one man in my life right now."

She stepped toward her friends. She was going to figure out just exactly what she wanted to do about Clint Gunderson later.

For now, Marin had an intent look in her eyes. One that told Maggie the other woman was up to no good.

MAGGIE WAS HOLDING UP WELL. PROBABLY BETTER THAN Clint was himself. She greeted her friends calmly, asking what they were doing there.

"This hot Texas guy and I came to see what you two need to get yourselves and Violet settled. I have groceries in the back. Dry goods, in case the power's not on out here yet. Donated by the waitresses of the diner—including Nikki and Em, who are filling in for Daisy and Dusty tonight. Enough for a week or so, at least."

Marin opened the back seat of the truck and started pulling out bags. Clint went over to help immediately. "Thanks, Marin. It's appreciated. I have a generator in the back, but need to run to town to grab some fuel."

He had planned to take Maggie and Violet to her brothers'. Either that or he had considered dropping her off at the largest Masterson ranch, where her cousin Pan lived. Whichever she had wanted.

She'd be safe there, with Levi Masterson's ranch hands surrounding her. That was the best option. She and Violet could've visited with her cousin, Pan.

But with Marin and Barratt there, she wouldn't be alone.

Barratt wore a gun in a holster on his shoulder. He'd carried it for years, he'd told Clint when he'd asked. Since someone had attempted to abduct his twin sister from right next to him when they'd been in college.

Brandt had stopped them—with his fists. Now he carried a Glock.

Maggie was already headed up the porch. "I need to make a list of everything we'll still need. I want to start with Violet, of course. Clint and I can make do as long as we need to, but I want her in a room of her own. She's had enough transitions lately. So we'll get hers first, then the baby's room, then ours. And the common areas."

Clint followed her. Making note of what he'd need to do to ensure the porch was safe as he did.

He'd stop off and grab some supplies at the hardware store and the lumberyard; he'd get started on that tonight. Jay's place had had the wiring updated six years ago— before Jay had gone to prison. There was a new HVAC unit installed, but it had never been used. There were no kitchen appliances and only a toilet, pedestal sink, and bare-minimum shower. That would have to be fixed in a hurry.

When Clint had inherited the house he'd done a quick walk-through of it, but he hadn't been focused much on Jay's property. Not at the time. Not with everything else he had going on. But there had been fresh drywall in two thirds of the house, at least.

It still needed painted. Maggie would be able to pick the colors she wanted.

He'd have to have her stay at the inn while he handled that. Just to avoid the fumes.

The floors had all been replaced with kid friendly laminate by his own brother. It wasn't exactly the color or the style Clint would've chosen, but it would work for the time being. They could change it out when the kids were all a bit older.

They had a roof over their head, they had a house to live in, and they would have what they needed for his kids. Clint would see to that. He would swing into town and grab a crib for Violet. He'd need two cribs, come to think of it. He had two nurseries to set up now.

There were dressers and rocking chairs at the other place. They'd need cleaned up and painted or sanded and stained. It might take him a few days, but he could get it all done.

He had one more stop to make in town, and that was with Joel Masterson and Rex.

There were going to be questions now. Lots of them. On both sides of the conversation.

He and Barratt grabbed the rest of the groceries—it looked like Marin had bought out the entire IGA—and carried them inside.

Barratt was a talker, more so than Clint was used to, but he was a very intelligent man.

Clint had to say that he liked the man, once he accepted that Barratt had no romantic interest in Maggie at all.

For a moment or two, he thought the man was interested in Marin, but after a few minutes, he revised that assessment. No, Barratt just seemed to be comfortable in the other woman's company, the same way he was Maggie's.

He also had a hard edge about him Clint hadn't yet figured out, but made him respect the younger man.

Barratt wasn't a pushover. It was in the way he spoke of his business plans. The man was rather tunnel visioned on building his own empire.

Clint just hoped the man didn't burn himself out.

Then again, Clint understood that fire. At one time, he wanted to make something of himself to. With the WHP and the Wyoming DCI. His plans had changed, but his determination was no less than it had been then.

Only now, his focus was on being the husband and father that Maggie and the babies deserved. He wanted nothing more than that for the rest of his days.

As soon as he convinced Maggie that he was the man meant for her.

But first, it was time he went hunting.

He and Barratt got the last of the groceries. Maggie was disconnecting the call on the new cell phone that had been in the bag of things Marin had purchased with Rex.

She looked up at him and smiled. "Augie is coming by. She and Junie are going to watch Violet this afternoon at their place while Marin, Brandt, and I make a list of everything we need. And get started."

"That sounds like a good idea. You might find things to use temporarily at the other place. Jay and I were both storing furniture there at one time." Clint looked at Marin and Brandt. "You'll stay with her until I get back? I have to go speak with Joel Masterson about what happened, and swing by the electric company to have power switched over to this address. I'll stop off and get some lumber for the porch and fuel for the generator. Then I'll be back."

"Don't worry, big guy. I'm not going to leave Maggie alone. No matter what," Marin said, a somber look on her face. "She has me."

One day, Clint would probably figure her out. But for

now, he was just glad Marin was there for Maggie when Maggie needed her. Marin had earned his undying loyalty for that.

Clint nodded. He kissed Violet on the forehead, then took a bold risk. He leaned down to kiss Maggie.

It thrilled him when she tilted her head back instinctively and rose on her tiptoes to kiss him right back.

He thought about what it meant, her willingness, on the way to town. Because something had certainly changed with Maggie.

He just couldn't figure out what it was.

## 54

CLINT HADN'T SEEN HIS STEPFATHER SINCE THE DAY HE'D driven his fist into the man's face out there on Wreck Curve Road. Seeing him in the jail's visiting center wasn't exactly something he wanted to do. But...

Clive could have the answers Clint needed.

Clive kept his eyes on Clint the entire time. He didn't even look at the two other men next to Clint. Even Joel Masterson.

"Son, what are you doing here?"

Clint gritted his teeth, wanting to yell at the man that he was not his son and never had been. A *father* didn't treat a child the way Clive had treated him—or Jay.

Had Clive been a better father, Jay would most likely still be alive. Pip and Perci Tyler wouldn't have nearly died, either.

But he contained himself.

Protecting Maggie depended on it. Rex pulled out a chair first. Joel and Clint followed suit.

"Someone's causing trouble. They burned down my

house last night. I almost didn't get my family out in time. You know anything about that?"

Clive's face tightened. He looked at Clint, an odd expression on his face. "I'm sorry about that. I heard you were involved with someone recently. Tyler girl, right?"

"Maggie. Martin Tyler's younger sister." He leveled a look at his stepfather. He didn't question how Clive knew about her—Clint understood how jailhouse rumors went. "She's eight months pregnant. It's a boy. My son. Someone broke in a few days ago, too. Maggie was there alone. That man knocked her down and hurt her. Terrified her. He said he was looking for something of yours. One of your case files, we think. I suspect it's the same man. Who have you pissed off enough that they would do this? They could have killed Maggie and Violet last night. And the new baby."

Clive just stared at him for the longest time. Then he rattled off a number. Rex wrote it down immediately. "That's the case file you're looking for. I suspect there are copies spread around. If you want to go lookin'." Clive looked at Joel Masterson. "How's that girl? The nurse."

It was the first thing he had said other than to greet Clint. First time he even looked at Joel.

"She's fine. Has recovered from what you did to her. She and Nate are happy," Joel said, a clear warning in his tone.

"That's good. Never truly did mean to hurt her. Never meant to hurt anybody, even before. Not really. Just... things got away from me. Lost control of myself."

Joel's face and fists tightened. Clint understood. He would never forget the sight of Perci Tyler's blood there that day. Ever. She had the same eyes as Maggie. He'd seen the fear in Perci's eyes that day, too.

But he had other things to worry about now. "Clive, what's that case have to do with you?"

Clive just smirked. "Go to your granddaddy's place, in the dining room. You take out the heat vent. Search around a bit. There will be a lockbox back there. No bigger than a book. You'll find your answer then. Speak to Jasper Grady and that assistant of his. Tommy Basroni. That's where you'll find your answers. Seems Grady has some secrets he wants hidden. Me, I don't care no more. I don't care about much at all any longer. But...that baby of yours is your mama's grandbaby. You happy about the new one? I don't like someone messing around with you. You are all I got left—you and your kids. So...you ask Grady about his secrets: that will clear all of this right up. Guy's harmless, mostly. Doubt he's ever hurt anybody. He always was too soft. Just wants to keep his secrets kept. But don't we all?"

"Blackmail?" Rex asked. Clint thought that was where Clive was heading. The man never would come out and say something. He liked leading people around. Making them work for it. Toying with them.

"Grady was involved in that case, just because he held his tongue when I told him to. And he never did anything against the law. Not really. But pretty boy Grady won't want any taint of it associated with him. Not with his plans. Real problem is his assistant. Basroni is the one yanking the mayor's chain now. Both came to see me, too. The younger one was cackling about his plan to get revenge for the past. Seems to think Grady could have done more than what he did. But what happened was an accident. I'm almost sure of it. I gave Grady the runaround, told him to go here. Go there. Playing with him. Grady never could handle that. Figured he'd finally put it together that it's Basroni pulling his chain. Handle it from there. Grady didn't do nothing that night. But maybe that's what Basroni's beef is—Grady didn't do anything to stop what happened to Basroni's mother. Didn't mean for them to cause you trouble, son. That was the last thing I'd want for your mama's grandbabies. I should've been better to you. To that girl of yours, too. You have any pictures? I'd love to see what she looks like now. That assistant of Grady's, he's been toying with him, enjoying himself, too. Have to admit, I can understand that. Some people just ask for it. He has been driving Grady a bit mad. I know mad when I see it. Basroni's flirting up Grady's youngest girl, just so he can get close to Grady, too. Don't know what Basroni is planning, but it'll be big. He always has wanted revenge for what happened to his mother. It was all that Art Talley's fault. All the trouble Grady ever faced was because of Art Talley. Well, Art... and that crush Grady had on Art's sister-in-law. Always knew trouble would come that way."

Clint stood.

He wasn't about to spend even a minute longer listening to Clive ramble. He had the names he'd been looking for. Now it was time to finish this and get home to Maggie.

Where he belonged. "Thanks."

That was all he owed the man in front of him.

"Son? You got any pictures? You and that kid of yours are all the family I have left."

He thought about telling him to go screw himself. He did. He just wanted to be a better man than that.

Clint pulled out his phone. Pulled up a recent photo of Violet in Maggie's arms. "She's almost sixteen months now. Just started walking this week."

Clint knew what it was like to feel all alone in the

world. And he couldn't ever do that to another living soul. Even the man who had done it to him time and time again.

Clive took the phone for a moment, stared at Violet. Ran one trembling finger over the screen as Rex and Joel headed for the door.

"Thank you. They are beautiful, Clint. Take care of your family forever. They are far more precious than you can ever know."

## 55

Maggie waited until the Grady sisters had left before turning to Marin and Brandt. Clancy and Cloe had brought enough baby clothes for Violet now, and had given her a good start on things for a newborn boy. She was starting to feel a bit more in control. But the arrival of Cloe and Clancy had delayed her plans. Maggie was determined to have a house for her family as quickly as possible. "I think this place will do nicely, but there are some things we need from the other place. It's twenty minutes up the road."

This wasn't the ranch house they'd lived in before, but it could be something *new* for the two of them. Someplace without the memories that had confused her so much. Today, this house, them—it could be a fresh start.

"You're staying with him," Brandt said. It wasn't a question. No one thought it was. Cloe and Clancy had just assumed she was involved with Clint. Maggie hadn't corrected them—because she was.

No more lying to herself. "Yes."

"Good." Brandt sent her a beautiful smile. "It's obvious

the two of you have the potential to be as annoying as Houghton and Mel. Just give it time."

Maggie liked the sound of that.

There was a formal dining room next to the kitchen. It had stacks of stuff piled in it that would have to be moved, but that was a minor thing.

Most of it looked like stuff straight from the 1980s. She would have someone move it to a spare bedroom—then she'd pick through it. See what could be sold online. That money could go into savings for the babies. The baby kicked, reminding her of their priorities. A formal dining room wasn't needed at the moment—but two safe nurseries were. Violet would need her space as soon as possible. "Let's get upstairs. I want to get Violet's room ready for her. We'll need to paint—"

"Not you," Marin said. "But I can recruit a Talley paint crew within a matter of hours."

"Good idea," Brandt said. "Because I think I stepped back into 1977 here."

"More like 1877," Maggie said, running one hand over the oak trim around one window. She half suspected it was hand-hewn. Beautiful—it could be a beautiful place with some work. They could fix it...and it would be loved again. So many of the Gundersons had been unloved for too long. She knew how that had affected him. Well—Maggie was going to change all that. "Clint told me this place has been in his family that long. I'm not sure which property was built first. There used to be a small town here on this property, but when the Gunderson family started to die out and the wars came and all of that, it dwindled. Got forgotten."

"Well, you and Clint can get started building it back

up," Marin said. "He still planning to do the other two houses out here?"

"Probably. These two, and that small one he has in town. He wants to fix them and rent them out. That was what he intended for this place, but…plans change." This house was close to thirty-five hundred square feet. And she thought there would be an attic and a basement—but she wasn't going to check them out yet. She'd leave that for Clint, thank you very much. No telling what was hiding up there. "So…Violet's room."

Maggie had a notepad. She made a list of everything that would have to be done to turn the fifteen-by-twenty space right across the hall from the master room into a room a little girl could be proud of. It needed new carpet—what was in there was thin and old, though it appeared reasonably clean. The walls needed a good wipe-down, just to get rid of the dust that had accumulated in the months between Jay hanging the drywall—he'd actually been pretty good at home repair and could have made a living at it, according to what Clint had said—and today.

That was easy enough.

The walls had been primed for painting. She'd have to get Clint to pick up some light pink or lavender paint. Probably lavender. That would be pretty. She'd told him to find white furniture, if possible. But that wasn't entirely necessary. They'd need to get some type of child-appropriate artwork on the walls. And Clint could build some bookshelves—he liked to build things, she knew that. He could build bookshelves for both of the babies.

She was running through the list as Marin and Brandt got started wiping down the walls and the two windows. Even without the paint, they could set up Violet's crib and a dresser. The Grady sisters had brought donated clothes that would fit. They'd been laundered and folded and were just waiting for a dresser to put them in. They'd also brought a bag of baby toys. She'd thought she'd seen a toy chest in the smallest room at the end of the hallway.

The toys had been in storage, so would have to be wiped down, but they could have Violet in a new room by bedtime. She said as much as she looked at Brandt expectantly. Within moments, he had been given clear instructions of what she wanted. "First, we need a lift to the second house."

There were other things, for both babies' rooms, that she wanted. She might be able to find them at the other house. Clint had said there was furniture left there.

Brandt obliged, like she knew he would, driving her and Marin to the house that had been Clint's grandparents'. Maggie took a long look around the yard. She could just see the roof of the house Clint had inherited from his brother in the distance. This one had a smaller front yard area, and it was a bit hillier and rockier than she'd like. And there was a pond too close to the backyard for her peace of mind. At least until the children were older.

That just reaffirmed what she and Clint had discussed earlier.

Jay's house was better for a family. Safer. But there were more modern supplies inside the one she had Brandt drive them to.

Jay's house was mostly empty, with a few pieces of antique furniture and almost two thirds of the house hung with new drywall. That still needed painted. Even the windows had been updated with energy-efficient, safer windows.

It was an empty shell—full of possibilities.

She was determined; the fire wasn't going to stop them

from building a life for their children. She wasn't going to let it.

She had made another list; this one of things she and Clint would need too.

They needed a bed frame and headboard. A sturdy one. For the master bedroom. Clint was a big man—he'd need a big bed. A small smile hit her lips. She was going to enjoy that bed with him, too.

She sent him a quick text, telling him where they were now—and that he needed to order a king-size mattress to be delivered tomorrow.

That meant... She turned back to Marin. "I think we'll be spending one more night at the inn, after all. There isn't a master bed ready." Maggie was determined—she wanted to sleep with his arms around her tonight. He wasn't getting away from her again. "We'll need to see what we have going on in there, see if we need to paint or anything. If nothing else, I'll recruit the Tylers and Talleys. Have a painting party. I'm sure we can get Darcey and Martin to be in the same room long enough to get some things done without killing each other."

She talked about what they could, as Brandt drove them to the other house up the road. As he started loading furniture for her right out of Clint's barn, near the back door of the house.

They could do this.

She was looking forward to it. While she had loved the way Clint had redecorated the ranch after the shooting, it had been *his* and Amy's house. She was going to turn Jay's former house into *their* house. For both of them. Where they could start fresh. Together. Just them, and their children.

Marin shot her a wicked look. "Making plans for what you want to go on in there?"

"You'd better believe it." Maggie unlocked the back door using the keys Clint had given her. "He isn't getting away now."

She pushed open the door, Brandt right on her heels.

Marin screamed, and grabbed Maggie's arm. "Maggie, no! Don't go in!"

Then Maggie heard the gunshot.

## 56

JASPER HAD SET IT UP SO PERFECTLY. THERE HAD BEEN NO room for failure. He'd called Basroni.

Told him flat out he knew exactly what the younger man had been doing. That he had enough on Basroni for the younger man to go away for years—if he didn't do what Jasper told him.

He'd done some digging; the internet was a wonderful tool. He had always thought so. He hadn't realized the woman's son had changed his name. He hadn't always been Tommy. Nor had he always been a Basroni. He'd thought the name had sounded so unfamiliar, but Tommy had made a point of telling him years ago that he had been born and raised in Masterson County. Had been proud of that.

Well, Jasper had made a point of knowing the people of his county. He should have seen the wolf in his own hen house.

Tommy Basroni had dated his daughter. Clancy had been head over heels for him for a few weeks just three months back.

Until she had ended it because they just weren't clicking.

Damn that bastard for daring to get that close to his daughter. That was what had really done it, sent Jasper over the edge.

Tommy had been too close to Clancy. And with careful investigation, Jasper had figured that out.

The back door slipped open. Jasper had been waiting for this moment for hours, with all the windows covered and him waiting in an old stuffed chair. Right there in the hall between the two doors. They were lined up so conveniently he'd pushed the chair between the two entrances, so Basroni wouldn't get away.

Someone stepped inside.

Jasper jumped to his feet and squeezed the trigger.

By the time he realized what he'd done, that he'd made a horrific mistake, it was too late. Far too late.

A woman stumbled; a man yelled out. He recognized her immediately.

He reached, one hand still holding the gun. Another shot discharged, like he was a rank amateur who had no business with a gun.

He was too late. Too, too late.

Maggie Tyler was on her knees in front of him. Leaning over the man Jasper had just shot. Jasper just looked at them. Stunned. She was moving, she wasn't hit. He hadn't shot an innocent pregnant woman.

But there was blood.

"Brandt! Brandt!"

There was a tall man bleeding at Jasper's feet. One he didn't recognize.

Jasper had just shot an innocent man.

He looked toward the open door.

*She* was there. Staring at him with horror in those blue eyes he loved so much.

Marin.

Heaven help him, Marin was there, too. Standing in the doorframe in one of those flowing skirts she'd favored and a bright red sweater.

Shock and fear covered her beautiful face.

She'd seen him. They had all three seen him. The girls, these two beautiful, wonderful girls, had recognized him. It was over for him now. "Don't move! None of you move!"

## 57

"Stay close," Rex ordered the young officer who he had paged to his office. He'd had two others he trusted accompany Joel Masterson to the home of Thomas Basroni, to ask him some questions.

Masterson had one of his deputies and one of Rex's out looking for the mayor now. Rex wanted to be there, but there was more he could do from his office than out on the street.

All they could really do at this point was ask questions. They didn't have enough for a warrant.

They needed warrants. They weren't going to get them just on Clive Gunderson's word. The idea was damned preposterous to begin with.

"What is this about, sir?" Claudia Grady wore her uniform proudly. And she looked good in it. If he wasn't a professional who would never cross those types of boundaries, he'd admit that. She had big green eyes. She actually looked too damned innocent to be involved in law enforcement, for one thing. Still, she was good at what she did. She had potential.

If her father was a damned criminal—and Rex believed all politicians were criminal at heart, at times—that could mean hurdles for her. It was just the way it was.

"I may need you shortly." It was a cop-out, of course. But she wasn't about to question him. At least not to his face. Perk of his position. He wanted her where he could see her while the questioned her father.

"Yes, sir."

His phone rang as she stepped out of his office. Rex checked it quickly. Joel Masterson.

*"Thomas Basroni is gone. Like he was never here, but he left us a nice little file filled with evidence of a cold case from twenty-two years ago. And it looks like it's just as Clive said. Basroni was tormenting Grady for weeks. Threatening his daughters. All three of them. Even had a gun pointed at that officer of yours. Could have killed her right there."*

Hell. That was going to complicate things. Why couldn't he have an *easy* weekend, for once?

Rex disconnected, then called Clint.

The last thing he needed was for Clint to go hunting Grady by himself. That could mean real trouble, but Rex would understand if he did.

Either Basroni or Grady was responsible for hurting Maggie. For burning down Clint's home.

How was a man supposed to just take that lying down?

Clint wasn't. It was time Rex went hunting. Before his friend did something stupid that destroyed everything Clint was working toward.

## 58

Clint got Maggie's text just as he was about finished ordering two cribs, two crib mattress, and two changing tables to be delivered to his brother's old place. He looked at the woman in charge of the store. "And add the best king-size mattress and box set you have. Plus a frame."

His checkbook was going to be pretty damned bruised after today, but he didn't care. He was going to get his house together for his family again.

"Of course. Tell Maggie congratulations on the new baby for me, too. She'll be a great mother. I bet her brothers are thrilled to be uncles, too."

He just nodded at that. Thrilled wasn't the word he'd use to describe the Tyler brothers.

Planning to roast him on a spit was more like it.

Clint didn't care at the moment. He had a family to provide for and a baby to prepare for.

Hell, maybe men nested, too.

He'd swing by his grandfather's house and grab Maggie. Wait for word from Rex.

He'd get his family settled tonight—and once that was

done, he was calling those five brothers of hers to come guard her. While he and Rex took care of the problem.

Rex and Joel Masterson had twelve hours to find the loose ends. Jasper Grady and that little shit-weasel assistant mayor of his. Whatever was going on between them had come too damned close to Maggie and Violet.

Clint was going to listen in while they interviewed Grady. Find out once and for all what was so damned important Grady would hurt a pregnant woman to keep it quiet.

Then he'd find whatever it was Grady had been searching for and turn it over to Rex. Be done with it.

He was sick and damned tired of cleaning up other men's messes.

## 59

MAGGIE HAD BEEN STUPID. SHE SHOULD HAVE TOLD CLINT what she felt. With everything between them as screwed up as it was, he had still deserved to know that she loved him.

She looked at Marin. The other woman's blue eyes showed her own fear. Jasper Grady stood behind her, a gun to Marin's head.

The living room was open, leading right into the large kitchen. The front and back doors were lined up perfectly. Two perfect ways of escape—and they couldn't get to either one.

"What is it you're looking for, Mayor Grady?" She wasn't going to cower down in fear. She wasn't going to do that. Maggie wasn't going to let *fear* rob her of anything any longer. "Take what you want and leave. Just like before. We need to get him help. You don't want to face a murder charge."

Panic threatened to sneak in.

She couldn't let panic happen.

If she lost control of herself, then she would lose control of the situation.

She took a deep breath and ran a hand over where her baby rested. "Get what you want and leave. We're not going to stop you. I don't care what it is or where you go when you leave. None of us are going to stop you."

He hadn't let go of Marin. His hand was splayed over her abdomen, directly below Marin's breasts. Like he was reaching. Holding *Marin* specifically, and not just because she was the most convenient hostage.

Something in the hold creeped Maggie out even more than the gun he held at Marin's temple.

It was so possessive.

"I didn't mean to shoot him. I was waiting for Tommy."

"Who?" Maggie asked.

"My assistant mayor. He's Bryce Thomas Johnson. His...mother...died during an investigation Clive worked. It was an accident, but enough to send Art Talley and that wife of his running for the hills. Even as pregnant as she was."

"My aunt was pregnant?" Marin asked. "We didn't know that. What happened to them?"

"Don't know. Art took off, and I said good riddance. His wife was about halfway along, I think. Hiding it, though. He took her and ran. Piss-poor father." Grady snorted after he spoke. He looked toward the window, then back at Maggie.

"No kidding," Marin said. "Let me go."

"No. As soon as I do, you two will cause trouble. I... need to think. I can't let it get back to my kids what I've done."

It was going to. That was inevitable. He had to know that, to realize…

Unless he killed them all and destroyed the evidence.

Before Clint came inside.

She'd heard his truck coming down the drive. Clint was out there.

Somewhere.

And he didn't know he was walking straight into hell.

"What are you planning to do with us?" Marin asked.

Maggie watched as the mayor tightened his hold on Marin. The gun in his hand trembled.

"I just want you two to stay quiet. I need to think." He looked at Maggie, but he never let Marin go. "I'm sorry about the fire. I panicked. Wasn't thinking straight. And there were so many evidence boxes, it was just more expedient to burn them all instead of searching for hours. I'm an older man now. I was getting tired. I didn't even see the trees behind the shed until it was too late. And that lumber on the front porch…"

Marin tried to step away but he stopped her.

He waved the gun around, then grabbed Marin's chin. He forced Marin to look at him over her left shoulder. Maggie stayed where she was, feeling beyond helpless. "You both know that I have used this before. Don't tempt me. I've always found you fascinating, Marin. You…haunt my dreams at night. Have for years. I don't want to hurt you, or Maggie. But I will if it becomes necessary. I need a few moments to think, to figure out what I need to do next."

Grady tied Marin to the old rocking chair in the corner of the dining room, winding a curtain cord around her wrists. He made Maggie stand in the opposite corner.

There was blood in Marin's hair. That image seared into Maggie's brain.

Brandt's blood had stained Marin's hair orange.

"That's too tight," Marin said. "Please…Mayor Grady…it's too tight. You're hurting me."

"That's the point, honey. I don't want you getting loose and causing trouble. You will, too. First chance you get. I've watched you, you know. When you weren't looking. Found you fascinating for years, since you were no more than twenty. Don't cause me any trouble. Please. I'm begging you not to make me hurt you. I really don't want to hurt you, honey." He cupped Marin's cheek. Caressed her lips with one finger.

Something about the look in his eyes had Maggie shivering.

When he pressed an exploring kiss to Marin's lips, Maggie almost gagged. He stood back up. "I always did like your mother, Marin. Something about the fire in her eyes. I love my wife, of course, but…there were quite a few what-ifs in my head. Sorry about her getting sick like that."

Marin didn't say a word. Grady just kept talking. Pacing. To Maggie's horror, he grabbed Brandt and dragged him out of the path of the back door and into the dining room. Brandt never moved.

Grady took the gun out of the holster Brandt wore and put it on an old table in the kitchen. Far from where they were.

"I really am sorry about having to do all of this to you both. And this boy here. I just…can't have some of that stuff getting out there. It would have ruined everything. Of course, it already has. Once people put it together that I'm responsible for this, well, I'm as good as ruined around here. I just hope my children aren't ostracized after this." He cupped Marin's cheek and ran his finger over her bottom lip. "Someone will have to make certain that doesn't happen."

He kissed Marin one more time, holding her head with his free hand when she would have pulled away. Marin had nowhere to go.

No one did. Grady blocked the only exit to the dining room with his body.

Then he turned to Maggie.

And reached for her.

She couldn't evade his hand.

"Come on, honey. You're going to help me look for a way out of this. And keeping you close will keep that girl in line. Keep Clint from shooting me where I stand. I saw that man of yours out messing with the furniture in that truck. No damned way for me to get out of here, is there? Not without him seeing. Unless we get really lucky."

Maggie had no choice. She shot a look over her shoulder at Marin.

Her friend looked more terrified than Maggie had ever seen. They were all alone with a man who had everything to lose.

Except for Clint.

Grady yanked her along behind him so fast Maggie went down to one knee again, crying out as she did so. Her arm went around the baby, and she tried to protect him as much as she could.

Grady just yanked her back to her feet, cursing.

## 60

There was a big Ford sitting in the drive in front of his grandparents' old place when Clint pulled in.

Barratt. The man had already loaded a few pieces of furniture Clint recognized from having been stored in the far barn into the bed of the truck. A dining room table that his great-uncle had made dominated. There were a few mismatched chairs in the bed, as well. He thought there were a couple more in the rear of the barn. He'd grab them, as they were harder to find. They might need stripped and stained, but they were sturdy chairs. They would hold up to a few more generations.

Thunder cracked overhead. It hurried him up. Clint stepped into the barn, looking for Barratt. The other man was nowhere around, most likely inside the house somewhere, at Maggie's beck and call. Barratt didn't seem to mind being ordered around. At least, being ordered around by Maggie and Marin.

Barratt had a calming presence and seemed to enjoy the almost fraternal role Maggie had him in.

He called out. Nothing.

Clint grabbed the last of the dining room chairs and tossed them into the bed. There was a tarp already spread over the table. He made quick work of tying it down, to prevent damage on the drive. The house Jay had been working on was only eighteen minutes away, if they took the back service road. Most people didn't even know that road was back there; the only place it went was to connect his three properties together, after circling around the old Gregory place behind him. Clint intended to buy the Gregory place when he had the money. It would make a damned fine rental, and he'd use the acreage around it for the horses he planned to raise.

But...his family's house was his ultimate priority now.

He'd grabbed paint swatches at the hardware store. He was going to show them to Maggie tonight, before Rex joined them for dinner with an update.

Rex and Joel Masterson were searching for Jasper Grady.

It was taking everything he had not to go out and join the search. Only that he needed this time with Maggie tonight kept him from doing just that.

Maggie's cousin Augusta had Violet for the night.

He was going to take advantage of that to work out a few things with the woman he loved.

But first, if she wanted that table, she would have that table. And the chairs.

He called out for her again.

Maggie was in that house somewhere. It was time he found her, chased off Barratt and Marin, and showed her exactly what he wanted their future to hold.

## 61

Jasper was sweating.

There was a back door and a front door fifty feet apart. They were his only real choices. He'd picked the front lock earlier. It was closest to his SUV. He'd hidden the SUV behind the smallest barn, where it wouldn't be visible from the front of the house.

He just had to get there. While Gunderson was still in that damned front barn, doing whatever it was he was doing. If Jasper beat him to the backyard, he could make it.

Maggie was damned awkward to drag along behind him. It would take too long with Maggie. And Marin…he could hear her yelling at the top of her lungs. Trouble. She would be trouble, that woman. "I should have gagged her."

Every possible scenario ran through his head; he discarded most of them. Jasper wouldn't be able to shoot a damned pregnant woman who'd once played Barbies with his daughters. He just couldn't do it.

"You would be better off turning yourself in," she said quietly.

Just as Marin yelled out again. Woman was loud enough to wake the dead. Or draw Gunderson's attention.

Which was what she was trying to do. Jasper just knew it. If the thunder stopped soon, she probably would.

Jasper cursed and tightened his hold on Maggie.

He dragged Maggie back down the hall to Marin.

"What are you doing?" He almost hissed it. He nudged Maggie toward the far corner. "Stay there."

He untied Marin quickly, then fisted the thin red sweater she wore in his free hand. He used it as a handle her to jerk her closer.

Just like that, he'd shifted one hostage for another. Marin—Marin would be a better hostage than Maggie. She could move faster, for one thing.

He'd take her, put her in his SUV, and drive. Canada was only twelve hours away. By the time anyone figured out he was involved, he could be gone from here. Or he could use her as a hostage if needed. Though he knew very well how that tended to turn out. Never good.

The life of a fugitive was a tough one, but it was better than being dead. It would kill his kids if he was dead.

Of course, it would kill his kids if they learned about this, anyway.

He had to get out of there and think. It might be best if he just took Marin with him when he went.

Maggie, as pregnant as she was, would be far too much of a liability.

Yes. Marin was best.

## 62

Maggie was a ranch girl at heart. She'd seen blood before, but she was definitely not equipped to deal with a gunshot wound. Or any of this. She fought the panic again.

She deliberately ignored Mayor Grady and knelt down next to Brandt. Tried to do what she could to help him.

Marin cried out next to her. Maggie glanced up at her. Marin looked terrified. She'd never seen Marin that afraid. Grady had a tight hold on Marin. He had to be hurting her.

Panic threatened. Marin—Marin never panicked. Marin could handle anything.

Maggie bit back her own terror. The mayor jerked Marin even closer.

Brandt shifted beneath her fingers, startling her. Maggie checked his face. His eyes blinked. He was still in there. Thank God.

Mayor Grady stood in the center of the hallway. Blocking the paths to the doors.

They had no other way out—except the windows.

She couldn't get out of here, not as big as she was now. Not safely.

And Brandt...she and Marin couldn't lift him. Not as big as he was.

They had to get the mayor and the guns he held out of the way. Somehow. And they had to get Brandt help, as fast as they could.

They were much too far away from the hospital now.

"I know you don't want to hurt us. You never intended that at all, did you?"

## 63

JASPER PUT HIS FINGER AT HIS MOUTH, AS HE WATCHED Gunderson from the window. The man spent too much time messing with that damned load of furniture. Jasper would have had time to run, had he not been so indecisive. "Don't say a word. Either one of you."

It would be Marin. She would be the troublemaker he had to worry about. He pulled her closer, put his hand over her mouth. She struggled. He put the gun next to her ear. "You have to be quiet. Be still."

Gunderson called out again. "Maggie! Marin! Barratt! Where the hell are you?"

Jasper put his hand over Marin's mouth.

Marin struggled. Pulling against him. Turned wild.

He didn't want to hurt her. He never would have wanted to hurt Marin. He was afraid that was exactly what would happen if she continued to fight.

He wouldn't hurt her like Clive had hurt Phil Tyler's girl. He wouldn't be that monster.

Jasper had no choice—he let Marin go.

He grabbed Maggie instead. Better *her* than Marin.

"Tie her up again." He couldn't handle both women at once. Jasper knew that. When there was more than one hostage, there was more room for error. But he wasn't going to hurt them. Either of them. He had to keep control of this situation. He had to. "Do it."

Maggie at least moved quickly. She had her little friend tied to the old kitchen chair in the rear dining room again fast.

Jasper grabbed Maggie again. "Come on. We're getting out of here."

He stepped toward the back door.

Just as it swung open.

"Clint!"

## 64

CLINT STEPPED INTO THE HOUSE AND FROZE AT WHAT HE SAW. Maggie was right there. A man stood behind her. Clint focused on the gun almost immediately.

Jasper Grady cursed. The two men eyed each other.

"Clint!" Maggie called again. She was crying, her big blue eyes wide and terrified. Jasper looked down at her. Stared.

Clint pulled his gun instinctively. Quickly. As fast as he damned well could.

"Grady, what in the hell are you doing here? Still searching?"

Grady flinched when he saw Clint's gun. "You know."

"Yes. So does the sheriff and the WHP."

He could hear Marin yelling from the dining room, which was off the kitchen. Nothing wrong with her lungs, at least. But why wasn't she right there, hovering over Maggie?

He didn't take his eyes off Grady, even though he saw the blood pooled in the rear hall. Saw a man's foot. He put it together fast.

"In the dining room. Brandt's hurt. And Marin, he made me tie her to the chair." Maggie pulled in a shuddering breath, one hand covering their baby. "Clint..."

"Put the gun down, son."

Clint looked at the mayor of Masterson County. "Why are you doing this? We know about Basroni. We even know you weren't directly involved in what happened to the guy's mother. Let Maggie walk outside, right now. You and I will figure out a way to fix this together."

"You got Tommy? He started off as such a good kid, Clint. I don't know what changed him." Jasper Grady's hand was trembling, but he had a vise on Maggie's sweater. "Hell, I don't know what changed any of us. Hold still, Maggie. I don't want anyone doing anything stupid."

Clint knew exactly how this situation would play out. And it wasn't good.

Not with Maggie in the way. "No one is going to do anything stupid. Rex and Joel Masterson have Basroni. Interviewing him right now."

"It'll finally come out then," Grady said morosely. "That's what I was trying to avoid. I don't want my past mistakes muddying things up for my kids. You understand that, right? Considering what Clive did to you. I can't ruin their lives like that. Guess I don't have any choice now, do I?"

"You are their father," Clint said, remembering his last look of the man who had raised him. The man who should have been the father Clint had deserved. "You have to do what's right. Make it right for them. Don't compound your mistakes."

## 65

HELL, JASPER KNEW HE WAS JUST DELAYING THE INEVITABLE. And Clint was right. He wasn't going to hurt these people —and that boy in the back needed medical attention. Quickly.

They were just...kids in the grander scheme of things. "How old are you, Gunderson?"

"Thirty-six as of last month."

"Four years older than my Cal. And Maggie here... she's the same age as my daughter Cloe. Did you know that?" He remembered her as a beautiful little girl. The red-gold pigtails. They were distinctive on Tyler girls. "She was such a pretty little girl."

He brushed the gun hand through the hair she'd left down. She smelled good. He tried to breathe her in over his own sweat. "It's ok, honey. Just stay still a few minutes longer."

He looked back at her man.

Hell, Gunderson's fear was right there on the man's face. "Put that gun down, Gunderson. We both know you'll never pull the trigger with Maggie here in between us."

They were cornered animals, he and Gunderson. With the prize, the prey, trapped between them.

There was one exit at his back through the kitchen. He had to drag Maggie there and outside of the house. Drag her out to his SUV. Let her go there.

Take off.

By the time Gunderson had someone after him, Jasper would be an hour or so away.

Not that that was much, but a smart man who knew the county as well as he did could probably disappear long enough out here.

He just had to get her to the truck.

Then he'd get away.

It was a desperate plan, but what else was he but a desperate man?

"Come on, little girl. You're coming with me. Gunderson...you just stay right where you are. Or it'll be your girl and that baby of yours that pays the price." Jasper deliberately dropped his hand from her shoulder—to cover the baby she and Gunderson no doubt already loved so much.

The baby kicked his hand in response, bringing back so many wonderful memories.

Tears hit his eyes. He'd never have those days again.

They were gone.

He'd never get the chance to see his girls as mothers, to see his boys as fathers.

He'd ruined all of that.

Time...it had been his enemy all along.

Time, and himself.

## 66

His shoulder was on fire. Brandt coughed as he woke.

"Thank God. Wake up, Brandt. You really need to wake up!" a frantic female voice said from near his feet. Brandt didn't remember falling asleep with a woman any time recently. His body definitely didn't feel like he'd had a good time lately, either.

Far from it.

His eyes flew open.

He stared into beautiful blue eyes and a terrified face. "What happen—"

She was tied to a kitchen chair. That's when he remembered. "Where's Maggie?"

"Jasper Grady took her." Marin was franticly trying to untie her hands. "He and Clint have her by the front door."

Brandt pulled himself up, one hand going to his right shoulder. It came away covered with blood. He coughed again. "Son of a bitch ambushed me."

"Yes. He ambushed us all," Marin said. "Hurry. Untie me."

He forced himself to his feet. His arm felt useless, but he did his damned best. He had her hands untied in less than a minute. "It's not that tight." He kept his words at a whisper.

She hopped to her feet as soon as the curtain cord fell to the floor. "He made Maggie do it. He didn't check how tight she'd tied me."

Brandt tried; he truly tried. But he fell to his knees behind her.

Marin came to him again. "You have to get up. We have to help. I need my gun."

"He has it. Put it in the kitchen. I can...probably get to it."

Brandt swore. "Let's go."

She started to the hall. "You stay behind me."

He wasn't about to let her go facing an armed gunman. It was never going to happen.

## 67

Maggie kept her eyes on Clint as Jasper forced her to walk backward through Clint's grandparents' house. The place was full of old boxes. Things. Trash.

Secrets, maybe. She didn't know. She didn't care.

Her hand rested where their son kicked against her. She pulled in a breath and tried to keep herself from freaking.

"Mayor, you have to let me go," she said as calmly as she possibly could. He didn't want to do this. No sane person would ever want to do this.

It was just circumstances. Dumb bad luck that he was here now. She knew that.

It didn't make it any easier. "This isn't the answer. Please."

"Just stay quiet, honey. We'll get out of here, and everything will be just fine." He patted her shoulder, awkwardly. "Just keep coming with me. Don't give the boyfriend time to even think about doing something he shouldn't."

CALLE J. BROOKES

Maggie looked at Clint. He was going to do something. She could see it in his eyes.

The mayor pointed the gun. And fired.

"Clint!"

Plaster flew around him where the bullet exploded into the wall. Clint ducked, instinctively.

"Clint!" She fought, tried to get the man to just let her go. "Don't do anything to make him shoot! Violet needs you!"

"I'm not going to let him take you from me," Clint said. "I can't. I love you too much to lose you, Maggie Tyler. There is nothing I won't do to keep you safe. From everything."

## 68

Clint saw the movement behind Jasper Grady, and he froze. His eyes met Barratt's for just a moment. The younger man nodded, though he looked damned unsteady on his feet.

Marin was there, too.

Behind Grady.

They had the man boxed in.

"Grady, look around you," Clint said quietly as Barratt pulled his gun and held it steady with one hand. "What is it you think is going to happen here? Let Maggie go, and we'll let you walk right out of here."

"I suppose that makes the most sense, doesn't it?" Grady said, glancing over his shoulder for just one moment. "Just walk away. Put this place behind me. Lose my kids. My girls, my boys. You're a father, Clint. Could you just walk away from your girl forever?"

"If it was what was best for her, in a heartbeat. I wouldn't even hesitate, if it meant she had a fighting chance."

"A father is supposed to protect. I thought that was what I was doing."

"Talk to me. Tell me why." Clint moved closer.

## 69

BRANDT WASN'T GOING TO BE ABLE TO DO A DAMNED THING, even with the guy's back to him. Not with the way his shoulder was going numb. But he was for damned sure going to try.

He was blocking the guy's only way out. Marin stood still, right there in the wide hallway. Right there, exposed. Brandt took a risk, took his eyes off the gunman long enough to check on Marin.

She stumbled. Far too close to the crazy bastard.

He reached out for her, to drag her back behind him.

Brandt was too late.

The gunman jerked around, yanking Maggie with him. "Don't move. Nobody move! Gunderson, we both know you won't be shooting that gun anywhere near your Maggie."

"I'll do what I have to do to protect my family," Gunderson said.

Brandt took a step closer.

"Marin, you just head up the stairs and stay there until all of this is over. Just go!" The guy looked at Marin with a wild look on his face Brandt would never forget. "You! Don't you touch her. Don't you ever touch her!"

Brandt froze where he was at. He felt like he was going to fall over at any moment. Sweat beaded on his forehead, threatened to drip into his eyes. He didn't know how much longer he could do this.

"Mayor Grady, I-I'm not going anywhere. Not without Maggie. Or the other people I care about. Don't do this! Please. I'm begging you."

Brandt would never forget the sound of her terror as she pled for them all.

## 70

SOMETHING ABOUT MARIN TRIGGERED THE SON OF A BITCH. Clint hadn't forgotten his years on the force. He knew had to read a man's tells.

Grady was holding himself together, for the most part.

He was just trapped.

But when he looked at Marin...he turned chaotic. Erratic.

Almost like an animal. A hungry one.

Someone without Clint's training wouldn't have seen it. But Clint did. Marin did something to Grady. Changed him, or drew him.

What in the hell that was going to do for them now, he didn't have a clue.

"Why do you want Marin to go upstairs, Grady?" Clint asked softly, risking taking another step forward. "Why don't you let her take Maggie upstairs with her? We'll talk this out down here. Man-to-man."

"I can't do that. Marin, you get upstairs now. I don't want to hurt you. I've always cared about you." Grady pointed the gun at Marin. His hand trembled on the trigger. Clint braced himself to attack. But there wasn't a whole lot he could do with Marin and Maggie right there, trapped. "And you tell my girls, and those boys of mine that I never intended it to be this way. Just…go. Get out of here. See to it that the town doesn't turn against them, will you? They are completely innocent of every one of their father's sins."

Clint waited.

Marin was frozen in the hall. Exposed. If Jasper squeezed the trigger, Marin wouldn't have anywhere to escape.

And neither would Maggie.

"I'm not going without Maggie."

"She's not going anywhere without Maggie, Jasper. We know that. Marin wouldn't leave her friend behind. Just let Maggie go with her. We'll work this out. Marin will leave if you just let Maggie go with her."

## 71

MAGGIE WASN'T STUPID. NO ONE WAS GOING TO DO anything to risk her. Her or the baby.

They couldn't stay like this forever. It was going to have to end. She just didn't know how. Not without someone she loved getting hurt.

The baby kicked her again, harder than he ever had before.

"Ooh!" She cried out and doubled over. Grady's hand yanked on her sweater so hard the knit rose up to choke her.

She coughed.

A cramp across her abdomen had her breath stopping for just a moment. Then it eased.

Intense.

The baby kicked again.

"Maggie, Maggie, honey…"

She looked up in time to see Clint step closer. They were almost within touching distance now. "I'm ok…just…"

Mayor Grady pulled her back a few steps.

Away from Clint. Toward Marin.

Just as Grady pulled the trigger again.

## 72

CLINT MOVED AS THE SHOT ECHOED THROUGH HIS grandparents' old place.

Marin and Maggie both screamed. Dove toward each other.

Barratt crashed to the ground with a yell.

It took Clint a moment to realize he'd somehow yanked Marin to oneside, and shoved himself in front of Maggie.

"Brandt!" Marin dove over the other man, her hand going to the wounds on his chest. "Brandt! Just stop this, Grady! Stop it now! Don't do this to your children! You're not a murderer! I know you're not!"

Grady yanked Maggie closer.

As long as Grady had Maggie in his hands, there weren't a whole lot of choices. Clint had to stay right where he was. And wait.

"What do you want, Grady? To end this now? So I can take Maggie home to our daughter? So I can get Barratt some help? The guy is bleeding out right before my eyes.

He's a nice guy who just wanted to help Maggie today. And Marin—she's now terrified of you. Just let them go, and we'll take a few minutes together. Let Marin get him out of here. Marin and Maggie. Do you really want it to go down like this? You a murderer? What will that do to your daughter's career with the WHP? It'll ruin Claudia's life if you kill someone. Don't do that to her. She's got a fair chance now. I'll talk to her commander myself. He'll protect her from some of this fall-out. I promise. You have my word. Talk to me about Clive. And what happened. Why does Basroni hate you so much?"

"I suggest you find Arthur Talley if you want the whole story," Grady said. "He always did like to play games with people. One time, one got to be too much. I came up after. Heard about what happened from Clive. Never saw anything more incriminating than a damned bloody scarf. That was it. That was enough to get Tommy's attention. I think he was the angriest with me because I stayed here. Made a life for myself. Never spoke up about the truth."

"I can understand that." Clint stayed where he was. But he never lowered his weapon.

He had to get some space between Grady and Maggie. That was the only real option. He had to get Maggie out of the line of fire.

And then he was going to take that bastard down.

Maggie cried out again.

She doubled over, clutching her stomach. When she looked up at him, Clint *knew*.

The baby.

She slipped to the floor. Grady cursed. Grabbed for her.

Clint dove.

Straight at Jasper Grady.

The bastard might shoot the hell out of him, but he wasn't getting a chance to put his hands on Maggie ever again.

## 73

A skinny arm went around her. Maggie was dragged across the old linoleum toward the back door. The sound of scuffling echoed around the kitchen. Grady yelled. Screamed.

As Clint pummeled him.

Maggie just watched, terrified the gun would go off again.

Marin's arm tightened around her shoulder. Maggie's hands rose to clutch the arm holding her. Her hand came away wet.

And crimson.

Her gaze flew to Brandt. He was ashen, barely moving. His eyes were open. He stared at them all.

Marin held Maggie tight. Tried to crowd her into a doorway, away from the fight.

Clint jerked Jasper Grady to one side with an audible thud. He slammed the man's arm to the floor. Grady's gun skittered across the linoleum.

Maggie didn't even hesitate. She reached for it.

Her hand wrapped around the grip. She lifted it. She had his gun. He couldn't shoot anyone ever again.

If he came toward her again, she'd shoot him, just like Martin and Michael had taught her to protect herself years ago.

It was practically over. It was almost over. It was almost over.

"It's almost over. It's…almost over…it's almost over," Maggie said, clutching her abdomen. The baby was going crazy. He must have felt her tension.

Her terror.

Marin still had her arm around her. Marin pulled Maggie to her feet, pulled her to the door. "Do the door, Mags. I can't. My arm…we have to get outside. Get help. My cell's in Brandt's truck. Get to Brandt's truck. Or Clint's. Go."

"I can't leave Clint. I can't leave him in there with Grady."Maggie turned back around.

Just as Clint shoved his fist into Jasper Grady's face, and the older man fell to the floor.

And didn't move again.

When Clint looked at her, she knew.

It was over. "It's over. Thank God it's over."

## 74

THE SCENE WAS UNDER CONTROL. JASPER GRADY WAITED IN the back of a squad car.

Grady's daughter stood next to a WHP detective, her face filled with horror. There were tears on her beautiful cheeks.

It would be burned into Rex's memory for eternity.

Movement caught his attention.

Madam Zelda was striding across the yard, straight toward Rex.

There was a determined look in her eyes that the red and blue of the flashers enhanced.

There was blood on the woman. She'd have to be processed. Her skirt and sweater were ruined. That thing was a monstrosity against modern fashion anyway. All flower-child hippie.

The sight of the blood covering her just pissed him off. That it was *her* made the anger far worse.

She kept coming at him.

He crossed his arms over his chest before he did something stupid like yank her close and lecture her on not tempting the devil.

Instead, he said nothing.

There was something in the way she was walking that kept his mouth shut.

She stopped right in front of him.

The next thing he knew, the fool woman hooked one skinny arm around his shoulders, and pressed her mouth to his.

Rex kissed her back, careful not to disturb the blood evidence on the damned woman.

He was a man. She was a beautiful woman, even if she was as nutty as a fruitcake. She wanted to kiss him. He would let her.

The kiss lasted less than twenty seconds. Then she jerked away and looked up at him, a completely broken look in those witch's eyes of hers.

"What the hell are you doing?"

"I just had to get the taste of that man out of my mouth. I'm not going to my bed tonight remembering *him* kissing me. Not tonight."

Madam Zelda turned and walked away, leaving Rex staring at her like an idiot. What in the hell was she talking about?

They loaded Maggie and that Barratt guy into the helicopter together. Clint climbed in last.

Rex would handle things from here.

He turned. Joel Masterson was around someplace.

Rex had work to do—time to erase the taste of that woman. It would be easier said than done.

That woman truly was a witch, in every way possible.

## 75

CLINT WASN'T EVER LETTING GO OF HER AGAIN. HE WANTED to tell her that, but the damned helicopter was too loud. Maggie rode in the back, holding Barratt's hand.

Barratt had been in and out, from the blood loss. He'd been struck twice. But he was holding on.

Barratt was out when they landed by the hospital on the pad that had been added after Clive had nearly killed Maggie's cousin.

Clint just hoped he'd get a chance to tell the man thanks for what he had done.

None of them had been doing this alone.

He hadn't missed that. Nor would he ever forget that. He hadn't been alone.

The hospital parking lot was filling up. Joel Masterson had made it to Clint's place through some private back road Clint hadn't even known existed. Word had gone out what had happened as soon as Marin had made the 911 call. But Joel and Rex had already been on their way to his place. They'd called for the emergency chopper crew within moments. In time, thankfully.

People were coming.

Tylers and Talleys. They would all be there as soon as they possibly could.

He wanted Maggie checked out before that happened.

He pushed the wheelchair with his woman in it himself. He needed to be the one to take care of her right now.

They hadn't said anything to one another since he'd first met her eyes over the shaking, crying body of Jasper Grady.

There was too much he wanted to say to her.

Marin's cousin Dixie was one of the nurses on duty in the ER. She met them at the entrance. Masterson must have radioed in. "Maggie, we've got exam room one set up for you now. Dr. Paterson is on duty tonight. And Nate and Perci are on their way."

"I'm ok, Dixie. It's just Brandt that we're worried about. He was shot twice, and he...I tried to stop the bleeding, but..."

"We'll take care of him," Dixie said as a team of physicians ran out to see to the gurney carrying the man in question. "I promise. Let's just get you and Baby Clint checked out while we wait to find out how your friend is doing."

"I'll need to call his family. He's pretty close with his sister and his brothers. His cousins. They're almost as bad as we Tylers. His twin Powell will want to be here."

"We'll take care of that. He's been staying at the inn. I'll have Darcey track them down. We'll handle it, ok?"

Clint just kept pushing the wheelchair closer to the first exam bay. Maggie needed to fuss over her friend—to distract herself from fear over their baby. He knew her enough now to see that. He helped her out of the chair and lifted her gently onto the exam gurney. "You'll be ok."

Her hands wrapped around his forearms and then she was looking up at him. For the first time since everything had ended at the ranch. "Clint."

Her eyes filled, her mouth trembled.

"I love you." He was vaguely aware of Dixie fluttering around the exam room grabbing a clean gown. It didn't matter. "I haven't said it enough, and I'm going to start right now. I love you, Maggie Tyler. And that will never change. You are my very breath. The last woman I said that to died and left me alone. I was afraid of losing you too, and that made me act like an idiot. More than anything in the world I am afraid of losing you. And I can't stand even the thought of it. You and the baby and Violet—you are everything that matters to me. I can't lose you. I just can't."

She stared at him for a moment as Dixie stepped out through the curtain. "Clint...I'm not going anywhere."

"You can't know that. I can't know that either. That's something today just shoved down my throat. None of us knows when anything will end for any of us." He was sounding like a ranting lunatic. And he wasn't keeping his voice down. He didn't need to be almost yelling at her, but that was what he was doing. Clint jerked away and turned. "I need..."

He turned back to the woman he loved more than anything. "I need *you*. That's all I can say. I need *you*, Maggie. With every breath I take."

## 76

THIS WAS THE MAN SHE WAS DESTINED FOR. IF SHE BELIEVED Marin that sometimes the stars aligned, and someone somewhere had something planned for certain people's lives.

Maggie was meant for Clint.

And had been forever. From that first time he'd brushed against her, and she'd realized that *he* could matter to her.

He did matter. He mattered more than anyone else on the planet. She had just been too afraid to see that at first. Or too young, too naive to go after what she wanted—to even see what it was she did want. "Clint, we're both stubborn idiots."

He stopped pacing. Dixie returned, a pair of thick socks in her hands. "Maggie, do you need some help getting changed into the gown?"

"Clint can help me," Maggie said as a sudden pain shot through her. The baby kicked. She focused on breathing, like her OB had told her. He took the gown and the socks and looked at them with an almost helpless look in his eyes. It had her melting. "Clint, you dork. I love you. In every way imaginable. I am not going anywhere, ever again."

Her eyes met Dixie's and she saw the approval as the other woman slipped out of the room to give them some privacy.

Maggie slipped out of her maternity top and pants, knowing that she would never be putting them on again. They had blood all over them. She wanted them gone. Out of sight.

So she could focus on what she had to do now.

She bent over to slip off her shoes, when a gush of liquid drenched her. She cried out.

"What? What is it?" Clint took a step toward her, pulling her closer. "Honey?"

"Clint, you'd better go get Dixie again. Fast." Maggie forced herself to remain calm. The man was two inches away from panicking as it was. "My water just broke."

"It's a month too early. At least a month too early." There was the panic. Right there.

"Clint…go get Dixie, ok? I'm going to change clothes. And while you're at it, call Junie and Augie, and have them bring Violet here. Then call Martin, let him know what's going on. My brothers will want to be here for this."

He was just staring at her. All of the fear he felt right there in his blue eyes.

Maggie walked toward him, and wrapped her arms around him, not caring that she was in her bra and wet pants. She hugged him as closely as she could. "We're going to get through this. Now, go."

Clint went.

## 77

REX KNEW SOMETHING WAS WRONG THE MOMENT JOEL CURSED and took off toward one of his deputy's SUVs.

Rex didn't question. When a sheriff started running, a commander followed.

He just followed. In time to see Madam Zelda collapse right into Deputy Lowell's arms.

The younger man scooped her from the ground.

"What in the hell?" Rex asked, reaching out for her himself without thinking about it. He didn't want to put his hands on that damned woman again, but he didn't like the idea of someone else touching her either. Not tonight.

"Her sweater's soaked," Lowell said. Rex reached out. Saw what he meant for himself. It was still tacky. Wet straight through.

"She's been shot," Joel yelled, yanking the red knit top up quickly. "Get me a first aid kit!"

All of the medical personnel had left when the helicopter pulled out. Rex looked around for anything to use to stop the damned bleeding.

There was an exit wound beneath the arm he had

behind her back. He could see the ripped fabric of her sweater right there on her front.

"Why in the hell didn't someone say something? Why didn't she? Damned foolish woman." Rex lifted her into the rear of the nearby open SUV. He looked at Lowell. "You're driving. Fast."

Rex pulled the rear door closed behind himself, shoving the rear seat down and out of his way. She was all damned long legs and elbows and blond hair everywhere. That damned flowing dress got tangled on his hand when he shoved the sleeve out of the way.

There.

"Through and through. She's tied a scarf around it." He'd seen the scarf, blue and red poppies all over it. The blood had blended in. He was so used to seeing her with scraps of silk tied around various body parts he hadn't even looked closer. Damned foolish woman. She had no business running around free like she did. "She needs a damned keeper. One with balls of steel and a damned whip or chain. And a roll of duct tape."

Lowell floored it. "Yeah, so I've heard. But what man is brave enough to step up? Tried myself. But women like her can terrify a man, and she wasn't all that interested. If she was…"

"No damned kidding." She'd been bleeding for a good hour or more. The scarf had slowed that bleeding some. But the inevitable had happened. There was no telling how much blood on her dress was hers and how much was Barratt's. Why? "Why didn't she say anything?"

"My guess? She was waiting to make sure Maggie was all taken care of before she did. She's a bit protective of the people she loves. The whole lot of the Talleys are, from what I can see."

Her head was resting against Rex's chest. Madam Zelda was a tall woman, thin. She looked a hell of a lot more vulnerable than Rex wanted to think about. His arms tightened around her gently. "Just get her to the hospital. I'll turn her over to her family there. Maybe they can do something to keep her out of trouble. Like put her in a straitjacket and lock her away in the attic of the inn."

He could still feel her lips pressed to his. Damn it.

She had a way of getting under a man's skin. But she hadn't deserved this.

He just held on during the forty-five-mile drive back to Masterson, his fingers wrapped around her wrist. Counting her pulse. Just in case.

Her eyes fluttered open ten minutes before Lowell yanked the SUV into the parking lot of the hospital.

Marin just watched Rex. He watched her face right back.

She never said a word.

Neither did he.

## 78

CLINT WAS HOLDING HIMSELF TOGETHER BY A THREAD, DOING the traditional call-in-the-troops call. He'd not gotten to do that with Violet. The only "troops" he'd had had with Violet had been Miranda and Rex.

He called Flo Talley first. Then Phil Tyler. He figured the two of them together could handle notifying the rest of the Tyler clan.

He called Miranda. That wasn't a call he was looking forward to making. No one probably knew what had happened to Maggie and Marin today. Not yet.

He didn't have time to say much more than what he did. "Maggie and Marin were held hostage today. Maggie's in labor, Marin is just fine. Get your ass here. I can really use some backup."

Between Miranda and Rex, they might just be able to keep the Tylers from killing him for what he had let happen to Maggie. If Miranda didn't kill him for what had happened to her sister, that was.

He hightailed back to Maggie's side, just as Dixie wheeled her out of the ER and to Maternity.

This was really happening.

Maggie held her hand out to him. Clint took it.

"Where's Violet? Is she here yet? What about Marin?"

"Not yet. They're on their way." He had no idea where Marin was, actually. He assumed Rex would handle that.

Rex. He should probably call the only man he considered anything close to his family.

He settled for texting instead.

Just as a Masterson County deputy ran through the pneumatic doors, Rex in his wake.

With Marin limp in his arms.

Maggie cried out, calling her friend's name. Tried to get out of the wheelchair to go to her friend. Clint stopped Maggie before she could rush to her friend's side.

"What in the hell?"

"She was hit today and never bothered to tell anyone. I don't know how much damned blood she's lost." Rex was furious. "How's Barratt?"

"I don't have a clue. They have him in surgery. Now Maggie's in labor."

Rex swore creatively.

Another nurse ran by, barking orders at a pair of orderlies. Rex put Marin down carefully on a gurney.

Then he turned back to Clint. "The damned Talleys can take care of her now. That woman needs a keeper. And a cage."

Clint kept his damned mouth shut. He had other things to worry about now.

"Clint, I…Marin…she pushed me out of the way. When we first walked in. She yelled at me right before I walked in and grabbed my arm. Pulled me to one side. Did he hit her then?" Maggie's eyes were wet and terrified. Her hands were resting on their son. "She...I didn't know he hit her."

Clint didn't know what else to do. He looked at Rex. His friend nodded. "I'll stick close to her. Keep you both updated on her and Barratt. You just get in there and get my godson born. I'm interested to see if he's as ugly as his old man. I'll take care of Madam Zelda. Just for today. Go."

## EPILOGUE

BIRTHING A BABY WAS THE MOST TERRIFYING EXPERIENCE OF her life. Even more so than being taken hostage by a maniacal mayor.

Maggie wanted to think she'd held up well. Even if it had taken an additional seven hours and forty-two minutes to accomplish the task. During that time, Marin had been treated and Brandt had come out of surgery weak, but he was expected to make a full recovery.

It was time to look toward tomorrow.

Their son now rested in his father's arms. Barratt Rexford Talley Gunderson had a lot of name to grow into, but at almost ten pounds, he was a bit closer to it than she would have expected. To her eyes, he looked just like his father.

He was perfect, with the requisite ten fingers and ten toes and a healthy set of lungs that demanded she nurse him immediately.

Clint slipped onto the bed near her knee, his gaze on their son. He'd barely looked away. "He's got your determination."

"I can work with that. He has your chin."

"Stubborn. We might as well get prepared." Clint looked at her. "He's perfect. You're perfect. I...what happened today just makes that clear. I love you. I'm never going to stop saying that."

"I'll never get used to hearing it. We could have lost each other. I think we both learned that today." Maggie slipped her fingers over his, where his hand rested on their son's small back.

Their son.

Their world, along with the little girl who had gone home with Flo and the rest of the Talleys.

Someone knocked on their door, and she leaned against Clint as he called for them to enter.

Two women walked in.

Miranda and Marin. Who walked on unsteady legs.

"Marin!" Maggie's eyes immediately filled. "I was going to come see you first thing in the morning."

"They've finally discharged me. I'm good to go. Stitches."

"And a bag of O-positive. She's part vampire now," her older sister said. "And she agrees never to get in front of a bullet again. I just can't handle the stress of worrying about her. I'm the one who is supposed to deal with bad guys—not you two. So just quit it, will you?"

"Heard Rex said she needed a keeper more than a few times," Clint said. "And a cage was mentioned."

"I heard she walked right up to him and planted one on him in your front yard," Miranda said. She hugged Clint quickly. He passed her the baby and she cooed over him. "Oh, he's gorgeous, Maggie. Looks just like...a cross between you and Clint."

"Barratt Rexford Talley Gunderson," Clint said. "We're calling him Barratt."

"Perfect." Marin slipped to the bed, exhaustion on her face. "How could he not be? He's Maggie's."

"He's perfectly healthy, even if he is almost four weeks early."

"At almost ten pounds, it's probably a good thing he came a little early," Marin said. She held out her arms and her sister passed Barratt to her. "He is as beautiful as I knew he would be."

"So why did you kiss Weatherby?" Miranda asked as Marin rocked the baby gently. "He's not exactly your type."

"Anyone would have been my type after this afternoon. Call him a palate cleanser. I needed to forget."

Her eyes met Maggie's.

Maggie knew the truth; they would never forget how they'd felt. It had changed them all. Today...they would never be the same.

It would take them all a long while to get over that.

"It's over now," Marin finally said. "Everything ever tied to Clive Gunderson has reached its conclusion. No more ghosts haunting Clint. You can move on now and know you're all safe. Weatherby is about to show up and confirm that, if you don't believe me."

"Getting spooky again, Marin," Miranda said, moving to the chair. "I'm going to buy you a cat and a crystal ball."

"I'll take it. I need a new one for my collection." Marin shot a tired smile at Maggie as she rested against the back of the chair. Maggie studied her for a long while—she was pale, shaky, but would be ok. They were safe now.

Miranda asked them questions about what had happened, as she and Clint spoke quietly. Easily.

It didn't matter to Maggie that he and Miranda had once loved each other. They still loved each other; it was obvious in the easy way they spoke with one another. The jokes. But there was no doubt in her mind that Clint loved Maggie, and always would.

She didn't doubt that now.

Miranda and Rex Weatherby were Clint's *family*. Even if he hadn't realized that. She had. She'd seen it. Family wasn't just biology. Or at least, it didn't have to be.

Marin drifted off. She probably should have been at home now, or in a hospital bed somewhere. But she wasn't.

Because she was family, too.

Miranda slipped out, to go grab herself some coffee and call her grandmother—who had Bentley, the child Miranda was in the process of adopting.

She'd asked Clint to be his unofficial godfather, like Miranda was Violet's godmother.

Maggie thought that sounded perfect.

She was nursing the baby discretely when another knock came at the door.

Marin didn't even stir to see that her prediction had been correct.

Rex Weatherby stood outlined in the door.

He stepped in. Clint stood. Maggie watched as the two men slapped each other on the back.

He turned to Maggie, his cheeks heating when he realized what she was doing. "I can step out."

"I'm good." Maggie was covered. It was definitely awkward, but they'd figure it out eventually. "Thank you, Rex. For what you did today. And for…getting her to help."

He grunted, then focused on the woman slumped in

the chair. "Damned woman needs a keeper. Should be in a hospital bed."

Right before Maggie and Clint's eyes, Rex slipped his arms around Marin's knees and behind her back. He lifted her effortlessly. Marin never stirred.

He promptly lowered Marin to the second hospital bed in the room and tossed a blanket over her.

He grunted, then settled into the chair she'd once occupied. "So...what's this kid's name and when does he get to come hang out with Uncle Rex so I can teach him about the real world?"

Maggie smiled, but said nothing. This was Clint's show —his choice. She passed him their now content son. Clint handed him to his godfather. "Meet your godson, Barratt Rexford Talley Gunderson."

Yes. Family was far more than just biology.

Now they were going to build one together.

# WHAT HAPPENS NEXT IN MASTERSON?

**There are many more things happening in Masterson. Stay tuned for more novels and mini-series in 2021 and 2022!**

And don't forget to check out the Masterson series in audio!

# ALSO BY CALLE J. BROOKES

ROMANTIC SUSPENSE

PAVAD: FBI ROMANTIC SUSPENSE

Beginning (Prequel 1)

Waiting (Prequel 2)

Watching

Wanting

Second Chances

Hunting

Running

Redeeming

Revealing

Stalking

Ghosting

Burning

Gathering

Falling

Hiding

Seeking

Searching

FINLEY CREEK SERIES

SERIES ONE (TEXAS STATE POLICE)

Her Best Friend's Keeper

Shelter from the Storm

The Price of Silence

SERIES TWO (FINLEY CREEK GENERAL)

If the Dark Wins

Wounds That Won't Heal

Hope for Finley Creek (bonus novella)

As the Night Ends

SERIES THREE (FINLEY CREEK DISASTER)

Before the Rain Breaks

Lost in the Wind

Walk Through the Fire

We All Sleep Alone

Stand Next to Me (Coming Soon)

MASTERSON COUNTY SERIES

Seeking the Sheriff

Discovering the Doctor

Ruining the Rancher

Denying the Devil

Facing the Fire (Coming Soon)

SMALL-TOWN SHERIFFS

Holding the Truth

SUSPENSE/THRILLER

PAVAD: FBI CASE FILES

Calle has several free reads available at

www.**CalleJBrookesReads.com**

For my grandfather, the best man I have ever known.

You will be missed.

Oct. 2015

For my grandmother, who gave me the courage to try. Without
you and your love of romance, I never would have made it
this far.

Feb. 2016

For my papaw, whose children loved him deeply, and will
always miss him.

Oct. 2017

**Calle J. Brookes** enjoys crafting paranormal romance and romantic suspense. She reads almost every genre except horror. She spends most of her time juggling family life and writing while reminding herself that she can't spend all of her time in the worlds found within books. CJ loves to be contacted by her readers via email and at **www.CalleJBrookes.com**. When not at home writing stories of adventure and wrangling with two border collies and a beagle puppy, CJ is off in her RV somewhere exploring the beautiful world we live in, along with her husband of she can't remember how many years and their child.